Ralph Broome

The Letters of Simkin the Second,

Poetic Recorder of all the Proceedings

Ralph Broome

The Letters of Simkin the Second,
Poetic Recorder of all the Proceedings

ISBN/EAN: 9783744716215

Printed in Europe, USA, Canada, Australia, Japan

Cover: Foto ©Andreas Hilbeck / pixelio.de

More available books at **www.hansebooks.com**

.THE.

LETTERS

OF

SIMKIN THE SECOND,

POETIC RECORDER OF ALL THE

PROCEEDINGS,

UPON THE TRIAL OF

WARREN HASTINGS, Esq.

IN WESTMINSTER HALL.

I——— curre per Alpes,
Ut PUERAS *placeas et* DECLAMATIO *fias!*
JUVENAL.

Enlighten'd Statesman! go through Toil and Strife,
And for thy Country's Good, embroil thy Life.
Go——*mighty Warrior!*——wide and wider roam,
To come at length, and be abus'd at home.   ANON.

LONDON:

PRINTED FOR JOHN STOCKDALE, OPPOSITE BURLINGTON HOUSE,
PICCADILLY,

M.DCC.XCI.

[Entered at Stationers Hall.]

DEDICATION.

TO THE

HONORABLE, AND RIGHT HONORABLE,

MANAGERS OF THE IMPEACHMENT

OF

WARREN HASTINGS, Esq.

YE far-fam'd Heroes ! greatest, best of Men,
Accept this Tribute, from your Poet's pen,
For gratitude alone inspires his lays,
And bids him sing each hardy Leader's praise.
Never did Warriors, *such a battle wage*,
In strife *so desperate*, ne'er did Chiefs engage.

B

What

What godlike qualities have all difplay'd ! !

The Knights of MALTA in a new crufade ! ! !

But thou, great EDMUND ! *whofe enlighten'd breaft,*

Glows with Philanthropy, above the reft,

Whofe endlefs labour, in an Empire's caufe,

Claims *what it ne'er receiv'd,* the World's applaufe, *

In future ages thy illuftrious Name,

Shall rival Cato's, in the field of fame.

But fay, fhall he, who does each day devote,

To ferve whole Nations, polifh'd, † tho' remote,

From fenfelefs Britons, find no prefent meed ?

What's *future* praife, for fuch a glorious deed ?

If Virtue then muft be *its own reward,*

The times we live in, *are extremely hard.*

The fuffering *millions,* they whofe caufe you try,

Difown their Patrons,—give them all the Lye, ‡

---

* In the firft ftage of the prefent Impeachment, Mr. Montague with great feeling, lamented the fituation of his poor friend Mr. Burke, and while he mourned the weaknefs of thefe latter times, faid, that Simkin's Hero muft look to pofterity, as other great men had done before him, for the reward of his labours.

† Mr. Burke defcribing the natives of Indoftan in the Houfe of Commons, faid, that they were " fam'd for all the arts of polifh'd " life, while we were yet in the woods."

‡ Though a very fincere admirer of Simkin, I fhould think it neceffary to advife him to change this line, or to expunge it totally, if a noble Lord, one of the Managers, had not repeatedly ufed the fame expreffion in the Houfe of Commons, during the debates upon the Regency Bill.

The

The crowded Audience, whom you entertain,
Opprefs'd by Taxes, of the Coft complain,
The watchful Senate murmurs at Expence,
And thinks the Charges of each year, immenfe——
EDMUND proceed,—'tis thine to perfevere;
Shall *clamour* ftop thee,* in thy bold career?
Still may thy Breaft o'erflow *with patriot zeal,*
Whilft vulgar fouls, *attend the public weal.*

Fox, tho' thy Speeches are but four Days long, †
Thy zeal, like BURKE's, is ftedfaft, bold, and ftrong,

* Alluding to certain filly afperfions out of doors—Firft, as to the enormous expence of the Impeachment—Secondly, as to the prefent ftate of India—And thirdly, a bold affertion hazarded by one Major Scott in the Houfe and out of it—that India is at this moment governed upon the fyftem laid down by Haftings, and condemned by the Managers.

† A great deal of moft aftonifhing eloquence, as Mr. Burke faid, was heard in the Houfe of Commons before Lord North could be driven from office; but thanks to the Impeachment, we have gone greatly beyond our forefathers.—In the time of Mr. Pulteney, a Speech of half an hour, would fet Country Gentlemen to fleep.—— Mr. Sheridan on the Begum Charge in the Commons, fpoke five hours and a quarter—Sir James Erfkine, who determined to go beyond him, with his eye upon the clock, and chin upon the table, continued upon his legs, *five minutes longer than Mr. Sheridan.*—Mr. Burke who fcorns to be outdone, made laft year a Speech of four days in Weftminfter Hall—Sir Gilbert Elliot followed this example in the Commons—Mr. Sheridan concluded laft year by a Speech of four days, and Mr. Burke began this year in the fame manner.

Im-

Impaffion'd,—eager,—vengeance in thy view,
The man who caus'd thy fall, to death purfue. *

, Encomiums fuited to the worth of GREY,
SIMKIN, alas ! wants language to convey ;
Whatever form, or character he pleafe,
GREY can affume, and act each part with eafe.
One minute fee him fhine, an able Pleader,
The next a Clerk like, monotonic reader,
The third, a Bottle-holder to his leader.

Advance, illuftrious Chiefs, renew the fight,
SIMKIN fhall each heroic act recite,
GREY, FOX, and SURFACE, with their General BURKE,
Shall ornament, and grace, a future work,
In the next year, fhould *ftars inferior fhine*,
Their rays fhall add, new fplendor to my line.

* Simkin here feems to allude to a prevailing opinion, that the partizans of Mr. Haftings at the India Houfe, firft raifed the alarm, upon the celebrated Bill of Mr. Fox, and he now juftifies the violence of that Gentleman, as perfectly confonant to the *lex talionis*—forgetting how ill this agrees with the character which Mr. Fox *has given of himfelf,*

Inimicitiæ placabiles, amicitiæ fempiterne.——

THE

THE

P R E F A C E,

To the P U B L I C.

IF I should not be reckoned a POET, *I may at least be held as* an Adventurer—*for no Writer ever stepped forward on ground less amusing, and where even the fictions of Poetry could not go beyond the fictions of* ORATORY ; *perhaps I may boast the Triumph of having kept some people awake : and am therefore as meritorious as*—the Gout.

If farther vanity I might indulge—it would be, that if my Heroes have not been HECTORS *or* NES-TORS—*nor I, a* HOMER,

> Still there have been contentions about
> My Works.   One pleasant Bookseller
> Has maintained, I do not know my
> Own writing so well as he does—that
> his——
>   " Is the true Mag-pie,"——

B 3

And

And that He, *and not* myfelf *am entitled to my*
Works. *But as I have no right to make any* obliging
Gentleman of this fort, *anfwer for my fins—fo will*
I fairly fay—that having committed my writing to
the WORLD, *when they are taken out of the World*
—as all Children muft die—my Undertaker is

Mr. JOHN STOCKDALE, BOOKSELLER,

in PICCADILLY.

THE AUTHOR.

A DE-

DESCRIPTION

OF THE TRIAL OF

WARREN HASTINGS, Esq.

LETTER I.

YOU have afk'd me, *dear* SIMON, a number of times,
To fend you fome more of my ludicrous rhimes;
Want of matter has hitherto check'd my endeavour,
But a fubject occurs which may laft me for ever.
   You muft know, *Mr.* BURKE, who was quondam a
        teacher,
An *ufher*, I think, is become an IMPEACHER;
In the Houfe he had rail'd againft HASTINGS fo long,
That the Commons believ'd, he had done *fomething*
        wrong;
So they articles voted, *not lefs than a fcore,*
Tho' EDMUND fays, he *cou'd have fram'd many more.*

                        As

As my hero afferted, and Hastings deny'd,
A day was appointed for him to be try'd.
But now for a time I muft make a digreffion,
To give an account of the court in proceffion.

The PROCESSION.

The Lord Chancellor's family firft came in view,
And the order obferv'd, was to walk two and two;
Then the Clerks and the Masters *in* Chancery
     came,
Then the Judges of England in duo's the fame,
With Adair the King's Serjeant, and then the Black
     Rod;
Then Heralds, and Barons, and Fathers in God.
After them were the Vifcounts, Earls, Marquiffes feen,
Then the *Dukes*, the *Archbishops*, and *Cryer* come in.
Next follows the *Chancellor*, and laft of all
Dukes—Cumberland, Glofter, and *York*, and *Cornwall*.
All after the *Heralds* walk fingly, alone,
And each as he paffes, bows low to the *Throne*;
So much for the *Nobles*, and now I'll defcribe
The proceffion of Burke and his *eloquent tribe*.
Firft Edmund walks in at the head of the groupe,
The powerful *chief* of a powerful *troop*;
What awful *folemnity's* feen in his gait!
While the nod of his *head*, beats the time to his *feet*.

Charles

CHARLES FOX is the fecond, and clofe to his right,

Whofe waddle declares he will never go ftraight.

The ruby fac'd SHERIDAN follows the third,

The oppofer of PITT and the Treafury Board;

His attention, 'tis faid, *has fo long been directed*

To the National *Debts*, that his *own* are neglected,

And on public affairs, *where fuch management's fhewn,*

No wonder a man *cannot think of his own.*

Next ADAM comes in with a fpit by his fide,

And ftruts like a turkey-cock fwelling with pride;

Then follows ANSTRUTHER that weathercock elf,

As a proof how a man may diffent from *himfelf;*

To the *Governor* HASTINGS his praife was profufe,

On HASTINGS the *pris'ner,* he pours forth abufe :

Then follows young GREY, an exact imitator

Of the fcurrilous BURKE,—a moft promifing prater;

Tho' all muft lament that he's under fuch banners,

As evil community injures good manners.

Then PELHAM, FITZPATRICK, and WINDHAM came

    forth,

With MONTAGUE, MAITLAND, with BURGOYNE and

    NORTH.

Chick TAYLOR and ERSKINE are join'd in the vote,

And as *Managers* known by a *bag* and *drefs coat.*

Then FRANCIS comes fneaking with grief in his heart,

At not being indulg'd with a *Manager's* part;

I

Tho'

Tho' he now and then fteals to the *Managers'* box,

To fuggeft a fhrewd queftion to EDMUND or FOX.

The Commons, all thofe who from riding have leifure,

Without order come in, and go out at their pleafure.

When the *Lords* and the *Judges* had taken their ftations,

The *Serjeant* at *Arms* utter'd three *proclamations*;

Then the charges and anfwers were read by the clerk,

And *fome* were got through *by the time it was dark.*

The *fecond* day alfo was wafted in reading,

But the *third* produc'd fomething of EDMUND's pro-
      ceeding :

He rofe and began—" You will find in the fequel,

" My Lords, to this tafk *I am very unequal* :

" But, the *Commons,* who hold me in high eftimation,

" Believe I am qualify'd *well* for the ftation.

" My *Colleagues,* whofe talents *refulgently fhine,*

" Will amply make up *for the failure of mine* ;

" Who fharing the trouble *of framing the ftory,*

" Have a right to partake with myfelf *in the glory.*

" My Lords, I forefee in the courfe of this trial,

" There will be much affertion, and alfo denial,

" And before I go farther, 'tis proper and fit,

" I fhould tell you what proof to rejeƈt and admit."

Here EDMUND attempted diftinƈtion to draw,

Between this high court, and the low courts of law ;

He

He laid down a doctrine of *evidence* found,

Which in no other treatise *could ever be found*;

The lawyer appear'd in whatever he spoke,

Than Blackstone more learn'd, more ingenious than
    Coke.

Rules of evidence *they* had the merit of stating,

But Edmund lays claim *to the praise of creating* :

Yet even this deed *by himself was excell'd*;

In describing the countries *he never beheld*;

To be sure, his descriptions were *vastly admir'd*,

The whole was his own, for his tongue was inspir'd,

With knowledge divine he expos'd to our view,

The religion of Hindoos, and Mussulman's too.

And he said Junghez Khan only seiz'd their dominions,

But that Hastings wag'd war with the people's opinions.

Here the orator bluster'd, at least for an hour,

About Warren Hastings, and absolute power,

Who according to Burke, has been forming a plan,

To map geographical morals for man.

Who to shew us his great geometrical art,

Fit climates for virtues has drawn on a chart;

That virtues and vices, that duties and crimes,

May change with the latitudes, countries, and climes.

Here Edmund committed his honor and word,

To prove *moral geography* vastly absurd;

And

And by way of a secret, *their Lordships* were told,
That truth's not affected, *by heat or by cold*;
" Far better," says he, " when the English went thither,
" Had they call'd the inhabitant natives together;
" And instead of subduing, or them over-reaching,
" Had busy'd themselves with evangelic preaching.
" No converts made they to the Christian religion,
" But pluck'd the rich blacks like the wing of a pigeon.
" For there was the Company's government built,
" Upon plunder, and rapine, and all kinds of guilt;
" In a system like this, 'tis no matter of wonder,
" If all were inspired by the spirit of plunder.
" There was not a captain, nor scarce a seapoy,
" But a *Prince* would depose, or a *Bramin* destroy;"
Here the *Hero* digress'd, and related some tales
Of a prince to be slain, as he thought, *by three seals*,
How *Nabobs*, and *Ministers* had been opprest,
And the innocent natives with famine distrest.
Now EDMUND returns to his well-belov'd theme,
To prove HASTINGS' power should not be supreme;
That Government rule 'twas his duty to draw,
From *Coke* upon *Littleton*, writers on law:
And whenever their *Lordships* shall come to decide,
BURKE hoped they would take *British laws for their guide.*
'Tis contended, says he, by the party accus'd,
We should govern by laws to which subjects are us'd.

But,

But, my Lords, I maintain, 'tis expedient and fitting,

To govern the world by the laws of *Great Britain*;

Nor do I conceive that it matters a jot,

With refpect to the laws, if they knew them or not.

And the pris'ner, I truft, will be try'd* and attainted

By thofe laws alone, with which I am acquainted.

When EDMUND grew faint, his auxiliar ADAM

Read letters, as oft as his principal bade him;

BURKE ended at length, with apprifing the *Lords*,

That he an œconomift was of his words,

That he fhould juft mention *the heads of each Charge*,

And leave it to others thereon *to enlarge*,——

Who would trace out corruption and bafe peculations;

Thro' all their meanders, and ramifications.

Here this letter ends, but expect, my dear Brother,

When EDMUND refumes, I will fend you another.

17th February, 1788.

LETTER

LETTER II.

AND now, my dear Brother, I take up the pen,
To tell you that BURKE has been ſpeaking again;
When the *Court* was aſſembled, thus EDMUND began,
" My *Lords*, I aſſert, WARREN HASTINGS's plan
" Has conſtantly been to get all that he can.

" For when NUNDCOMAR gave the Board information
" Concerning his bribery, and peculation,
" Inſtead of confronting the charge and denying,
" He caus'd his accuſer *to ſuffer for lying*;
" That is, NUNDCOMAR was for *forgery* hung,
" Which ſilenc'd for ever his *garrulous tongue.*
" Twenty thouſand pounds ſterling the criminal took
" From the Begum, I find, *by the Company's book*;
" To the truth of this action, her *ladyſhip ſwore*,
" And a *Rajah* too gave *twenty* thouſand pounds more;
" And this by the *Rajah* was certainly done,
" For the favour which HASTINGS conferr'd on his ſon:
" But, *my Lords*, he was guilty of further abuſe,
" For he took many bribes *for the Company's uſe*;
" The Company, *tho' they receiv'd them, and kept them,*
" Were deſirous to aſk, *why did* HASTINGS *accept them.*

" To

" To this queftion the criminal made no reply,

" So to this very moment, *we cannot tell why.*"

Here EDMUND minutely defcribed to the *Lords,*

The modes of collection, and *Revenue Boards.*

On farms and on diftricts, the changes he rings

Till he happens at length to get hold of the *Sings;*

He talk'd about Contoo, and Deby, and others,

All Hindoos in caft—in iniquity, brothers.

Here EDMUND launch'd out, and prefented to view

Such a picture, as none but himfelf ever drew.

" Of culprits whom DEBY SING fentenc'd to ride

" On a pillory ox, with a drum on each fide,

" And whilft he and his party were bufy'd with pillage,

" This terrible bullock paraded the village.

" The natives alarmed at this horrible fight,

" From their villages made a precipitate flight.

" This has I admit an incredible look,

" And would not be believ'd, *were it not in the book.*

" From the Company's records, the ftory I drew,

" From records, which are inconteftably true ;

" And he, who collected this ftrange information,

" For humanity's fake, would fupprefs the relation.

" But however his wifhes might go to conceal it,

" In difcharge of his truft, he was forc'd to reveal it :

" To him in a body *the* RYOTS complain'd,

" That their houfes were burnt, and their cattle diftrain'd.

" That

" That when Deby, the plunderer settled their rent,
" In taking the balance, he was not content
" With any thing less than six hundred per cent,
" And those who the cash were unable to raise,
" Were cruelly tortur'd in different ways."
The cruelties here, which the *Orator* stated,
Are more than in verse can be justly related:
He describ'd to the audience *in language obscene*,
New *sockets* for *candles*, and *glasses unclean*;
From these *filthy cups*, some were drinking the waters,
Whilst others were ravishing mothers and daughters;
For tearing off nipples, a *Bamboo* was cleft,
And the suffering female was stripp'd of her shift;
Whilst EDMUND these cruelties horribly painted,
Some ladies took salts, others wept, and ONE fainted.
And indeed, my dear Brother, I'm free to confess,
As EDMUND described it, they could not do less.
Some people, however, who perfectly knew
The true state of the case, said 'twas mostly untrue;*
On this subject farther, I've only to add,
The surprising effect which his eloquence had,

Not

* The story of Deby Sing having attracted the attention of this country, and indeed of all Europe; we think it right to add Major Scott's *prose* account of that celebrated story.—He has published two letters to Mr. Fox, in which he details it at length, refers to the do-

cuments

Not only on thofe, *who ne'er heard it before,*

But on BURKE, who had read *it a hundred times o'er.*

In the annals of painting, *'tis certainly new,*

For the *artiſt* to faint, *at the piƈture he drew;*

But BURKE was fo touch'd, that he fainted away,

Like Siddons, the Tragedy Queen, in a play.

Some think *'twas his conſcience that gave him a ſtroke,*

But thofe *who beſt know him, treat that as a joke:*

'Tis a *trick* that ſtage orators have at their need,

The paſſions to roufe, *and the judgment miſlead;*

And *Dick,* who is ſkill'd *in theatrical painting,*

Had given his leader *ſome leſſons on fainting.*

cuments neceſſary to prove all his aſſertions; and we can with con‑
fidence affirm, that he has proved the following faƈts;

1ſt. That at the time Mr. Burke told the ſtory, *he knew* from direƈt
and pofitive evidence, that it would be impoſſible to implicate Mr.
Haſtings direƈtly or indireƈtly, in any criminality that might attach
upon Deby Sing.

2d. That Mr. Burke *knew* he was ſtating what *was not true,* when
he affirmed that Deby Sing was appointed farmer of Rungpore and
Dinagepore, by Mr. Haſtings.

3d. That he ſtated certain aƈts of great cruelty as faƈts proved,
though *he knew* they were mere aſſertions, *then in the courſe of in‑
quiry.*

4th. That many of them, upon the fulleſt inveſtigation, have turned
out *to be falſe;* and to conclude, the final decifion of the Bengal Go‑
vernment, after the fulleſt inquiry, proves, that Deby Sing was inno‑
cent of all the moſt dreadful crimes charged againſt him, and that no
Engliſhman, of whatever rank or ſtation, is implicated in ſuch of the
criminality (trifling as it is) which attaches upon Deby Sing.

Now BURKE from his horror a little compos'd,

To the gallery ladies a fecret difclos'd ;

He faid, that the men whofe induftrious hands

Had been tortur'd, and fcrew'd, were the tillers of
      lands,

And owing to them he affirm'd it to be,

That the ladies drank morning and afternoon tea.

Here EDMUND ftruck a more loud deprecation

Againft the effects of divine indignation,

And demanded that HASTINGS be made to atone

For the crimes *of all others, as well as his own.*

Juft here was the fpirit of eloquence damp'd,

For the ftomach of EDMUND was fuddenly cramp'd.

When FRANCIS beheld his dear orator ftop,

He fprung twenty feet at two fteps and a hop ;

Affa-fœtida drops he apply'd to his nofe,

But tho' EDMUND recover'd, the fpeech had a clofe.

LORD THURLOW long filent, now thought it his turn

To fpeak to the *Court,* fo he mov'd *to adjourn.*

   21ft February, 1788.

LETTER

LETTER III.

Dear Brother—

You aſk, why was Francis diſtreſt?
Why he fear'd for the cauſe ſo much more than the reſt?
To anſwer this queſtion as well as I can,
I muſt give you a ſketch of this wonderful man—

Some certain things riſe from the dark:
Our hero ſtarted firſt a clerk—
In office, that was ſtill impreſſing
On tender youth this uſeful leſſon;
Thoſe that would thrive, muſt learn to cringe,
" *To turn like door upon a hinge;*"
To flatter thoſe that favour ſhew ye;
To ſpurn at thoſe that are below ye;
Francis, by acting well this part,
Completely won his patron's heart;
Who made him, by a ſudden ſpring,
The fifth part of *a potent King;* *
That is, he was to *Bengal* ſent,
The under limb of *Government.*—

* Francis's definition of himſelf and his power to the people in India.

Let

Let yonder beggar mount a horfe,
The Proverb tells " which way his courfe ;"
So FRANCIS, who had been a hack
Of office, 'midft a fervile pack,
Saw thoufands tremble at his nod,
And like a Philip's fon, became a god.
His fortune had been great indeed,
If HASTINGS had not check'd his fpeed,
And to his profpects put an end,
By calling from *Lucknow* his friend.
This FRANCIS never can forgive,
As long as he and HASTINGS live ;
And from that time, has been purfuing
Means to effect his total ruin ;
But fruitlefs finding oppofition,
He form'd—like fome— *a coalition :*
But *coalitions ftill muft fall,*
One certain fate *o'ertakes them all.*
Tho' his—a novel kind of plan—
To join, and then betray the man ;
But HASTINGS' genius was awake,
And ere he ftung, it fcotch'd the fnake.
This to the fire but added fuel,
Until it ended in a duel.——
When FRANCIS faw his fchemes all fail,
For England's fhore he fpread his fail.——

No

No sooner on shore had our PHILL set his feet,

Than he drove, like a *Post-boy*, to LEADENHALL-
STREET;

In the flames of his Malice, he burnt to disclose

A tale, which had cost him some years to compose;

But he got a rebuff from the Court of Directors;

They were HASTINGS's *friends*; they were Virtue's pro-
tectors:

They paid just regard to their honor and glory;

They read not PHILL's papers: they heard not PHILL's
story;

Tho' like lightning to England from India he came,

In speed he was greatly surpass'd by his fame;

They knew, how the measure of HASTINGS he crost,

How near his advice COROMANDEL had lost;

By the Court of Directors, it clearly was seen,

That the man was a compound of envy and spleen—

    Then away to the mongers of Boroughs went he,

    To try, if with some one he could not agree;

    And find a fit corner—for once—to his use,

    For speech unrestrain'd, and for licens'd abuse.

But when from himself an abusive oration

Could produce no effect on a sensible nation,

His attention was turn'd to the *Quixote-like* BURKE,

Who is fond of engaging in *Quixote-like* work;

C 3

He

He told him long ſtories of damſels diſtreſs'd,

Of extirpated nations, of RAJAHS oppreſs'd;

Of HASTINGS's having compell'd the NABOB,

His kindred, his mother, grandmother to rob—

" Shall the eloquent BURKE, who by pleading the cauſe

" Of *Powel,* and *Bembridge,* gain'd laſting applauſe;

" Shall the man, who to wretches like theſe was a friend,

" The rights of old damſels refuſe to defend?

" Oh! let not the children of ASIA beſeech

" Thy mercy in vain; but the tyrant impeach;

" I myſelf will find matter, do you furniſh ſpeech."

Then away poſted BURKE to his CHARLEY and SHERRY,

Who were toping at BROOKES's, pot-valiant and merry!

" I have ſomething, my boys, upon which we may

    " prate,

" 'Tis time we ſhould ſpout, leſt we grow out of date;

" Againſt a Nabob, I am furniſh'd with matter—

" When matter is found, we can all of us chatter;

" Warren Haſtings is he—you remember, his friends

" *Prevented* us lately, *from gaining our ends.*

" That ſtock-holding-crew the late change brought

    " about

" In adminiſtration, and turn'd us all out:

" Let us try, in our turn, if we can't over-reach him,

" Then hilloa, brave boys, let us on and impeach him!

" Perhaps

" Perhaps the rich rogue, when he finds himfelf under
" Our lafh, may prefent us fome part of the plunder."
Then CHARLEY, who found himfelf not in a cue,
So wild, fo romantic a fcheme to purfue,
Who found by a balance, juft made of his books,
Himfelf better paid by attending at Brookes',
Requefted, that BURKE would be pleas'd to defift
From the bufinefs, or ftrike his name out of the lift.
And SHERRY, who now holds theatrical ftuff,
Declar'd on the ftage " there was acting enough,"
And begg'd, that if BURKE had this farce at his heart,
HE might be excus'd from the taking a part.
BURKE ftarted, and fwore, if you do not think fit
To fupport me in this, I'll go over to PITT.
Then CHARLES, who began to forefee the reduction
Of his force at St. Stephen's might prove his deftruction,
Engag'd for himfelf, and the whole of his party ;
Tho' fome people think, CHARLES is not very hearty.
Three years have elaps'd fince the fuit they began, ⎫
They may work many more, let them do all they can, ⎬
Before they will conquer this much-injur'd man ! ⎭
You afk'd me what caufe had the Houfe to refift
Adding FRANCIS's name to the MANAGERS' lift ?
Why moderate men to exclude him agreed, ⎫
Tho' BURKE pledg'd his honor, he could not proceed ⎬
Without FRANCIS's aid, to fupport him in need. ⎭

Then

Then, EDMUND! thy zeal ſtruck the guard from thy
    tongue,
And betray'd the baſe ſource, whence the charges all
    ſprung.
Great part of the Houſe, which till then had believ'd
The ſtory, now find themſelves groſſly deceiv'd;
How many good men, now are griev'd to the heart,
To think they were talk'd into taking a part.

But FRANCIS triumphantly laugh'd in his ſleeve,
To think he ſo long could the public deceive.
As he walk'd along Bond-ſtreet, he ſaid to a friend,
" Tho' my foe be acquitted, 'twill anſwer my end;
" Oppreſt with fatigue, and o'erburthen'd with coſt,
" His health will be broken, his fortune be loſt;"
Then he ſwore, by the Lord, he would not ceaſe pur-
    ſuing,
Till death and damnation had finiſh'd his ruin.
Tho' ſo ſolemn an oath, he confeſs'd gave him pain,
To come from a boſom ſo *kind* and *humane*.

I conclude for the preſent:—but if, *my dear* BROTHER,
You like this epiſtle, I'll ſend you another;

February 23d, 1788.

LET-

LETTER IV.

As the Orator now had recover'd his ftrength,

Which had fuffer'd from fpeech of immoderate length,

He return'd to the tale he had often repeated,

And told us how ill the poor natives were treated.

Thofe natives who furnifh'd the Ladies with tea,

Were as gentle and mild as poor creatures could be;

But as patience like all other virtues is bounded,

They all flew to arms when the trumpet refounded:

But, alas! th' infurgents contended in vain,

They fought, they were conquer'd, were routed, and
  flain.

Here Edmund broke forth in a ftrain fo fublime,

No poet can do him ftrict juftice in rhime—

" I charge Warren Hastings, and thofe he employed,

" With (in practice and theory) having deftroyed

" All government—And with endeavouring to draw

" Depravity into a fyftem of law—

" Peculation to rules of arithmetic brought,

" This curfed High Prieft of iniquity taught.

" In

" In the name of the COMMONS and PEOPLE at large,

" With *high crimes and strange misdemeanors I charge*

" WARREN HASTINGS.——— —

" I charge him with *treachery, fraud,* and *abuse,*

" And with *robbery* too, for the *Company's use*—

" I charge him with *cruelties* and *devastations,*

" Such as never were practis'd on innocent nations.

". I charge him with leaving in those wretched climes

" Not *money enough* to *atone for his crimes.*"

But now the *sublime* being suddenly ended,

To the *pathos* my versatile Speaker descended,

" I spy a *religious respectable band,*

" Who all holy mysteries well understand,

" Who from duty should save our religion from sink-
  " ing,

" Of HASTINGS, what must be their manner of think-
  " ing?

" I spy on the *woolsack* the JUDGES *profound,*

" Who can find out the *law* and at pleasure expound,

" With so much uprightness and justice, I wonder

" What must be *their* thoughts of *extortion* and *plunder.*

" Of NOBLES I spy an *illustrious train,*

" Whose honor can suffer by no spot or stain ;

" All those must undoubtedly favor the work,

" And cry, *Bravo, bravissimo, rare* Mr. BURKE !

" In

" In the *name of religiou*, which he has difgrac'd ;

" Of our *Conftitution*, which he has defac'd ;

" In the *name of thofe millions of Indians deftroyed*

" By HASTINGS, and others whom he has employed ;

" In the *name of humanity* and *human nature*,

" All ftabb'd to the heart by this terrible creature,

" I IMPEACH WARREN HASTINGS ! Nor let me com-
   " plain,

" That pleadings fo ftrong fhou'd be offeted in vain."

Here ended great EDMUND, and CHARLEY arofe,

A *mode of conducting the caufe* to *propofe* :

A contrivance of his, or fome lawyer, perhaps,

Who has fpent all his life in the laying of traps.

In Æfop you've read of that *fubtle old Fox*

Who liv'd by deftroying *hens, pullets* and *cocks,*

Who one night on his ramble had faften'd his eye

On a cock and his family roofting on high,

Who made fuch a *flattering treacherous fpeech*

To prevail on the poultry to come in his reach :

With *fimilar motive* did CHARLEY propofe

His method to make WARREN HASTINGS difclofe

The *reply he will make to their charges,* and thence

To enable themfelves to *foreftall his defence* ;

But DALLAS and PLOMER, and vigilant LAW,

Perceiv'd his defign, and the evil forefaw.

They

They oppos'd him with arguments weighty and found,
But CHARLEY with firmnefs difputed the ground.
After much altercation their LORDSHIPS withdrew
To determine on what was moft proper to do.
And here, my dear Brother, this Letter I end,
And when the Court meets, I another will fend.

February 25th, 1788.

LET-

LETTER V.

ONCE more, my dear SIMON, I take up the pen
To record the exploits of thofe eloquent men.
The LORDS met, and we heard that the *Court wou'd not*
  clofe
With the method which CHARLEY was pleas'd to *propofe*;
Then CHARLES and the MANAGERS begg'd to retire
To hold confultation——they had their defire.
After fome fhort adjournment, the heroes came back;
Some faces were long, and fome others look'd black.
Fox faid, " We fubmit, yet beg leave to proteft
" That we ftill muft confider *our mode as the beft*,
" And though for the prefent, we *privilege* wave,
" The *Rights of the Commons* we carefully fave.

" My LORDS, the firft charge we are going to bring
" Is the *conduct of* HASTINGS *concerning* CHEYT SING."
Then CHARLEY with gefture emphatic avow'd,
That HE of his rank was exceffively proud,
As being commiffioned to open the *firft*,
And indeed he appeared as if ready to burft;
But whether his *fwelling* were *wind*, *fat*, or *pride*,
Is a queftion too grofs for myfelf to decide;
         " Our

" Our fine Conftitution," fays he, " is a creature

" Of which WE compofe the *diftinguifhing feature*,

" And the beft things the *Commoners* have in their reach,

" Is, *whenever they like, whom they hate to impeach.*

" I would have you, however, this inference draw,

" That impeachment's *not founded, or governed by Law;*

" Our judges, my LORDS, I am free to aver,

" Are much better men than their anceftors were;

" But what makes them fo? 'tis not praying or preaching,

" But the dread they are conftantly in, *of impeaching.*

" My LORDS, we have been in minority long,

" But in this point we had a majority ftrong;

" All claffes of people, all parties agreed,

" That we were engag'd in a praife-worthy deed;

" For, my Lords, we this difficult tafk undertake

" For no other caufe *but for juftice's fake,*

" For the fake of a people *who never complain'd*

" To us of the injuries *they had fuftain'd,*

" And from whom no reward *can be ever obtain'd.*

" The man againft whom all thefe charges we bring

" Made a treaty, my LORDS, with one RAJAH CHEYT

      " SING,

" And from documents which we fhall read, it appears

" That the treaty inviolate lafted three years;

" But I beg I may not do the Criminal wrong,

" For it was not his fault that it lafted fo long,

" It

" It was FRANCIS, who being concern'd in the making
" The treaty, prevented *the Culprit from breaking :*
" For HASTINGS break treaties, and fets them afide
" Ere the ink on the paper is perfectly dried.
" In this cafe the Pris'ner may fhelter his name,
" In the branches wide fpreading of FRANCIS's fame,
" But when the *French* threaten'd Bengal with invafion,
" And finances were low, HASTINGS took the occafion,
" In breaking of treaties, his fkill to exhibit.
" And demanded of CHEYT an *additional tribute.*
" WARREN HASTINGS, my LORDS, to facilitate breaking
" Of treaties, was bufy'd with *dictionary making ;*
" Explanations by JOHNSON, it feems, would not do,
" So he made fome himfelf which are perfectly new."
Here CHARLEY defcanted for more than an hour
Upon HASTINGS's new definition of power,
And 'tis certain, that CHARLEY threw many new lights
Upon Sovereign Princes and Sovereign Rights.
At length he this ultimate inference brought,
That the *Sovereign is all, and the People are nought.*
" This tribute," fays CHARLES, " CHEYT neglected
        " to pay,
" And a thoufand pretences he made for delay ;
" But HASTINGS again with law dictionary, new,
" Proves, that money *as foon as demanded—is due.*

" The

" The money was paid—CHEYT gave HASTINGS a fum,

" To excuse him from paying for ages to come;

" And HASTINGS accordingly took the amount,

" And carry'd the fame *to the public account*;

" But this notwithstanding, he could not difpenfe

" With the tribute demanded on any pretence.

" The RAJAH refifted—and HASTINGS defign'd

" The delinquent should therefore *be heavily fin'd*,

" That is, as the vaffal his mafters withftood,

" His crimes should be turn'd *to the Company's good*:

" But the RAJAH and HASTINGS were ftiff in opinion,

" And the former in confequence loft his dominion."

Here CHARLES a vaft number of arguments brought

To prove that the RAJAH *was never in fault*;

That when HASTINGS the tribute prefum'd to exact,

" He committed a curfed, iniquitous act;

" That no ftate neceffity *ever could be*,

" For a deed fo flagitious, *an adequate plea.*

" My LORDS, it is faid, *a great man* in this ftate

" Thinks HASTINGS is like *Alexander the Great*.

" But the only fimilitude I can difcover,

" Is in the rafh act of that defperate lover,

" Who when with ftrong liquors *made damnably drunk*,

" Perfepolis burnt *for the whim of a punk.*

" My LORDS, I conceive that you need not be told,

" That the eyes of all Europe your actions behold,

" That

" That if all our charges are pleaded in vain,

" You will render Great Britain as odious as Spain;

" But I cannot, however, the notion admit,

" That your LORDSHIPS can ever the Pris'ner acquit;

" But fhould it be fo—we have this fatisfaction,

" WE *can fafely difclaim any fhare in the aftion.*"

CHARLES ended his fpeech and their LORDSHIPS ad-
	journ'd,

And home the delighted fpectators return'd.

February 26, 1788.

LET-

LETTER VI.

THIS day, my dear friend, I've the pleasure to say,
For the *first time* we had an oration from GREY:
For the MANAGERS follow an excellent line,
And alternately suffer each other to shine;
Chief Painter is BURKE, and the head of the trade,
He teaches the use of light, colours, and shade.
Some people will have it, that EDMUND is teaching
His nineteen disciples the *art of impeaching*;
And if this be a truth, I with justice may say,
He has not a scholar more *docile* than GREY:
But in spite of his *training*, BURKE would not confide
Too much on a *Steed*, that had never been try'd:
So he prudently order'd, that GREY should go o'er,
The story which CHARLEY *related before*,
And indeed he exhibited proof of his strength,
By detailing the RAJAH's misfortunes at length;
But as he could add nothing new to the charge,
On the *system of feuds* he was forc'd to enlarge,
And with infinite learning, the Orator shew'd,
That the RAJAH's possession was *not like a feud*;
And the town of Benaris, he seem'd to believe,
Was the *Paradise ancient* of ADAM and EVE;

That

That HASTINGS, like *Satan*, was fond of expelling

The innocent folk from their beautiful dwelling;

And the principal pleafure which HASTINGS enjoy'd,

Was feeing their elegant manfions deftroy'd.

CHEYT SING, in one letter, call'd HASTINGS the
     Mirror

Of the World, but GREY thinks, that it muft be an
     error,

Or if not, it *reflected no object but terror.*

After this, he came forth with fome Latin quotations,

Which are beauty fpots common in modern orations.

Then he humbly requefted, their LORDSHIPS would not

Be offended, at feeing him *angry and hot;*

For a man muft be callous, or worfe than a fool,

Who on fuch occafion is *temp'rate and cool :*

" No *perfonal malice,* no *paffion* I feel,

" Save for *Juftice's fake* an *inordinate zeal;*

" Nor have I, my LORDS, the leaft fhadow of doubt

" Of HASTINGS's *guilt,* or *of making it out.*"

Two hours he dilated, yet faid little more

Than CHARLES had a hundred times utter'd before;

'Twas mere repetition of phrafes, and thence,

I have taken the liberty here to condenfe

The fpeech, and, I hope, without *lofing the fenfe.*

Then papers and witneffes roundly afferted

Some facts, *which have never been yet controverted.*

Next a *charter was read,* by whofe friendly affiftance,
It was prov'd that the *Company has an exiftence.*
Here ended *one day,* and the hearers complain'd
With reafon, of not being much entertain'd.
The next day, the MANAGERS fpent all the time,
To prove againft HASTINGS a radical crime,
Which of all forts of crimes, is affuredly worft;
That the *Prifoner* with *animus malus is curft;*
That his words, and his actions, the MANAGERS find,
Arofe from a *natural badnefs of mind:*
This natural *badnefs,* fome doctors have taught,
Is a human misfortune, inftead of a fault;
And therefore did HASTINGS's counfel contend,
That a proof of this nature could anfwer no end;
But as neither the matter difputed would yield,
The LORDS were of courfe beaten out of the field:
They return'd, and my heroes were fuffer'd to add
New proofs, that the *Prifoner* is *mentally bad.*
Then ANSTRUTHER open'd—A queftion arofe,
(Among the fpectators, as you will fuppofe)
It was, *which is dulleft,* the *Clerical reading,*
Or his *monotonical manner of pleading ?*
This queftion would furnifh an infinite theme
For argument, both being *dull in extreme;*
To decide on this queftion, then baffled the fkill
Of the beft connoiffeurs, as it conftantly will.

Six

Six days in examining proofs were expended,

And I thought with the reft, it would never have ended;

But with pleafure and joy, I was quite overcome,

When ANSTRUTHER faid, *he was going to fum :*

The fummary too was fo *barren* and *dull,*

There was not *one flower* for SIMKIN to cull;

And what muft furprife you ftill farther indeed,

Curiofity found not *one paffable weed.*

And here, my dear Brother, this letter would end,

Were it not for my worthy poetical friend,

Who contended, that BENN had been wickedly joking,

When he fwore that *fnuff taking was equal to fmoaking.*

At the fame time BURKE ftarted a comical notion,

Of a CHANCELLOR *being found deep in devotion;*

This would be it was thought, a ridiculous fight,

The BISHOPS *all laugh'd,* as with reafon they might.

But now, my dear SIMON, I finifh this letter,

With a hope that my next will be longer and better.

February 28th, 1788.

 LET-

LETTER VII.

AS the MANAGERS, Brother, adhere to the plan
Of changing each day, and relieving their man,
This day, Mr. ADAM arose to declare,
That to open the *second Charge fell to his share* :
" My LORDS, I well know 'tis a difficult task,
" And one that I had not the courage to ask :
" I am confcious, indeed, of too many defects,
" But still *I must do*, what *my Gen'ral directs*.
" Friend SHERRY, who formerly open'd this caule,
" In the *Senate*, obtain'd such *uncommon applaufe*,
" That I'm almoft afraid to exhibit my fkill,
" Leſt the people fhould laugh at my fpeaking fo ill.

As lawyers are fond of *nice legal precifion*,
He purfued the profeffional mode of divifion,
And the Charge was *with art anatomical fplit*
Into feveral heads, as the Speaker thought fit;
That OUDE had good things in great plenty and ftore,
But now is reduc'd and exceedingly poor;
That the BEGUMS were *Ladies of quality regal*,
And that their eftates and poffeffions were legal;

And

And next, that 'twas HASTINGS's duty to fee
No infringement was made upon his guarantee,
That though HE in *the name of the Company made it,*
He himfelf was the firft who prefum'd to *invade it ;*
That HASTINGS compell'd the reluctant NABOB
His *Mother, Grandmother, and Kindred to rob ;*
That thefe Princeffes and their defcendants muft rue it,
That they all were diftreft, and that HASTINGS well
     knew it :
That to find fome pretext for this *damnable action,*
He accus'd the poor innocent ladies of *faction ;*
That IMPEY his colleague, collected a pack
Of ftrange affidavits, to prove *white was black.*

    " 'Tis feldom, my LORDS, that an advocate needs,
" To prove criminality latent in deeds,
" Except in *Impeachments,* and there we muft fhow,
" That fome things *are bad,* not *inherently fo :*
" But in HASTINGS a number of actions are *bafe,*
" That would *not be fo,* in *another man's cafe :"*
Next ADAM difplay'd geographical knowledge,
(Which he pick'd up, perhaps, when a *ftudent at College)*
Of the province of *Oude,* he defcrib'd the dimenfion ;
Its *latitude, longitude, fite,* and *extenfion :*
From *Anglefea Ifle,* to the mouth of the Humber,
Is a great many miles, and he ftated the number ;

                        But

But it was not fo long, he moſt folemnly vow'd,
Nor was Ireland fo *wide*, as *the province of Oude*.
" My LORDS, tho' this province was fertile and rich,
" And formerly rais'd to a very high pitch,
" No fooner with us had it form'd a *conneƈtion*,
" Than it paid very dear for our *purchas'd proteƈtion*;
" Of that treaty with us, th'extravagant price,
" Was the *Robilla War*—and 'twas EDMUND's advice
" An *additional Charge* againſt HASTINGS to make it,
" But we could not prevail on the COMMONS to take it."
Here ADAM to ſhew his *rhetorical powers*,
Gave their LORDSHIPS a handful of brilliant flowers;
He faid, that the Sun which on *avarice roſe*,
Its meridian was *cruelty*, *horror*, and *woes*,
And in *blood was its ſetting*, and *ultimate cloſe*.
And next he proceeded, with care to defcribe
The BEGUMS *of Oude*, and their *dignify'd tribe* :
He detail'd an account of their *Siſters* and *Brothers*,
Of their *Uncles* and *Aunts*, of their *Fathers* and *Mothers*;
After which, it was clearly and learnedly ſhown,
That the caſh which they legally had was *their own*;
" But, my LORDS," faid the Speaker, " I told you before,
" That the NABOB through us grew *exceedingly poor*,
" And having for money no other refource,
" From his parent he wanted to *take it by force*,

" But

" But HASTINGS, my LORDS, it appears at that time,

" *Prevented the Son from committing the crime.*"

Next ADAM in raptures proceeded to quote

A letter, which one of the Princeſſes wrote,

He ſaid, *Queen* ELIZABETH never wrote better,

Nor could CECIL her Miniſter pen ſuch a letter;

It was *ſo pathetic, ſo moving, ſo pretty,*

That HASTINGS's breaſt was *affeéted with pity.*

" When HASTINGS," ſays he, " ſpeaks the *language of*

   " *nature,*

" There is not a more *intelleétual creature :*

" But when he would cover ſome *aétion impure,*

" His ſtile is *perplex'd,* and his language *obſcure :*

Then ADAM diſplay'd in the language of *thunder,*

How the BEGUMS *had ſuffer'd* from HASTINGS's *plunder;*

But it chanc'd in the midſt of this violent prating,

He the *Priſ'ner accus'd* of *a letter miſdating,**

Who whiſper'd, 'TIS FALSE, to ſome friend that was

   near,

But lów as it was, ADAM happen'd to hear :

Not *lightning,* which burſts from th' eleétrical cloud,

Not the *voice of the Heavens,* when it *thunders aloud,*

Not the *burſt of a gun,* not a *mine that is ſprung,*

Could in any degree match the MANAGER's *tongue.*

---

* This error in which Mr. Adam was involved, he might have eſ-
caped, if the Managers who had authority to ſend for perſons, papers,
and records, had examined Sir John Macpherſon, or Mr. Auriol.

" My

" My Lords, when I make an addrefs unto you,
" Shall any man dare to *fuppofe it untrue ?*
" In the high fituation in which I am plac'd,
" Shall a whifper efcape from that *Being difgrac'd ?*
" I cannot fupport it—I cannot endure it—
" I am ftung to the quick, and there's nothing to cure it;
" *Oh fave me, protect me,* my Lords, if you can,
" From the *whifpers and words* of that *infolent man :*
" 'Tis far, far below me, to afk *fatisfaction*
" In private of him for this *damnable action :*"
No perfon could judge where his paffion would lead,
If his temperate friends had not hinder'd his fpeed;
He recover'd a little, and went on to draw,
Conclufions from *arguments founded on law ;*
He belong'd to the law, and he freely allow'd,
'Twas an honour that made him exceedingly proud,
That the Begums *in Court* fhould be *publicly try'd,*
He faid, was a point that could not be deny'd,
Before Hastings and Impey their property took,
As is written in every juridical book :
Some perfons who heard what the Manager fpoke,
Burft out in a laugh at his ludicrous joke;
They faid, that the pleader in fury of diction,
Forgot the extent of the law's jurifdiction :
Others *fmil'd with ineffable pity, and then*
Reflected too hard on profeffional men;

I have

I have to obferve, that in ADAM's oration
Came frequently in an *old Latin quotation*;
But I could not diftinguifh, fo quick was it faid,
The *language alive*, from the *language that's dead :*
At length, my dear Brother, this mafs of confufion,
After *four hours fpeaking*, came fafe to conclufion.
Here then for the prefent, my letter I end,
But you'll foon hear again from your Brother and Friend.

April 15, 1788.

As my heroes all thirſt for the *making orations*;
Mr. PELHAM this day roſe to make obſervations:
He ſaid, he was *order'd to comment at large*,
Upon HASTINGS's *anſwer to this preſent charge*;
That the labours they had to get over, were more
Than any Committee had ſuffer'd before;
For the Pris'ner poſſeſs'd an *extenſive connection*,
And *friends* who afforded him *mighty protection*;
This, however, he could not conſider a crime,
Except at the *preſent* unfortunate time:
'Tis our pride to have friends, but in HASTINGS's caſe,
The converſe of this propoſition takes place.

And indeed, my dear Brother, I can't but remark,
There is ſomething in HASTINGS exceedinly dark;
For that which in others is reckon'd a *merit*,
Is in HASTINGS a ſign of *malevolent ſpirit*:
In his *words*, in his *actions*, and even his *thoughts*,
The MANAGERS ſee *unatonable faults*:
To return—PELHAM ſaid, that all HASTINGS's friends
Were *wretches, who ſerv'd his deteſtable ends*;

'Twas

'Twas a comfort, howe'er, that the MANAGERS had

Some witneffes, not fo *corruptedly bad :*

" 'Tis faid, that in feizing the Princeffes' treafure,

" Neceffity urg'd and dictated the meafure ;

" But fuppofing it fo, he committed a blunder,

" In drawing refources from rapine and plunder :

" Befides, I can prove beyond all contradiction,

" That this *ftate neceffity* is but a fiction ;

" But fuppofing it real, all people agree,

" State neceffity is a tyrannical plea."

Here fome who remember'd *what came from that quarter,*

When the party fell foul of the *Company's charter,*

Who had not feen much of the tergiverfations

Of Orators modern, when making orations,

With wonder were ftruck, *that they now fhould deny*

That plea, upon which they wifh'd *then* to rely.

Then PELHAM attention requefted to call,

To the fate of the ladies lodg'd in the *Khord Mhal;*

A picture of horrible fuff'rings he drew,

Which his confcience declar'd were infallibly true ;

Thofe dames, the compaffionate MANAGER faid,

Were *driv'n to defpair* by the *wanting of bread* ;

And he fadly lamented that damfels fo fair,

Should from *wifhes ungratified fink in defpair* ;

At the centinels pofted, the ladies threw dirt,

Who were frighted, it feems, but not mortally hurt;

They

They threaten'd to throw themselves over the wall,
And to dash out their brains by the force of the fall;
Within the Zenana, no longer would they,
In a *starving condition* impatiently stay,
But break out of prison, and all run away:
One night they had fram'd some uncommon designs,
And had form'd and arrang'd themselves into three lines;
In the firft line their children, so pretty, so dear,
In the second the ladies, their flaves in the rear,
But what they intended, did never appear:
One day when the ladies were difmally weeping,
Letafut Darogah, who had them in keeping,
To filence their noife had no other recourfe,
Save driving them into the Convent by force:
The Sepoys were call'd, and a battle enfu'd,
The ladies were warm, and the Sepoys were rude;
The former threw bricks, and the latter threw ftones,
Without breaking of heads, without fracturing bones.
At length after fighting, and ftriving in vain,
The ladies return'd to their prifon again:
Soon after this difmal, this fhocking adventure,
The Begums apartment they wanted to enter;
But the Begum hard-hearted deny'd them admiffion,
So they went back again in a mournful condition;
But what was the worft of this accident new,
The Sepoys, alas! had the Ladies in view.

Here

Here PELHAM's fpeech ended, which from the beginning,

Had taken *three hours*, in the carding and fpinning.

Then SHERRY arofe, and complain'd of the trouble,

Which HASTINGS's counfel were rendering double;

That making to evidence *frequent objection*

Did harm to their ftories, and broke their connection;

That themfelves were of evidence *Judges the beft*,

As to *what fhould be read*, and *what fhou'd be fupprefs.*

Then they call'd Major SCOTT, who is HASTINGS's
 friend,

And afk'd him *by whom the Defences were penn'd:*

He was *help'd by his friends* being *ftraighten'd for time,*

Which proves, like the reft, *an additional crime;*

Thus ended this day, and at meeting the next

We heard SHERRY preach upon quite a new text:

And in order to cover the Pris'ner with *blame,*

He offer'd in evidence *general fame;*

Common fame, he allow'd, was indifferent proof,

But in HASTINGS's *cafe, it would do well enough:*

And tho', fays my hero, it does not appear,

The report fpread fo far as to HASTINGS's ear,

Yet whether he *heard it or not,* 'tis the fame,

He might, had he liften'd, have heard *common fame.*

Then witneffes many were call'd to the bar,

Till at length EDMUND call'd upon *Prince Cantemar,*

Whofe

Whofe evidence, LAW and his brothers withftood,
But their LORDSHIPS declar'd, it was evidence good :
BURKE took up his book, and proceeded to read
A chapter intitled *Sultana Valide* :
He read how the Sultans their mothers refpected,
That maternal injunctions were never neglected ;
In Mahommedan countries, the Mother Sultana
By cuftom prefides o'er the Sultan's Zenana ;
For the ufe of her fon, the kind matron provides
A plentiful ftock of young beautiful brides :
In the feaft of Bairam, a frefh Virgin is led
Each night by the Mother to Royalty's bed ;
And tho' Virgins are fent by a three-tail'd Bafhaw,
He cannot, according to Muffelmen Laws,
Touch one without making a wicked *faux pas :*
If the Sultan, perchance, has a mind for fome other,
And gets her unknown to the Emprefs his mother,
It highly reflects on the Dowager's honor,
And fixes difgrace everlafting upon her.
Here ended this day, and their LORDSHIPS arofe,
So my Letter in confequence draws to a clofe ;
But permit me to tell, e'er I lay down my pen,
How the ftory affected the women and men ;
Thofe thought it a *wafteful profufion of charms,*
To fleep but *one night* in the *Emperor's arms,*

And

And lamented *their* fortune who after *one night,*
Were *for ever secluded from tasting delight :*
These *envy'd the Prince,* and would fain introduce
A custom so good into general use :
To the trial our Ladies impatiently run,
And expect repetition of similar fun.

April 19th, 1788.

E   LETTER

LETTER IX.

Y OU complain, my dear Friend, of the time which
    is paſt,
Since you and your friends were amus'd with my laſt;
But pray how am I to regale you with fun,
When BURKE and the MANAGERS treat us with none?
Beſides, I've been troubled ſo much with the vapours,
At hearing the Clerk read ſuch *bundles of papers*;
I aſſure you, ſo many dry tales have been read,
So many inſipid tautologies ſaid,
That I ſeldom am free from a pain in my head :
And alas ! 'tis with infinite ſorrow I ſay,
Six weeks in this manner are ſquander'd away :
But to ſhow you I'm yet in the land of the living,
And able to write, I'm determin'd on giving
Of the Queſtions and Anſwers a ſlight intimation,
As a ſpecimen only of examination :
As ſoon as the Court is prepar'd to begin,
SHERRY riſes, and begs to call MIDDLETON in,
A name at whoſe ſound there's a *general grin*.
Five days has poor MIDDLETON ſweated and ſtew'd;
Their queſtions are *artful*, his anſwers are *ſhrewd* :

He

He was afk'd if the Eunuch ADMAS *had a child*;

Lord THURLOW look'd *black*, and the *Ladies all fmil'd*;

The witnefs made anfwer, I really can't fay,

The powers of his mem'ry were melted away.

Q. Have you *e'er feen the* BEGUMS ? He anfwer'd I've
not.

Q. Pray *mention* their perfons.—*A.* Indeed I've *forgot.*

Q. What may in rebellion your principles be,
Or can you the probable confequence fee
Of men rifing in arms and o'er-running the nation ?

A. Indeed 'tis a queftion of deep fpeculation.

Q. When the Eunuchs were fetter'd, pray what did they
feel ?
Were they thinking of poifon, the rack, and the
wheel ?
Or what do think you might have been their intentions ?

A. I concern not myfelf about their apprehenfions.

Q. How many young damfels liv'd in the Khord Mhal?

A. I do not believe I can recollect all.

Q. Say, what were their wifhes and what was their view?

A. I cannot remember that ever I knew.

Q. When they threaten'd to throw themfelves over
the wall,
What induc'd them to hazard the getting a fall ?
A. I do not remember they did fo at all.

                    Q. Why

Q. Why did GORDON addrefs to the BEGUM that Letter?

A. He himfelf is in Court and can anfwer you better.

Q. You were at Lucknow in the year eighty-two;

A. I'm inclin'd to believe what you fay may be true.

Q. Have you any doubts of it? And if fo, how many?

A. I believe not: I think that I cannot have any.

Q. The Pris'ner's defence, did you pen part or not?

A. I had fome converfation with Major John SCOTT.

Q. With the counfel of HASTINGS, were your at the
  Hall?*

A. I might accidentally give them a call.

Q. What, go accidentally with Major SCOTT?

A. I really don't know, if I did I've forgot.

Q. Do children in India their Parents efteem?
  Do they love their Mammas'? and how ftrong do
   you deem
  Their affection may be? Or pray can you tell,
  If Papa and Mamma are lov'd equally well?

A. Some perhaps love their Father and fome love their
  Mother,
  And fome children love neither one nor the other.

Q. Does the Son by the Laws of the *Coran* fucceed
  To the Father's eftates?—*A.* Yes: the eldeft indeed.

* Drapers' Hall.

Q. May

Q. May the Mother that property legally keep,

Lodg'd where she and her husband did usually sleep?

A. I am rather inclin'd to be led, I confess,

To believe that the wife no such right does possess.

In this manner was MIDDLETON badger'd and flurry'd,

Like a bull at a stake by fierce animals worry'd :

Mean while the severest satiric remarks

Were made on his words, by those *critical sparks :*

Till at length LAW requested their LORDSHIPS would

take

Compassion upon him for *Clemency's sake.*

In the vast heap of questions I almost forgot,

To relate SHERRY's *conduct* to *Major John* SCOTT;

This witness he press'd very hard to produce

Some private remarks for the MANAGER's *use,*

Private Letters and all, this inquisitor keen,

Maintains by themselves may be *properly seen.*

But in this the arch MANAGER did not succeed;

It was thought by the LORDS an *indelicate deed :*

Sir ELIJAH was call'd, and a number of men,

All examin'd and question'd again and again :

But as there was nought entertaining and new,

It could answer no purpose to write it to you :

So weary was I with this Examination,

That I almost resolv'd to desert my narration :

At length, SHERRY fuddenly ended my forrow,
By declaring he meant to fum up on the morrow;
He will fum up the whole of the Charge as he goes, ⎤
But amidft all the fummings up, *under the rofe*, ⎬
I would afk when he means to fum up what he owes. ⎦

May 5th, 1788.

LETTER X.

THE IMPEACHMENT.

YOU ASSURE me, *dear Brother*, the comical tales
I've related, amufe our *acquaintance* in WALES;
You beg me, as SHERRY proceeds to Impeach,
To give you in rhyme the *contents of his fpeech.*
The tafk is too hard—for the fpeech is fo fine,
It efcapes fuch a dull underftanding as mine.
Howe'er, to oblige you as far as I can,
I'll begin an oration as SHERRY began.
When the LORDS were affembl'd, and fet in their places,
He rofe up, *brimful of theatrical graces :*
" Permit me, my LORDS, ere I fpeak more at large,
" To difclaim every *motive* for making this charge.
" Has the NABOB complain'd ? Is the Prifoner accus'd
" At the fuit of *thofe ladies* we fay he abus'd ?
" 'Tis the caufe of mankind, led by EDMUND the brave,
" His object is man, from *man's bafenefs* to fave.
" The MINISTER PITT fays, " *the Treafury is drain'd ;*"
" But all muft admit *they are much entertain'd.*
" However, I'd have it be well underftood,
" If we have *any motive*, 'tis certainly good.

E 4

" My

" My LORDS, you expect proofs *conclusive and strong*;

" But in that expectation, *your Lordships are wrong* :

" From documents written, no proof can we draw,

" Nor can *any one* swear—to what *nobody saw*.

" I'm not pleading excuse for our failing in proof,

" For tho' we bring none, *we* can make out *enough* :

" I shall make out enough from the Pris'ner's defence,

" By giving *my* meaning, and taking *his* sense.

" 'Tis said, when the House *a delinquent impeaches*,

" The MANAGERS should be correct in their speeches;

" That is, they should make a plain simple narration

" Of facts, well attested, without aggravation :

" That *legal chicanery* should not assist,

" To give the *plain sense* an *ingenious twist*.

" But, *my* LORDS, by your leave, the distinction I'll
       trace,

" Betwixt *misdemeanour* and *capital case* ;

" For unless we were certain your LORDSHIPS would
      " hang him,

" The MANAGERS' tongues claim a *licence* to bang him.

" The PRISONER, my LORDS, under various pretences,

" Has set up at times a long string of defences :

" My LORDS, there *was one* to the COMMONS address'd,

" But that to *your Lordships* is reckoned *the best* ;

" It seems that the former was *hastily* penn'd

" By those that would do it—*acquaintance* or *friend* :

" And

" And as all common men are but commonly wife,
" For the COMMONS, a *common defence* would fuffice—
" And finding *our charges* divided and fplit,
" Each *journeyman* took what the MASTER thought fit.
" My *fkill in finance*, Mr. SHORE, is your lot :
" My *confiftence* to prove, I rely upon SCOTT,
" And on MIDDLETON's *memory*, when I've forgot.
" He thought, as the COMMONS themfelves were de-
    " puted,
" The COMMONS, by deputy, might be confuted;
" But now that your LORDSHIPS have call'd him before
    " you,
" At your Bar it behoves him to tell his own ftory.
" But, my LORDS, we object to this fhifting of ground—
" For the conduct of journeymen mafters are bound.
" Would it not be, my LORDS, moft furprizing and
    " ftrange,
" If EDMUND our CHIEF, *his opinion fhould change ?*
" If having perfuaded the COMMONS to join
" In a vote, he fhould take up a different line,
" And fay, " *The impeachment was* yours, and *not* mine :"
" That he ever was HASTINGS's *friend* in his heart,
" Tho' compell'd to accept of a MANAGER's part ?"

While SHERRY was fpeaking, I could not conceive,
Why the LORDS and the COMMONS all laugh'd in their
    fleeve :

Why

Why Burke fear'd that Sherry was out of his track,
Why Fox's dark face look'd a little more black—
But fince I have learnt, that the picture he drew,
Was the *likenefs of fomething* that moft people knew—
That Burke and Charles Fox had conjointly brought
    forth
The very fame arguments—*verfus*—Lord North.
That Charles would not " truft his dear perfon a
    " minute"
Alone with Lord North, fo much danger was in it.—
And Burke, with *impeachments* the Houfe to fupply,
Carry'd fome in his pocket, " cut ready and dry."
1 am told, it has long been his cuftom to take 'em
Wherever he goes, like a Prieft's " Vade Mecum."
St. Stephen's refounded with Scaffold and Block,
North fell from the Treafury Bench with a fhock.
" Throw a bone to a dog, and no longer he fnarls,"—
So North threw a bone out to Edmund and Charles;
That is, they determin'd, if Pitt had not feen 'em,
To fhare all the *loaves and the fifhes* between 'em.
From that moment have Charley and Edmund
    agreed,
That North muft be honeft and noble indeed !
Burke fearches for elegant phrafe to commend :—
And Charles too is happy to call him his friend.

I

As

As Sherry in fpeaking is fond of precifion,

He adopts the *theatrical mode of divifion :*

That is, he arranges the *plot* and the *facts,*

And the play will confift of a *number of acts.*

One act was gone through when the poft-bell was ring-
     ing,

Which unluckily puts a full ftop to my finging.

Howe'er, if this letter can add to your pleafure,

I'll fend you another as foon as I've leifure.

June 5th, 1788.

LET-

LETTER XI.

AGAIN, *my dear Brother*, I take up the quill,
My debt to *difcharge*, and my promife fulfill.
Thus SHERRY began :—" Now, my Lords, I proceed
" Some loofe and confus'd affidavits to read :
" I'll allow to be true every word they contain ;
" But permit *me* their *meaning* and *fenfe* to explain.
" My Lords, there was fwearing by foot and dragoons ;
" By *vollies* fome fwore, and fome fwore by *platoons* ;
" Thefe fwearings I call, SIR ELIJAH's *collection*,
" Intended to prove a well known infurrection :
" But, my Lords, you fhall prefently fee me victorious
" Over this infurrection, however notorious ;
" After what I have faid, will the *counfel* infift
" That any rebellion did ever exift ?
" This point being fettled, I now take my courfe
" To ASOPH UL DOWLAH's attendants and horfe :
" That he had two thoufand, the *counfel* contended,
" But that's a pofition that can't be defended.
" My Lords, I infift that *two hundred's* the moft ;
" The reft had deferted, were jaded, or loft :
" Befides, I requeft it may not be forgot
" The rate ASOPH travell'd, *full gallop* or *trot* ;

2

" And

" And 'twas right that the NABOB ſhould travel *incog.*
" By poſt or by *Dáuck*, without baggage or clog,
" To ſuppreſs, like himſelf, *a rebellion incog.*
" But I'll give them two thouſand, with *Bhangies* and
   " *Coolies*,
" With elephants, camels, with *hackrees and doolies!*
" The *counſel* ſome proof have endeavour'd to bring,
" That the BEGUMS lent aid to the RAJAH CHEYT SING,
" One thouſand *Nejeebs*—but I boldly avow
" They were fellows with *matchlocks*, detach'd from
   " LUCKNOW;
" But where ever they came from, I care not about
   " 'em,
" For your Lordſhips ſhall ſee, in five minutes I'll rout
   " 'em.
" SADUT ALLY, they ſay, in conſpiracy join'd,
" And I aſk'd Sir ELIJAH, why HE was not fin'd?
" Sir ELIJAH, my Lords, gave a very good reaſon,
" —The man who is *poor*, can't be *guilty of treaſon.*
" His ſafety was then to *inſolvency* due—
" *An axiom, I find, inconteſtably true.*
" My Lords, I ſhall prove this commotion and riſing
" Was not of my Ladies the BEGUMS' deviſing;
" And their *Eunuchs*, poor creatures, ſo gentle and mild!
" Are unable to injure man, woman, or child.
" Colonel

" Colonel Hannay himfelf, I can prove, was the man

" From whofe cruelties all the difturbance began :

" And this to eftablifh, *no witnefs* I call,

" Save the elegant letters of *Naylor* and *Hall*.

" The Begums' Jaghire, Major *Naylor* march'd thro',

" 'Twixt the *Goomty* and *Gogra*, his route to purfue;

" Where for fome little time his battalions were halted,

" Some Rajah to quell, who, he fays, had revolted.

" This revolt, I prefume, muft have been a miftake,

" So I pafs over that, for his memory's fake.

" But when to the country of Hannay he came,

" He found nothing elfe but combuftion and flame.

" The army of rebels the *Major* o'erthrew ;

" He frighted their heroes ;—he wounded and flew.

" Thefe poor dying wretches, that made no refiftance,

" He offer'd to cure :—They refus'd his affiftance.

" The *counfel* may fay, 'tis from prejudice ftrong,

" Thofe men their exiftence refus'd to prolong ;

" That a *foreigner's touch* would a Bramin pollute ;

" But prejudice *now* 'tis my turn to difpute.

" Thefe folks were from fuch foolifh prejudice free—

" They were patriots, my Lords, of the higheft degree ;

" They died that their blood to *their* Gods *might afcend*,

" Who till now to their cries did not chufe to attend !"

Four hours and a half, ere he came to a clofe,

Did SHERRY declaim on fuch topics as thofe:

He ended at length with a compliment fine

To BURKE, whom he ftil'd " fomething more than

    " divine !"

For giving himfelf this occafion to fhine.

And BURKE, to whom nothing's more odious and hate-

    ful,

Than the man who for favour conferr'd is ungrateful,

Opportunity found, with *large int'reft* to pay

The compliments back, on the very fame day.

One man had, it feems, the prefumption to ftate,

The IMPEACHMENT *Expence* was enormoufly great:

When BURKE, in a moment, fprung up in his place,

And cry'd, as he ftar'd the man full in the face,

" *Such ftinginefs, Sir, would a nation difgrace !*

" After all the fine things we've heard SHERIDAN fay,

" He's a pitiful wretch who *refufes to pay:*

" Now that genius has blinded our eyes with its flafh,

" Can we *look at accounts ?* Can we fum up our cafh ?

" After foaring above all the regions of fenfe,

" Can we tumble fo low as to *think about pence ?*

" Has not SHERRY, this morning, expos'd to your view,

" All the beauties of *Thefpis,* and *Cicero* too ?

" To the BISHOPS, he gave an example of preaching ;

" To the COMMONS, a model of future impeaching ;

" HIS-

" Historians, hereafter, fhall copy his di&ion,

" And Poëts themfelves may learn *leffons of fiction* :

" Rhetoricians are taught the arrangements of *flowers*,

" To the *bufkin* and *fock* he has given new powers;

" The Painters may learn finer pictures to draw,

" And the Judges new Modes of *interpreting law.*

" From him may the Orator learn to prevail,

" By action and found, when his arguments fail:

" The Philosopher too, may learn nature to fift;

" The Attorney, to cloak a bad caufe with a fhift.

" Now fince ev'ry profeffion fome benefit draws,

" Can we think for a moment of *ftarving the caufe !*"

No fooner was Edmund fat down, than a *fpark*
Arofe in his place, and begg'd leave to remark,
" That himfelf and fome others remember'd the day,
" When the Man *who fo freely votes thoufands away,*
" For hearing a fpeech, or for feeing a play,
" Was once in his Majesty's *Kitchen* fo fparing,
" As to *weigh out the cheefe,* nay, to *pocket the paring !*"

And now, *my dear* Brother, I lay down my pen,
Which after next Tuefday I'll take up again.

June 8th, 1788.

LETTER

LETTER XII.

DEAR BROTHER—

WERE it not that I fear you would deem it neglect,
Or accuse, me, perhaps, of the *want of respect*,
I would pass o'er in silence the Speech of this day;
For SIMKIN, like SHERRY, wants something to say.
The PEERESSES thought there would rise a *new Sun*,
And that former out-doings would now be out-done!
At *Six* in the morning, 'tis said they arose—
By *Eight* dress'd their heads, by *Nine* put on their
    cloaths—
By *Ten* took their places, in high expectation
Of seeing this SHERIDAN *act an oration*.
By *half after Twelve*, or at farthest by *One*,
The PEERS were assembled—the PLAY was begun.
Two hours, he harangu'd, but I little remember,
" Save IMPEY and DAVY, and 12*th of December*."
He describ'd a circuitous string of suggestions,
And put to *the Counsel* some very close questions.
He knew he might safely their answers defy,
Since the forms of the COURT *would not let them reply*.

F

As

As the sense of his speech was but ill understood
By myself, I conclude 'twas uncommonly good.
When his genius inflammable rose to its height,
Like Lunardi's *Balloon*, it escap'd from our sight :
As when some Balloon at its equipoise pitch,
Loses part of its air by the *break of a stitch*,
The *high-flying* Hero no remedy knows,
And the car tumbles down with more speed than it rose :
So the high-flying Sherry discover'd at length,
That an Orator may soar too high for his strength :
For just as his voice was rais'd up to its top,
The Court, with surprize, saw him suddenly stop.
Then Adam stepp'd forward, and said, " *that his friend*
" *Was seiz'd with a--a--trifling—and therefore must end.*"
This accident, Brother, must greatly diminish
The length of my letter ; and here I should finish,
Were it not that I heard some *odd jocular sparks*
Conversing together, and making remarks.
A *trifling !* said one, as he laugh'd very hearty,
Has long been the common *disease of the party.*
Lord Crop, who is one of your old fashion'd Peers,
That wants to find Meaning *in all that he hears,*
Said, " Orators *now* were not fram'd to his taste,
" They carry no *weight*, they're constructed for haste ;
" And like our *Mail Coaches*, that travel so fast,
" Must now and then get an unfortunate cast."

One

One Gentleman faid, " where he reafons on facts,
" *We find* SHERRY *dull*; but whenever *he acts*,
" In five minutes time he difplays to our view,
" The *Tragic*, the *Comic*, the *Pantomime* too,"
He added, that all the great men of our nation
Would adopt a new plan for their fons' education ;
They find it now ufelefs to lay in a ftock
Of logic, by reading *fuch authors as* LOCKE ;
They find *graceful action* and *elegant diction*
More pow'rful than reafon to carry conviction :
So a new fet of tutors they mean to engage——
The very beft actors they find on the ftage ;
Some *Mafter*, like SIDDONS, whofe pathos excels——
Or whofe leffons fhall imitate *nature* like WELLS.
And the lawyers, it feems, who attend the King's Courts,
No longer will trouble themfelves with reports.
The Student finds COKE *upon* LYTTLETON dry,
And with *Johnfon* and *Shakfpeare* his place will fupply ;
In fhort, the *old* ORATOR's * anfwer is true——
" That *Action*, and *nothing but* ACTION, will do !"
Here then I conclude, and fhall filent remain,
Till SHERRY begins his Oration again.

  June 13th, 1788.

---

* Alluding to the Philofopher, who being afked what was the firft
qualification of an Orator, anfwered, *Action* ; what the fecond, *Action* ; what the third, *Action* ; meaning thereby, that *Action* was
enough for an Orator.

F 2

LET-

LETTER XIII.

DEAR BROTHER, at laſt I've the pleaſure to ſay,
That the Orator clos'd his Oration this day.
Tho' EDMUND *his chief*, who ſuppoſes the ſtrength
And effect of a Speech correſpond with its length,
In a whiſper obſerv'd—" Now you find yourſelf ſtronger,
" You might as well ſpeak for a *week or two longer.*"

Thus SHERRY began :—" Much indebted I own
" Myſelf to this COURT, for the favor they've ſhewn ;
" My LORDS, you'll excuſe my again going o'er
" The ground I have travers'd ſo often before ;
" Your LORDSHIPS remember I left off with reading
" The *narrative part*—and I now am proceeding
" To bring from behind the thick miſt of confuſion,
" *A fraudulent friendſhip*, and *friendly colluſion.*
" Theſe things came to light from the reading a letter—
" A *private epiſtle*, and ſo much the better—
" When in private and public we find contradiction,
" That letter which tends to the *Priſoner's conviction*—

" That

" That Letter alone we bring forward to view—

" Convinc'd that none elfe can be poffibly true.

" The Pris'ner, it feems, thought it matter of wonder,

" That MIDDLETON gave him no part of the Plunder;

" That the diff'rence 'twixt him and his Agent was wider

" Than that between LION and *Lion's Provider :*

" That at leaft it became an *obedient Jackal*

" To remember the *Lion,* and not fwallow all.

" My LORDS, tho' we make out no *pofitive Proof,*

" That thefe were his thoughts, we've fufpicion enough ;

" And I truft that this Court will give ready admiffion,

" In *failure of Proofs, to* ASSERTED SUSPICION.

" My LORDS, there have been many Letters fuppreft,

" Some made for the purpofe, and fome better dreft.

" There was one from the NABOB, by which it appears

" He wifh'd not to take the BOW BEGUM's *Jaghires.*

" Thefe PRINCESSES had (what our Ladies would think

" Not uncommon) a *whim for good victuals and drink*—

" Too long in the habit of cutting and carving,

" To relifh the Fafhion of pinching and ftarving.

" Now the Pris'ner, who wickedly wanted to force

" Thofe Ladies to follow fome defperate courfe,

" Thought nothing fo likely to ftir up a riot,

" As to *weaken the Tea,* or to *alter their Diet.*

" Not all the tyrannical acts of paft Ages,

" Not TACITUS, *No !* not the luminous Pages

F 3

" Of

" Of GIBBON *himself,* can an inftance produce

" Of Authority turn'd to fo wicked a ufe;

" No cruelties equal were exercis'd in .

" This World, fince the days of ORIGINAL SIN,

" To the forcing a tender affectionate Son,

" To act by *his Mother as* ASOPH has done.

" He forgot in our SHAKSPEARE that precept divine,

" *Let thy mind be untainted, and nothing defign*

" *Againft thy dear Mother !* No, this he forgot—

" Or if he remember'd, regarded it not.

" 'Twas hoped, that the BEGUMS would openly rife,

" And affemble a Hoft by the found of their cries;

" That HASTINGS might find fome excufe for the
        " meafure

" He meant to adopt with refpect to their Treafure;

" But the BEGUMS, my LORDS, tho' of millions bereft,

" *Could live pretty well upon that which was left :*

" They are ftricken in years, they are gentle and meek;

" No refentment they feel, and no vengeance they feek,

" E'en now that ourfelves with fuch zeal are purfuing

" This Man, THEY *would weep* if they heard of his ruin.

" 'Twas expedient, my LORDS, that thefe Dames fhou'd
        " rebel,

" Or be thought fo at leaft, which would anfwer as well.

" So IMPEY fet off, and collected a pack

" Of ftrange *Affidavits,* fome white and fome black,

" And return'd with a budget brim full in a crack.

" One

" One day, the CHIEF JUSTICE was travelling post—

" The next at LUCKNOW, when, like *Old* HAMLET's

    " *Ghoſt,*

" *Swear! Swear!* you muſt *Swear!* was *Old* TRUE-

    " PENNY's cry,

" To thoſe who ſtood near, and to thoſe that paſs'd by."

" My LORDS, this great Man, in aſſeſſing the rate

" Of Crimes, had an eye to the wants of the State:

" JUSTINIAN and TIMUR he treated as fools;

" And was guided by COCKER's *Numerical Rules.*

" *Ye* GUARDIANS *of Juſtice,* to you I appeal—

" Shall *Private* give way to the *General Weal?*

" *Ye* PRELATES, to whom our Religion belongs,

" Our Country to ſave, may we do private wrongs?

" To decide on this Queſtion, my LORDS, is your lot,

" Whether HASTINGS's conduct was uſeful or not?

" Let the TRUTH *but* APPEAR, and the Battle is won,

" The Verdict is ours!—Now, my LORDS, *I have done!*'

The *Gallery folk,* who, miſled by the ſport,

Conceiv'd 'twas a *Play-Houſe, inſtead of a* COURT;

And thinking the Actor uncommonly good,

They CLAPP'D, and cry'd " BRAVO!" as loud as they

    could.

Then EDMUND gave SHERRY a hearty embrace, ⎫

And cry'd, as he ſputter'd all over his face, ⎬

" *At Supper this night thou ſhalt have the* FIRST PLACE!" ⎭

            On

On thy Leader's right hand be thy dignify'd feat;
Fat Beef and fat Mutton shall garnish thy Plate;
And when thou hast supp'd, to enliven the soul,
Shall Claret and Burgundy fill up thy Bowl!
The HEROES, who long and successfully fight,
From the *Edicts of* HOMER establish a right
To enjoy the rich Feast with BRISEIS at night.

And now, till the Court shall think fit to renew
The Trial, *dear* BROTHER, I bid you adieu.

June 18th, 1788.

BROTHER SIMON IN WALES

TO

SIMKIN THE SECOND IN LONDON.

FORGIVE me, *Dear Sim*, if I'm not deeply fmit-
    ten,
With your half dozen Letters fo fluently written;
And fince, after SHERIDAN's heart-ftirring fummons,
A paufe is judg'd *prudent* by LORDS as by COMMONS:
And leifure may leave you to liften inclin'd,
I embrace a fit moment to tell you my mind.

Methinks, *Brother Sim*, your adventure was bold,
When you ftepp'd forth an ape of *your Namefake of old;*
That Simkin fo pleafant, whofe well-mingled fatire
Ow'd no poifon to Party, no gall to ill-nature;
From Talents and Virtue withholding his fneer,
At folly HE laugh'd, and the laugh was *fincere:*
In Vanity's Vortex his models he chofe,
And *Coxcombs* and *Pedants* alone were his foes.

I

But

But you, *my dear Brother*, with feelings more nice,
Find ridicule lurking in—horror of Vice;
And efforts of Genius acute and refin'd,
That honour our Country, our Age, and Mankind,
Deform'd in your Verfe, take a farcical mien,
Where pleafantry check'd, wears the features of Spleen,
Too angry for Humour, for Cenfure too gay,
Your irony dies in plain ftory away.
And, while we lament that your Arrows are fhot,
Where Envy and Party in vain feek a blot,
We cannot avoid, *Brother Simkin*, be fure,
Sufpecting your motives may not be quite pure.
And thus, when you tell us you're glad to the heart,
" * *That the* ORATOR SHERRY *has finifh'd his part;*"
When you fay " *that fome Letters are meant for* CONVIC-
" TION,"
We own that you there drop the *language of Fiction.*
Beware, *Brother Simkin*, this Painter fublime,
Who has lately engrofs'd your befpattering Rhyme,
In a playful effufion of Fancy has fhewn,
A PORTRAIT that fome may miftake for *your own:*
A *Plagiary Author*, Retailer of Scraps,
Purloin'd from a Brother—from ANSTEY perhaps:
All Candour without, all Envy within,
A fmile ill concealing the horrible grin;

* Vide Simkin's 6th Letter.

Who

Who fain would be witty and archly fevere,
While from eyes fwoln with rage, gufhes forth the hot
    tear.
The *Picture in* PARSONS yet gladdens the fcene,
Nor need I repeat, 'tis SIR FRETFUL I mean.

  Then warn'd, *my dear Brother*, with SHERRY have
    done,
Nor hang up your Blanket 'twixt us and the Sun;
Fot lo! through the pores of your thread-bare defign,
The rays of the God more refplendently fhine.

    July 1ft, 1788.

LETTER XV.

SIMKIN THE SECOND,

NOTICING SIMON.

SOME fellow, *dear Brother*, affuming your name,
My Letters to you have thought proper to blame;
His Cenfure's convey'd in a diffonant Chime,
With *one Line for Senfe*, and *another for Rhyme !*
He talks about " SHERIDAN's heart-ftirring Sum-
　　　" mons,"
For no other ufe but to *jingle* with *Commons ;*
Then he fpeaks of " *Old* SIMKIN, whofe well-mingled
　　　" fatire
" Ow'd no Poifon to Party, no gall to ill-nature."
Such uncouth ideas in every line
Prove clearly, the Writer's *no Brother of mine.*
He tells me, forfooth, " that he's not deeply fmitten
" With my half dozen Letters fo fluently written;"
Were he not below notice, fome lines I would write him,
That, if he can feel, fhould effectually fmite him.
One moment *he thinks*, and the next *he is fure*,
That " my motive for writing is not very pure."

If Simkin *the Second* he really knew,

He would own, with a blush, his *Suspicion untrue.*

By his boldly obtruding *Suspicion* for Knowledge,

One would think him a *Student of* Sheridan's *College;*

But when I consider how feeble his Pen,

Sherry never could own him—*as one of his Men.*

Once more then, *dear Brother,* I bid you adieu,

And will write nothing more till *requested by you.*

P. S.—As to Sherry himself—just to fill up the void,

 In suppressing all Theatres, now he's employ'd;

 And having in Acting accomplish'd some Fame,

 He's preventing all others—from doing the same.

 For that excellent Precept has ne'er met his eye,

 " *Do to others, oh Man! as thou wouldst be done by.*"

  July 8th, 1788.

LETTER XVI.

THE
REAL SIMON IN WALES,
TO
SIMKIN THE SECOND IN LONDON.

MY *dear Brother* SIMKIN, with heartfelt concern,
From reading *The* WORLD *of laſt Monday*, I learn,
That ſome impudent Knave had the boldneſs to ſend you
Some lines *in my name*, with a view to offend you.
The work I diſclaim, and 'tis my reſolution,
If I find out the rogue, to commence proſecution.
No, BROTHER, your Letters muſt always delight us,
And we hope, you will ever continue to write us.
When the *Simpleton* call'd you " Retailer of Scraps,"
One would think that he meant to give SHERIDAN ſlaps,
Of novelty careleſs, *you* only profeſs
To give SHERIDAN's *ſpeech*, a *poetical dreſs*.

Sir LAWRENCE LLEWELLYN, return'd to his ſeat,
Laſt night gave his friends, the electors, a treat;

Sir

Sir LAWRENCE, you know, is a man of high breeding,

And exceſſively fond of *theatrical reading*;

He ſaid, " SHERRY's *Speech* was an excellent piece

" Of *patch work*, with ſhreds brought from ROME and

   " from GREECE ;

" But ſhould Poets and Orators try him for theft—

" Like the *jackdaw* of old, would a feather be left ?"

Sir LAWRENCE obſerv'd, 'twas exceedingly odd,

To hear of an actor becoming a God.

But he thinks this *new* GOD, ſhould in gratitude foſter

And ſupport his Creator,—this Simon *impoſtor*.

Sir LAWRENCE conſider'd the ſcribler's obtruſion

Of Sir FRETFUL, a very unhappy alluſion.

Now, I bid you farewell, till the PARLIAMENT ends,

When I hope, *my dear* SIMKIN will viſit his friends.

  July 15th, 1788.

LETTER XVII.

SIMKIN to his DEAR BROTHER SIMON,

IN WALES.

HUZZA, *my dear Boy! Renovation of* FUN!
The curtain's drawn up, and the Play is begun!
You have read in POPE's *Homer,* how *royal* ATRIDES
Used to summon to council, that *bully* TYDIDES;
MENELAUS, *the cuckhold*—block AJAX; old NESTOR,
ULYSSES, the knave, and THERSYTES, the jester:
With *worthies,* like those, he was wont to debate,
How to conquer *old* PRIAM, and ruin his state.
To each separate leader such part he assign'd,
As suited the pow'rs of his body and mind.
For sloth and remiffnefs, he *some* reprehended,
And some, for their courage and zeal, he commended.
So, (*the* POST and *the* HERALD announce to their readers,)
Has EDMUND, *great* EDMUND, that *leader of leaders,*
To council conven'd the whole *corps of conductors,*
With *Attornies* and *Counsellors, legal instructors.*
When they all were assembled,—BURKE rose to explain
The plan he had form'd for the op'ning campaign.

" Ye

" Ye *lingual champions*, would the ALMIGHTY blefs
" Our unremitted labours with fuccefs,
" Soon fhould we ftretch this EASTERN VICTIM low,
" And proudly triumph o'er our hated foe.
" But HEAVEN, alas ! to us its aid denies,
" HASTINGS, e'en yet, is favour'd by the fkies;
" *Eight tedious years* have paffed, fince I began
" To war with this unconquerable man;
" All means, all arts, all ftratagems I've try'd,
" And fought with FOX and PARTY on my fide;
" For terms opprobrious, ranfack'd JOHNSON through,
" Till JOHNSON's *learning yielded nothing new.*
" I tax'd my brain, inventive, to traduce
" The foe, by ftrong diverfify'd abufe:
" But vain my toil, the public ftill admire
" The man who boldly braves a PATRIOT's *ire.*
" Oft has defpair excited me to yield,
" And leave my foe the honour of the field.
" But now I fee *one ray of comfort fpring,*
" While NOBLES mourn *the ficknefs of the* KING.
" *Come then, my* HEROES, be the fight renew'd,
" And WARREN HASTINGS may be yet fubdu'd."

Here EDMUND ceas'd—th'affembled Chiefs agreed,
'Twas *theirs* to follow, as 'twas *his* to lead.

G

Then

Then BURKE refum'd—" *My friends*, bear well in mind,
" The part to each bold leader I've affign'd;
" *The Heaven-born Lawyer*, Fox, fhall fingly ftand,
" Oppos'd to yonder formidable band;
" His powerful eloquence fhall over-awe
" DALLAS and PLUMER, with *their leader* LAW,
" *Their* weaker notes, *his* thund'ring voice fhall drown,
" His *eye-brows* fright them with terrific frown.
" By fome fhort turn toward a dang'rous hit,
" Or gall the enemy with ftrokes of wit:
" To paint the Matron's wrongs, or caufe to flow
" The tear of pity, for *fictitious woe*;
" The various beauties of the STAGE to cull,
" Give life and fpirits, when the COURT grows dull;
" To pleafe the Ladies, make the audience merry,
" My hopes and confidence are plac'd on SHERRY:
" But let him heedful of the darts he fends,
" Wound not *obliquely*, as before, *his* FRIENDS.

" To prove in TACTICS, HASTINGS' want of fkill,
" His *military plans*, concerted ill;
" To prove that long, unparallel'd *fuccefs*
" Makes, if well underftood, *his merit lefs*;
" That 'tis not CONQUEST ftamps the *Hero* GREAT,
" Since *honours, wealth*, and *fame, attend* DEFEAT:
" This be *thy* glorious tafk, *oh, great* BURGOYNE!
" And NORTH and ERSKINE, if they pleafe, may join.

I   " AN-

" ANSTRUTHER, ADAM, TAYLOR, MAITLAND, GREY,
" May as occasions rise, come into play.
" Should SHERRY's wit, or CHARLES's reasoning fail,
" They, to consume the time, may storm and rail :
" With dirt and mud, bedawb the PRISONER thick,
" *Perchance some fragments on his coat may stick.*

" You, *brother* DICK, shall be our *serjeant Prime,*
" The *fugal-man,* to watch, and give the time.
" When sparks of wit illuminating shine,
" I'll *tip the wink*—do you *repeat the sign,*
" And, in loud laughter, let the Phalanx join.

" DOUGLAS, the *green bag* I consign to thee ;
" Let LAWRENCE hand *the documents* to me.
" I trust the banquet to th'ATTORNEY's skill ;
" TROWARD shall tax, and pay the *landlord's bill.*
" These, COADJUTORS, be your separate tasks,
" These are the duties which *your* LEADER asks."

He said—and bursts of general applause
Presag'd their future ardour in the cause.
The *meaner part* to *youthful* GREY assign'd,
Corrosive prey'd on his aspiring mind :
His pride was touch'd, his vanity was hurt ;
A SCAVENGER, *forsooth !* and *deal in dirt !*

G 2

With

With eye indignant, viewing *Marſhal* BURKE,

He cried, " My ſoul diſdains ſuch paltry work ;

" For *throwing mud*, and all ſuch vulgar ſtuff,

" Thou need'ſt no aid—*thyſelf canſt throw enough !*

" No—let the part *I* take be *nobly large*,

" I *ſingly* claim the *conduct of a* CHARGE ;

" I pant, I burn, for Oratoric fame,

" With FOX, with SHERIDAN, to join *my* name.

" If this my juſt requeſt ſhall be deny'd,

" EDMUND *farewell ! I take the better ſide.*"

BURKE, in reply, thus ſooth'd his *teſty friend :*

" Thy warmth I pardon, and thy zeal commend ;

" To thee hereafter, I'll a CHARGE conſign,

" And thou, *another* SHERIDAN ſhalt ſhine !

" When *change of pow'r* puts PITT within my reach,

" Or NORTH, or *I*, will *that raſh Boy* IMPEACH !

" Not PITT *alone*, but *more* we have in view—

" ALL who approv'd *the* * *Phantom*, we'll purſue,

" Of aid like thine, we then ſhall ſtand in need,

" And various cauſes thou ſhalt have to plead."

* See the Debates on the Regency Bill.—When this letter was written, the Managers were in daily expectation of filling the higheſt offices of the State.

Here

Here *the meeting broke up*, and I've only to add,
It is ftrongly fufpected, that EDMUND *is mad!*
For he means, as we hear, to bring forward a charge
Againft PITT, *the two* HOUSES, and NATION at large!
LORDS and COMMONS he reprobates loudly, for clofing
With PITT's *limitations*, and PITT for propofing:
In his *moments of phrenfy*, his rage he expreffes,
'Gainft thofe COUNTIES and TOWNS that have fign'd
      the *addreffes*.
Like CAIN, he has made HUMAN NATURE *his foe*,
And at all who approach him, he levels a blow.

Here my Letter I clofe, but fhould EDMUND's *pro-*
      ceeding
Supply me with aught that is worthy your reading,
Be affur'd, I fhall quickly difpatch you another;
For the prefent, I reft your affectionate Brother.

    February 16th, 1789.

LET-

LETTER XVIII.
SIMON IN WALES

TO HIS

DEAR BROTHER SIMKIN IN LONDON.

WHAT a ftrange world it is, BROTHER SIMKIN!
    we're in,
Of lies and confufion, of folly and fin!
And *the right* and *the wrong* feems fo twifted about,
That I'm fure at this diftance they can't be found out.

But PARTY I fear is the caufe of the *baftings,*
So lavifhly given to poor WARREN HASTINGS.
And I oftentimes think all the MANAGERS cruel—
That their FIRE is *refentment,* and MALICE the *fuel;*
Elfe why fhould DICK SHERRY, and old MASTER
    BURKE
On the fubject of *plunder* and DEBTS make fuch work?
Dire fpectres of MASSACRE call up to view,
When they furely might know, *not a word of it's true.*
Indeed I muft own that I pity the ears
Of their LORDSHIPS, the BISHOPS, and DIGNIFIED
    PEERS;

I pity

I pity thofe Ladies, fo modeft and nice,
Who heard all the *filthy defcriptions of vice,*
And which, while the SPEAKERS fo lavifhly paint,
Some Ladies fuppos'd the beft thing was—*a faint*;
But even for HASTINGS a *fomething* I feel,
Which by chance may be wrong—but my heart is not
      fteel;
For I fee him furrounded, by foes, in his chair,
Who attack him like maftiffs that *worry a bear*;
While he's nothing to do but obferve what they fay,
And expend the NET SUM OF THREE HUNDRED A DAY!

As for EDMUND, who *fickens the Senate with prate,*
I have not a doubt but he's crack'd in the pate;
For whether 'tis BEGUMS, or WARS, or the NATION,
He's fure to come forth with a *ftrange botheration,*
While his fpeech is fo crowded with tropes and allufion,
With logic, and metaphor, wit, and confufion;
Is fo gay, and pathetic, or folemnly deep,
That *his* FRIENDS run away, and *his* FOES *fall afleep.*
A fimile oft I've endeavour'd to find
For this man, but could never get one to my mind.
Yet I think—he refembles a *rufty conductor*
That *points* to the HEAV'NS, but is *fix'd to a ftructure,*
That *hourly* contends with the elements' rage,
But a *flafh of true* LIGHTNING gets *once in an age.*

G 4

Well,

Well, I truſt WARREN HASTINGS has worth to defy all
The bitter attacks of his foes, at his trial;
That truth and integrity, plac'd in the ſcale
'Gainſt dark perſecution, will ever prevail;—
But hold—let me ſtop—what a race have I run,
Dear SIMKIN! another ten words, and I've done.

   I hope very ſoon you'll ſend me a letter,
Confirming the news that His MAJESTY's better;
But the STOCKS will inform me, in ſpite of diſguiſe—
For they fall when HE's *worſe, when he mends, why they*
       riſe;
Yet never before was ſuch great conſternation
Betray'd,—from the dread of a *new* 'MINISTRATION;
One would think from the general terror, I ſwear,
That their conduct, and characters, ar'n't very fair.
But of this I know nothing, and heedleſs of ſcandal,
I value plain truth in a TURK, or a VANDAL.—

   Sure PITT merits praiſes, in proſe as in rhime,
For the ſtand he has made at this critical time;
And of HIM and his PHALANX we proudly may ſing,
For *their guard of the* COUNTRY, and *care of the* KING.
Yet ſtories by ſome ſpread abroad of the PRINCE,
A ſpirit of cruelty rather evince—
For ſurely, *my* BROTHER! it ne'er could have been,
That his HIGHNESS each night at the OP'RA was ſeen!

That he gave himſelf up to the Follies *of* Fashion,
And loſt in *wild riot the* Tears *of* Compassion :
That when thro' the country ſwift ſorrow had run,
The Father *was pity'd by* all, *but the* Son !—
That *clubs,* and *gay parties,* and *muſic,* and *glee,*
Were the types of that feeling, *none wanted but* He,—
That by Regency *cares* not a moment oppreſs'd,
As uſual, he drank, and he ſung, and he dreſs'd :
And mocking propriety, graſp'd at dominion,
But ſcorn'd *e'en to flatter* the public opinion.

Such ſtories as theſe are the work of the devil,
Contriv'd by the baſe, for the purpoſe of evil,
And far other treatment he ought to have prov'd,
As doubtleſs he wept for the Parent he lov'd,
In *decent retirement* has kept out of ſight,
And loſt in his anguiſh *the taſte of delight* ;
Has duly conſider'd the proſpect before him,
And taught all the people t'admire and adore him.
Dear Simkin *adieu !* I have nought more to ſend——
But remain your affectionate Brother and Friend.

SIMON

February 23d, 1789.

[This Letter was by another hand.]

LET-

LETTER XIX.

AT length, *my dear* BROTHER, with pleasure I tell
Yourself and my friends, that His MAJESTY's *well !*
The MONARCH whose sickness *his subjects* deplor'd,
By the *blessing of* HEAVEN, again is RESTOR'D !

Your remember, perhaps, that I formerly said,
'Twas suspected that EDMUND was *touch'd in the head ;*
Some thought my assertion was matter of sport,
But now all the papers confirm the report ;
They describe him one day full of spirits and gladness,
The next like a *spectre,* dejected with sadness,
In the BOOKSELLERS' SHOPS, seeking *Books* upon
  MADNESS ;
At St. LUKE's and in BEDLAM inspecting the cells
To see in what comfort INSANITY *dwells.*

Till his friends can provide a fit keeper, they say,
He is under the care and tuition of GREY ;
Who permits not *his patient* to join in debate,
Without *feeling his pulse,* to *discover his* STATE.

So

So knowing is GREY, he can tell by the touch,
If EDMUND's in danger of faying too much;
When his vifage grows red, or his pulfe becomes ftrong,
GREY knows, if he fpeaks, 'twill be *flamingly wrong:*
One day, when BURKE fpoke, and GREY fail'd to attend
      him,
To the *Tower* fome whifper'd a motion to fend him;
But others more tender, lamenting his cafe,
Thought BEDLAM by far a more fuitable place.

   You will afk, to what caufe is his malady owing?
In this, like yourfelf, I am very unknowing;
Difcufs'd it has been, but as yet undecided,
On this his acquaintance and friends are divided.
Some fay, that his fpirits, inflammably hot,
Boil and bubble at times like a SOAP-BOILER's *Pot,*
And that the eruptions which happen'd of late,
Were nothing in fact, but *the fteam of his* PATE.
The DOCTORS, to fhew their deep learning, explain
How ideas by friction may wear out the brain;
And compare the infide of *the Orator's head*
To an old woman's *carding cloth* worn to a thread.
The METHODISTS fay, that his confcience is ftung
By his conduct political, when he was young;
But others will have it—to this very hour,
He would ruin the kingdom, if 'twas in his power.

The

The CLERGY believe his diforder a fign,
Of *juft retribution*, and *vengeance divine*;
But the major part think, his finances disjointed,
His ambition all humbled, his hopes difappointed,
Have occafion'd a *fever malignant*, and thence
They account for the frequent PRIVATIONS *of fenfe*;
But if it be true, that the MONARCH's neglect
Of merit, can caufe fuch a difmal effect;
Were it certain, a lucrative office would cure him,
And enable the COMMONS *again to endure him*;
We all fhould folicit his MAJESTY's *grace*,
And if poffible, get him a PAYMASTER's *place*.

But when you reflect on the wonderful change
In political profpects, you'll not think it ftrange,
That BURKE fhould go out of his mind, or perhaps,
If you hear by next poft of CHARLES FOX's *relapfe*,
Or of SHERIDAN's creditors *op'ning their throats*,
Having touch'd upon fome *moft unmufical* NOTES.

[This SHERIDAN, Brother, obferve, is the fame,
Who affumes in the papers JOE SURFACE's *name*;
This laft to adopt is henceforth my intention,
Juft honour to do to the *author's invention*;
HE *himfelf* gave the *name*, and the character drew
As he look'd in his glafs—So the LIKENESS *is true*.]

To

To return—*this* TRIUMVIRATE, scarce a week since,
Were coming in *Ministers* under the PRINCE,
And there can be no doubt but the general voice
Had loudly applauded His HIGHNESS's *choice*;
For who like JOE SURFACE is skill'd in *finance* ?
Or can equal CHARLES FOX in the *doctrine of* CHANCE ?
Less judgement it needs in this critical age,
To *govern a* KINGDOM, than *manage a* STAGE.

That invention is ever the daughter of need,
Is one of those truths in which all are agreed;
And those who beheld the most difficult scenes,
Have quickest conceptions of WAYS *and of* MEANS;
What exhaustless resources *that genius* displays,
Who neither the *interest nor principal pays* !
Who even additional credit can get,
From ad INFINITUM *increasing his debt* !

Now, since to the Nation her debts are distressing,
Such MINISTERS must be a NATIONAL *blessing* :
And BURKE, when in humour and office, was fit
To amuse the *young members* with sallies of wit;
With some funny story a laugh to create,
And divert their attention from matters of state.
Indeed I must think, tho' I dare not aver,
ROYAL WISDOM in some points is subject to err,

For

For no men of judgement would e'er have expected,

That talents fo ufeful fhould be fo neglected.

Howe'er, as the KING is reftor'd to his health,

They muft bid adieu to HOPE, HONOUR, and WEALTH.

Their *dreams* of AMBITION delufive are fled,

For the Minifter's yet not OFFICIALLY *dead*;

PITT falfifies JOSEPH's *prophetic expreffion*,

Concerning his " laft dying fpeech and confeffion."

The TRIUMVIRATE now may go feparate ways—

JOE SURFACE again to the writing of Plays;

CHARLES FOX on the Continent finifh his ramble,

Or teach the *young* PRINCES at BROOKES's to gamble;

And BURKE, if he ever recovers his fenfes,

May harangue to the LORDS, when the TRIAL com-

    mences.

SIMKIN.

P. S.   The LORDS and the COMMONS of IRELAND

    have fent

COMMISSIONERS here, an addrefs to prefent,

To make the PRINCE *Regent*, which now, to be fure,

Proves rather precipitate and premature;

This, however, affords little matter for wonder,

As the IRISH have *Leave* by prefcription to BLUNDER.

    March 10th, 1789.

LETTER

LETTER XX.

YOU tell me, *dear* SIMON, the *lads of the leek*
Expect me to fend them a letter a week :
The tafk is too hard, but I would not refufe 'em,
Could I find out new matter enough to amufe 'em :
At prefent, I take up the pen to relate,
What is faid to have paft at *a whiggifh debate* :
When the WHIGS were inform'd, 'twas His MAJESTY's
  will,
A ftop fhould be put to *the Regency Bill,*
The concern, which they felt at *not getting their places,*
Was meafur'd exact by the *length of their faces* :
One day and one night they devoted to *forrow,*
And a council was held at his GRACE's the morrow,

DIALOGUE.

DUKE.—" Well this to be fure is exceedingly hard ;
   " Why, CHARLES, did you play that unfor-
    " tunate card ?
   " Had you never brought forward *that Claim for*
    " *the* PRINCE,
   " We had all been in office thefe *many weeks fince.*
       BURKE.

Burke.—" With your Grace in opinion, I fully agree,
   " This comes from his not being *guided by me* ;
   " 'Tis feldom or never that Charles conde-
      " fcends,
   " In making a fpeech to confult with his friends."
   " To be guided by you"—(faid Charles Fox
      with a fneer)
   " By old Counfellor Burke, pray, my Lord,
      " did you hear ?"
Burke.—" Yes, guided by me, and I boldly aver,
   " When you act from yourfelf, you do nothing
      " but err."
(Fox *fneering again)* " I can make no defence,
   " But muft bow to your honour's oracular fenfe."
Burke felt from the manner in which Char-
     ley fpoke,
The keen edge of this cutting, ironical joke :
He fir'd in a moment, th' explofion was louder,
Than a mine when the match is applied to the
     powder.
   " *Perdition* and *death !* have I liv'd to thefe
      " years
   " To be flouted and huff'd by unmannerly jeers ?
   " Can a man of *my dignity* ever fubmit,
   " To be treated with *fcorn*, or infulted with *wit* ?
      " You

" You know very well, that if EDMUND withdraws
" His aid and fupport, there's an end of your
  " caufe :
" His aid from the *Greeks*, when ACHILLES
  " withdrew,
" Remember how HECTOR their armies o'erthrew,
" What numbers he captiv'd, what thoufands he
  " flew.
" Were the party of *my reputation* bereft,
" There would not be a rag of good character left.
" By the public what right has the *fon to be trufted*,
" Whofe father's accounts *are as yet unadjufted?*
" Who poffefs'd of large property, threw it away,
" Upon women and wine, or difpers'd it by play :
" From the party fhou'd I, like ACHILLES fecede,
" They would be contemptible wretches indeed."
JOE SURFACE, lefs patient than CHARLES, or the
  . DUKE,
Was ftung to the quick by this pointed rebuke ;
He began in a manner farcaftic and taunting,
" A truce, Mr. BURKE, with Thrafonical vaunting ;
" Why fing your own praife, when we own there
  " was never
" *A hero more bold,* or *a ftatefman fo clever.*
" We feel ourfelves honour'd by EDMUND's *con-*
  " *nection,*
" And in fafety fight under his friendly protection.

H

" Thro'

" Thro' him we have purchas'd immenſe reputations,

" By pleading the cauſe of unquerulous nations,

" Of Dowager Begums *that never complain'd*

" Of Hardſhips and cruelties *never ſuſtain'd.*

" How highly the people applaud us for ſhewing

" Our zeal, to affect a late Governor's *ruin,*

" To whom, as all parties unite in confeſſion,

" Britain owes at this day *all her Eaſtern poſſeſſion;*

" With gratitude mov'd, they admire our depriving

" *That man of ſubſiſtance, by whom they are thriving;*

" *Popularity, credit,* and *fame* we obtain,

" From the deeds of Achilles this preſent campaign.

" How gen'rous, how bold, how heroic a thing,

" *'Tis to treat with contempt an unfortunate King !*

" In terms of reproach, and in language diſloyal,

" To animadvert on the *malady royal :*"

In this manner ſarcaſtical Joseph was ſhowing,

What vaſt obligations to Edmund *are owing :*

When Edmund thus anſwer'd—" This language

       " from Joe,

" Makes good what I propheſy'd ſome months ago;

" I ſaw as in favour he grew with *his Highneſs,*

" *He treated his friends with ſatirical dryneſs.*

" And now the ungrateful is rais'd to the top,

" He thinks he's no longer in need of a prop,

" *But I truſt I ſhall ſoon ſee him ſuddenly drop.*

I.

" I'll

" I'll *leave oppofition*, this day, I affure ye,

" I'll refign you a prey to the *Minifter's fury.*

" When Pitt is no longer in dread of my thunder,

" What hero can keep his audacity under."

Joe.—" You may go when you pleafe, we can do well

       " without you,

" *Not one of the party cares fixpence about you.*"

Then Courtenay obferving, the ftorm that was

       brewing,

Unlefs guarded againft, muft involve them in ruin.

Thus fpoke—" 'Tis with infinite forrow I fee,

" That the heads of a party can thus difagree.

" When I think of the Orator's tergiverfation,

" And leaving us all in a perilous ftation,

" My arteries fuffer a ftrong palpitation."

But now as the heroes were cutting and fooling,

A fervant announc'd that the *dinner was cooling* ;

The agreeable news put an end to debating,

And like Homer's heroes they all fell to eating.

The Port and the Claret went merrily round,

And difcord itfelf in a bumper was drown'd.

    March 28th, 1789.

H 2

LET-

LETTER XXI.

I TOLD you, *dear* BROTHER, a month or two back,
That BURKE was preparing another attack.
After fixing, unfixing, refixing the day,
The LORDS have at length put an end to delay,
So EDMUND came forward attended by GREY.
You have frequently heard, that with men of the FIST,
BOTTLE-HOLDERS, like SECONDS, make part of the lift·
And thence the new fafhion, 'tis probable, fprung
To appoint BOTTLE-HOLDERS *to men of the* TONGUE:
So EDMUND, intending to batter the ears
Of the CHANCELLOR, JUDGES, and *dignify'd* PEERS,
Has his *bottle-man* alfo, and frequently fips,
To wafh out his mouth, and to moiften his lips.

    Thus EDMUND began—" We are come from a place
" Where we heard a great deal about MERCY and
      " GRACE;
" About *thanking the* LORD for reftoring the KING,
" Which moft people think a *defirable thing*;
" But, my LORDS, the beft praife we can offer to GOD,
" Is freely to exercife JUSTICE's *Rod* :
                  " Some

" Some impertinent men, in another place, afk

" In how *many years* more we fhall finifh our tafk ?

" My anfwer is fhort—that I cannot pretend

" To form an idea of *when it will end.*

" When the purpofe for which it was firft undertaken

" Is anfwer'd, *'tis likely* it may be forfaken.

" But I cannot conceive that the duty is hard,

" Since *labour for labour* is ample reward.

" If much of the feffions already is fpent,

" It arofe from a late moft afflictive event.

" What with *mourning, rejoicing, thankfgiving* and *preach-*
   " *ing,*

" We have not had time to proceed with IMPEACHING ;

" But I truft that *both* HOUSES will now be at leifure

" To hear me go on, and I'll do it with pleafure.

" The ftory, my LORDS, which I now have to tell,

" 'Tis probable may not be relifh'd fo well.

" No BEGUM of fierce violation complains ;

" No RAJAH groans under the weight of his chains ;

" And forry I am, that I cannot regale

" Your ears with a RAPE, or *fome delicate tale.*

" 'Tis but feldom indeed, in thefe liberal times,

" Opportunity ferves of committing *fuch crimes.*

H 3

" But

" But before I the fubtle diftinction defcribe

" Between Peeshcush, and Nezer, and Rishwet,
    " a bribe,

" You muft know that the people whofe caufe we are
    " pleading,

" Have tranfmitted Petitions to ftay our proceeding :

" They roundly affert, *that* they *never fuftain'd*

" *Thofe cruel diftreffes of which* we *complain'd.*

" The petitions, I grant, are *authentic* and *true* ;

" But, *my* Lords, what is that to *the* Commons, or
    " You ?

" It can't fave the Pris'ner, I venture to fay,

" Since all muft allow we know better than they ;

" And like the Old Bailey, in this cafe, I hope,

" Good *character clearly* presages *a rope.*"

    Juft here, Burke was feiz'd with a drought on his lip,

So he juft faid, " My Lords," and repeated his fip—

" The Pris'ner, my Lords, while he fill'd that high
    " ftation,

" Was the fource of corruption and bafe peculation ;

" All kinds of corruption were of his contrivance,

" Or fupported at leaft by his purchas'd connivance :

" For when the Dewanny, my Lords, was withdrawn,

" From the Nabob's inftructor, Mahmed Reza
    " Cawn,

" Not

" Not a man could be met with fo virtuous and juft,

" As to fill that important refpectable truft:

" Not a man could be met with fufficiently wife :—

" Then to whom do you think he directed his eyes?

" To *a female*, my LORDS, the DEWANNY he gave,

" To a *dancing girl* truly, that fprung from a flave.

" I do not allude to thofe *elegant dances*

" Whereby *a fair lady her beauty enhances*;

" But to that kind of dancing which young men admire,

" In Ladies that fkip it and dance it *for hire.*

" MUNNY BEGUM, the object of HASTINGS' election,

" Sole Regent was made, without any *reftriction.*

" *No reftrictions, my* LORDS ! fhe was perfectly free,

" As *Regents*, I think, *fhould in general be.*

" But the powers of Regent alone would not do,

" He made her ARCHBISHOP, and CHANCELLOR too.

" The NABOB's *dear perfon*, his army and treafure,

" Were all at *this* BEGUM's, the dancing girl's pleafure.

" And here let me afk, can your LORDSHIPS fuppofe

" That *he* was not paid for it—*under the rofe ?*

" Was it likely that HASTINGS thefe offices gave her

" Without *fome return* from the PRINCESS's *favor ?*

" And we could eftablifh againft him, with eafe,

" *Three hundred and fifty odd thoufand* RUPEES,

" If the man who inform'd us that HASTINGS was fee'd,

" Had not *died on the gallows*, for *forging a deed.*

H 4

" The

" The counfel may urge, that no credit is due

" To a wretch that *was hang'd*—that it *cannot be true.*

" But let them beware how on this they infift,

" Left I add a new charge to the *criminal lift*—

" That Hastings and Impey concerted a plan,

" *To* Murder *a noble, an innocent man.*

" Suppofe that fome fcandalous fellow fhould fay,

" An Archbishop in robes had robb'd on the Highway,

" Or a Chanc'lor been publicly guilty of *plunder,*

" We all fhould receive it as matter of wonder ?

" But whenever we hear of an *Eaftern* Nabob,

" We annex the idea of *plunder* and *job.*

" We *prefume* on his guilt from this circumftance ftrong,

" And 'tis not in nature that we fhould be *wrong :*

" The pris'ner's vaft ftomach, your Lordships will

  " find,

" Occafion'd a *famine,* wherever he din'd ;

" And, indeed, it is wonderful how he could eat

" *Up two hundred pounds, at a fingle day's treat !*

" Munny Begum, who fed him, would frequently fay,

" It coft her two hundred pound fterling a day.

" Hastings eat *in three months* what was meant to fup-

  " port

A *hundred black Peers* at the Princess's court ;

" And whilft this *ftrange glutton* was lavifhly fed,

" A hundred old nobles were ftarving for bread.

" Like

" Like a *vulture* he fnatches the food from the grave,

" Nor preys EAGLE-*like*, on the *living* and *brave*.

" Ye PRELATES and BISHOPS, fuppofe if you pleafe,

" An intruder fhould lick up *the fat of your* SEES;

" Or fuppofe that a man without any pretenfion,

" Should devour at a meal any *nobleman's penfion?*"

As EDMUND was earneftly putting thefe cafes,

It fomewhat affected their reverend faces.

Howe'er, BURKE went on with his pleafant oration,

Till, as ufual, he ftopp'd to repeat his potation.

Whene'er he grew dry, to his DOCTOR he beckon'd,

Who acted this day BOTTLE-HOLDER and SECOND.

When his patient was tir'd, GREY would read us a letter,

By way of amufement, till EDMUND was better.

Thus being alternately BUTLER and *Reader*,

Four hours he fupported his eloquent leader.

But to finifh the fubject—When EDMUND had rail'd

Four hours againft HASTINGS, his energy fail'd;

And in fpite of his *bottle*, and *frequently drinking*,

He found that his ftrength and his fpirits were finking;

But indeed I muft own, he poffeffes more vigour

Than one could expect from his *manner* and *figure*:

At length quite exhaufted, the LORDS he addrefs'd,

On the MANAGER's *part*, with an humble requeft,

That

That they would be pleas'd, for that day to adjourn,

To give time for his fpirits and ftrength to return.

I hope you will like this epiftle, *dear* BROTHER,

And if EDMUND finds matter, I'll fend you another.

SIMKIN.

April 25th, 1790.

LET-

LAST WE'NSDAY, DEAR BROTHER, I went to the
    COURT,
Expecting from BURKE *a renewal of sport*;
Where, like others, I found myself *much disappointed*
By the Orator's faculties being disjointed.
The cause of his illness I wanted to find,
And heard many whimsical reasons assign'd :
Some said the disease was increas'd in his head ;
Some said he was drunk, and lay stretch'd on his bed ;
Some thought he was seiz'd with a fit of the vapours,
At something that morning *in one of the papers*—
That a certain GREAT PERSONAGE meant to insist
On expunging his name from the COUNCILLORS' LIST,

    Being thus disappointed, I hasten'd away
To ST. STEPHEN's, to hear what the COMMONERS say :
There I found MAJOR SCOTT, by Petition, was trying
To restrain able Speakers from wilfully lying ;
But I hope, that by Parliament privilege pleading,
They'll hinder this lover of truth from succeeding ;

For

For if Burke's not allow'd to say more than is true,
He'll furnish no matter for writing to you,
And I muſt, of neceſſity, bid you adieu.

When Edmund recover'd, the Papers gave warning
Of his ſpeaking again the next Saturday morning;
So I went to the Hall, and reſum'd my old ſtation,
Expecting another moſt brilliant Oration—
But, alas! *my dear Brother*, you muſt not accuſe
Me of *Dullneſs* this day, if I fail to amuſe:
For Burke, tho' he ſpoke for three hours, or more,
Only *travers'd the ground he had travers'd* before.
His language was *beautiful*, vaſtly *ſublime*,
And I wiſh I could do it *ſtrict juſtice in rhyme*:
He drew a ſtrange picture of Hastings's diet;
Of his feaſt on diſgrace, of his *infamy*-riot.
In Corruption, the Pris'ner's delight is to lie,
And " *in excrement wallow, like pigs in a ſtye.*"
" To your Lordships already it muſt have appear'd,
" With Corruption the Pris'ner's all over beſmear'd;
" With Corruption *this* Hastings is cover'd ſo thick,
" When I ſee him, my ſtomach turns ſuddenly ſick:
" The diſeaſe of Corruption has been ſo neglected,
" The Company's *Settlements* all are infected;
" Not Hastings *alone* is corrupted, *but all*
" *Who breath the* pestiferous air *of* Bengal!

" Yet

" Yet tho' 'tis fo bad, that I cannot endure it,

" I fear 'tis impoffible ever to cure it.

" We *have no direct proof of Corruption*, 'tis true,

" But in failure of that, *ftrong prefumption will do*.

" Corrupted he was by the *Dancing Girl's* treat,

" And you can't have forgotten the dinners he eat.

" *Two hundred pounds fterling*, this gluttonous finner

" *Three months unremittedly eat at a dinner*;

" But the thing at which I am fo highly offended,

" Is the manner wherein the large fum was expended;

" No part was expended on mufic or finging,

" On *Dancing Girls, Illuminations*, or *Ringing*:

" No friend ever tafted the milk or the honey,

" *'Twas a feaft of corruption*, a FLOW OF DRY MONEY,

" To a defert, a jungle *this* TYGER withdrew,

" To prey on this victim his avarice flew.

" But, my LORDS, if this circumftance is not enough,

" I'll give you another to ftrengthen the proof:

" When his much *honour'd Colleagues* in Adminiftration

" Accus'd him of bribery, and peculation,

" *Their Prefident* would not fubmit to his trial,

" Nor confeffion of guilt would he make, nor denial;

" Inftead of expofing himfelf to conviction,

" He difputed their power, and ufurp'd jurifdiction."

Here

Here EDMUND a number of reaſons aſſign'd,
Why HASTINGS the *Honour of Trial* declin'd;
Why has yet the DIRECTORS no anſwer had got,
Whether NUNDCOMAR's *Stories* were founded, or not.

(Here 'twas whiſper'd, that EDMUND to ſtate had
    omitted,
That HASTINGS conceiv'd himſelf fully acquitted;
For to NORTH, or Directors, if doubt had appear'd,
By one Queſtion alone, every doubt had been clear'd—
No ſcruples remain'd, for his frequent Election,
By Miniſter, Parliament, and the Direction,
Proclaim'd to the World their united opinion,
That HASTINGS deſerv'd, and was fit for Dominion.)

Now EDMUND, more loudly returns to his cry,
Of " *Preſumption, Conviction,* and HOG *in a* STYE."
Not a man ever went to that infamous place,
But is deeply involv'd in this Culprit's diſgrace,
All, all—His *Accomplices,* wicked and baſe.
I do not, however, ſaid EDMUND, intend
To include PHILIP FRANCIS, *my worthy,* DEAR *Friend,*
Nor his *honeſt Aſſociates;* but barring *theſe Three,*
They are *all* KNAVES or ROGUES, in the higheſt degree.
And indeed, my *dear Brother,* you cannot but think,
That ſo much Corruption muſt *horribly ſtink;*

And

And believe me, I fmell it whenever I meet
An *Indian* NABOB, as I travel the ftreet.
The Nobles, I truft, will this Seafon recal
Their *Relations* and SONS, from *contagious* BENGAL ;
What a horrible thing, if fuch bafe peculation,
Were imported from thence to an *innocent Nation !*

Three hours and a half on this fubject alone
The wit of the Speaker refplendently fhone:
He refembl'd *a Colt*, in his circular lunging,
Now *walking*, now *trotting*, then *kicking* and *plunging !*
In like manner did BURKE run his circular Race
Two days, without *changing* or *fhifting his place :*
" *'Tis an excellent Pad !* as your *Horfe-Dealers* fay,
" That can pace *on a Trencher* the length of a day."
If this can a merit in ORATORS be,
'Tis BURKE's, all allow, in exalted degree :
On PRESUMPTION, CORRUPTION, the changes he rung,
Till at laft it exhaufted, and wearied his tongue.
He faid he had more than *half open'd* his Charge ;
That his Friends would hereafter explain and enlarge.
With this declaration their Lordfhips were ftruck,
And thought themfelves born to exceeding *good luck,*
That THEY fhould *be Peers* in fuch turbulent times,
Of enormous *long Speeches*, IMPEACHMENTS, and
    CRIMES ;

When

When Speakers, like Bruifers, make trial of ftrength,
And the Worth *of Oration depends on* their Length.

'Tis reported, *dear Brother*, that fome of the Peers,
Who think they can't live a *vaft number of years*,
Direct that their Sons fhould the Trial attend,
That their Titles and *that* may together defcend.

I obferv'd, that though Edmund was frequently dry,
No Bottle appear'd—but I cannot tell why.
I took notice of fomething more ftrikingly ftrange,
To his Corps, his behaviour has fuffer'd a change:
His Language this day was *more gentle* and *mild*,
And he fpoke like a Father addreffing his Child;
But before, when he fpoke to his humble adjutors,
'Twas the ftyle and the manner of *Ufhers* and *Tutors*.
As he finifh'd, it ftruck me, Fox fhrugg'd up a fhoulder,
And Grey fhew'd *his teeth*, on being call'd—Bottle-
    Holder.

April 30th, 1789.

LETTER XXIII.

YOU remember laſt ſeaſon, that JOSEPH foretold,
With a ſpirit prophetic, that EDMUND the bold
Would one day or other th'IMPEACHMENT condemn,
And declare to the COMMONS 'twas owing to them;
That he ever was HASTINGS' friend in his *heart*,
Though compell'd to accept of a *Manager's* part.
I thought ſuch a change could not poſſibly be—
JOSEPH knew him, however, much better than me;
It ſeems, that they ſwindled him into the taking
Of a part, which he is on the verge of forſaking.
But I cannot conceive at what people are aiming,
By the preſent circuitous mode of diſclaiming.

I ſaid in my laſt, that the MAJOR was trying
By *Petition*, to lay an *embargo on Lying*;
This was owing, I find, to the Orator's quoting
Some Articles not of the Commoners' voting;
Miſdemeanors they voted, but EDMUND went further,
And in two or three inſtances charg'd him with *Mur-*
  " *ther* ?
So HASTINGS the Houſe has addreſs'd by Petition,
To know whether THEY authoriſe *the addition* ?—

This

I

This occasion'd laft *Monday* a curious Debate—

In a hafty fhort fketch, all the points I'll relate.

When EDMUND heard PITT and fome members confefs,

That HASTINGS's Cafe call'd aloud for redrefs,

And SCOT *pledg'd his word*, that the Orator knew

At the moment he fpoke, that *the Charge was untrue*;

His feelings, long callous, now fenfibly ftung,

In a moment unbridled his virulent tongue.

" Indeed, Mr. SPEAKER, 'tis vaftly abfurd,

" To expect me to anfwer *for every word*—

" When an Orator's Speeches are rapidly flowing,

" He often muft fpeak, *without thinking or knowing*;

" Do you think, in the hurry of cutting and flaying,

" That *we* can find leifure, for gauging and weighing;

" Or pray, are the Managers here to be treated,

" Like *Shylock*, whom *Portia* fo knavifhly cheated?

" Or can a Diffector fo able be found,

" As to cut human flefh, to *exactly a pound*;

" To cut juft a pound, and there inftantly ftop,

" Without drawing blood, without fpilling a drop?

" If that be your meaning, I freely proteft,"

(At that moment applying his hand to his breaft)

" 'Tis more than a *Catholic Chriftian* can do—

" (Then pointing to CHARLEY) *or even a Jew.*

I

" And

" And juſt as the Criminal felt himſelf pinch'd—

" *You* might have complain'd, *had the Managers flinch'd;*

" Had they ſuffer'd a cauſe ſo important to drop,

" Or fall on their heads for the want of a prop.

" Let them point out the time, if we have been remiſs—

" Did we ſpare him in that? Did we ſcreen him in this?

" No, Sir, where the Cauſe was deficient in ſtrength,

" *Our Speeches have amply ſupply'd it by length.*

" But, Sir, 'tis my wiſh to be fully inſtructed,

" In the mode that this Trial ſhould *now* be conduct-
      " ed:

" If when we perceive *our own evidence failing,*

" Are we not to ſupport it, *by ſtorming and railing !*

" Nundcomar's Accuſation muſt certainly ſink,

" Unleſs we prevail on their Lordships to think,

" That he of his life was unjuſtly depriv'd,

" And that Hastings and Impey the Murder con-
      " triv'd—

" But, Sir, if the Commons think fit to deny,

" Or give *Amplification* the name of a *Lye* ;

" If the Managers' conduct the House ſhould con-
      " demn,

" I can prove *all I utter'd, proceeded from* them ;

" As they heard my Oration, and let me proceed,

" They not only *approv'd,* but *committed* the deed.

I 2

" 'Tis

" 'Tis the COMMONS of ENGLAND, *the People at large,*

" Who HASTINGS and IMPEY as *Murderers* charge;

" When they forc'd me to take the *Chief Manager*'s part,

" (An Office I always diflik'd in my heart)

" When they coax'd me, and fwindled me into this
  " fcrape,

" *(Where they leave me alone, that themfelves may efcape)*

" 'Tis certain that they, whether waking or fleeping,

" *Their confciences left to the Managers' keeping—*

" Mr. SPEAKER, I fay 'tis a terrible cafe,

" If I am to be try'd, and expos'd to difgrace,

" And ftand in my turn in the Criminal's place.

" Thofe who fit in this Houfe, and my perfon behold,

" Muft fenfibly feel that I'm rather too old :

" That life is already too far in advance,

" For me now to join in the *ludicrous dance :*

" My legs and my heels not fufficiently light,

" Befides I'm too aged to turn *to the right.*

" Shall I, *the firft figure* that's feen in the groupe,

" Who with dignify'd *ftep* have conducted the troop—

" Shall I lay of a fudden thefe honours afide—

" For exceeding my duty fubmit to be try'd ?

" No, no—to myfelf I will ever be juft,

" Though the Houfe fhould think fit to deprive me of
  " truft :

" And,

" And, indeed, 'tis a favour I now have to afk,
" To be kindly reliev'd from a difficult tafk;
" But if I'm to finifh the work I've begun,
" And allow'd to proceed as I've hitherto done,
" You fhall never complain that I'm idle or flack,
" Or in any way backward to lead the attack;
" You fhall foon fee the Criminal *bare to the bone*,
" While I *tear off his flefh* by the *fod*, or the *ftone*.
" But if on the other hand I am difgrac'd
" In the eyes of all Europe, by being difplac'd,
" Pofterity's praife fhall compenfate the wrong,
" I have fuffer'd from thofe who have known me too
   " long."

But, alas! my dear SIMON, in fpite of this pleading,
The Commons approv'd not of EDMUND's proceeding,
And therefore they voted, t'appoint him a day,
As perhaps he might have fomething farther to fay;
But EDMUND conceiv'd it was groffly mif-fpending
His time and his words, to go on with defending,
So he fent them a Letter, inftead of attending.
On HASTINGS and *Friends* 'twas extremely *fatyric*;
On *Himfelf* and his *Party*, a high *Panegyric*;
But MONTAGUE, when he had done with the Letter,
An Eulogy made that was ftronger and better.
He enlarg'd on thofe talents which EDMUND has got,
And defcrib'd many virtues—*fome fay, he has not.*

         Th'

Th' *Encomiaſt* concluded his friendly Oration
With pronouncing aloud, a *ſtale Latin Quotation* :
That BURKE's Underſtanding, tranſcendently fine,
Graſps all that is Human, and all that's Divine !

    You muſt know, my dear BROTHER, a notion prevails,
That SIMKIN is *not a true Native of Wales.*
That SIMKIN and SIMON are old faſhion'd Names,
That never a *Taffyland Gentleman* claims ;
But moſt people think that *my Letters* are writ
By a DUCHESS of SCOTLAND, renown'd for her wit,
And zeal for the *Adminiſtration* of PITT.

    The queſtion CADWALLADER wants to propoſe,
" Is JOSEPH or BURKE the beſt Poet in Proſe ?"
The next time I attend at the *Weſtminſter Forum,*
It ſhall be debated *Judicibus coram.*
And indeed the beſt Critics are free to confeſs,
Their Speeches aſſume a poetical dreſs.
'Tis thence without trouble or waſte of much time,
I give the contents of their Speeches in rhyme.

    Dear BROTHER, adieu ; but I'll write you again,
Tho', as matters now ſtand, I can ſcarcely ſay when.

      May 5th, 1789.

LETTER XXIV.

AT length, *Brother* SIMON, the bufinefs is ended,
For which HASTINGS's *Trial* was lately fufpended.

When the LORDS were affembled, *great* EDMUND
    came in
With a countenance woeful, th'effect of chagrin,
Which put me in mind of *the Picture of* SIN.

" *My Lords*, the laft time I appear'd at your bar,
" I told you a ftory about NUNDCOMAR.
" I faid, he by IMPEY and HASTINGS was hung,
" In order to filence his garrulous tongue.
" *They murder'd the Man*," " was the term that I us'd,
" A term *good enough* for the Pris'ner accus'd ;
" But the COMMONS, *my Lords*, have been fuddenly feiz'd
" With a Naufea, I find, and are vaftly difpleas'd.
" Their *Confciences tender*, can't bear a tranfgreffion
" Of TRUTH—and laft night they difclaim'd the Ex_
    " preffion.
" But, *my Lords*, notwithftanding the COMMONS reprov'd
    " me,
" I am proud to declare that they have not *remov'd me :*

I 4

" My

" My conftituents, perhaps, may be fomewhat difgufted,

" Yet ftill they believe, I am fit to be trufted.

" And I foon will convince them by Arguments ftrong,

" That their judgement is neither ill-founded nor wrong.

" Tho' I am not permitted to add a new charge,

" On thofe which I have, I will dwell, and enlarge ;

" Tho' I lower my ftile, and new-model my diction,

" According to this late invented reftriction :

" Tho' of *Amplification* I'm partly bereft,

" I will make the beft ufe of the *little that's left* ;

" And here by the bye, I've been often complaining,

" That the SENATE of late is too fond of *reftraining* ;

" Should your *Lordfhips* inquire, why the freedom I took,

" Of ftating a fact that was *not in the Book ?*

" The reafon is plain, I moft perfectly knew,

" That HASTINGS would tell you no credit was due -

" To the bare *ipfe dixit* of one who was try'd,

" And for FORGING a *Paper with infamy dy'd,*

" I call'd it a *Murder,* but 'twas at a time,

" When *I wanted a* WORD to diftinguifh the crime ;

" Our language is poor, and our words are fo few, ⎫
" Their *meaning fo weak,* that they never can do   ⎬
" For HASTINGS's crimes, *fo atrocious and new.* ⎭

" I wanted a word juft diftinction to draw,

" Betwixt *moral Murder,* and *Murder by Law* :

" 'Tis

" 'Tis a *fort of a murder*, that's no where defin'd,

" Tho' I've got the idea fomewhere in my mind :

" But, *my Lords*, it behoves me to make fome excufe,

" For the prefent apology long and diffufe,"

(Here he gave us a fpice of his annular fpeaking,

And *apologies made, for apology making !)*

" But as foon as the final apology ended,

" And his conduct approv'd by himfelf and defended,

" He obferv'd to *the* LORDS, he had told them before,

" The Charge was half open'd, or probably more :

" That only two days were employed in revealing,

" What HASTINGS had fpent many years in concealing—

" But no longer to build on the grounds of *Sufpicion*,

" I now fhall make ufe of the Prifoner's admiffion :—

" In Seventeen Hundred and Seventy-three,

" The KING and his PARLIAMENT made a decree

" 'Gainft the Company's fervants *accepting a Fee* ;

" That whoever took money, the fame muft produce,

" And give it all up for the COMPANY's *ufe*.

" This claufe by the Pris'ner was fo underftood,

" As to let him take bribes for the *Company's good*.

" Imprefs'd with this notion, it feems that his coffers

" At all times were open to liberal offers."

Here EDMUND with infinite humour defcribes,

A *new Court of* EXCHEQUER for taking in Bribes,

Where

Where FRAUD the high office of *Treasurer* took,
And OBLIVION kept the *Remembrancer's Book*;
EXTORTION affefs'd the refpective amounts,
And CONFUSION, the *Auditor*, pafs'd the accounts:
His agents were vile *Banyans* and *Gentoos*,
A fpecies, indeed, of *black Brokers* and *Jews*.
Now EDMUND cafts up all the feveral fums,
By Units, Tens, Hundreds, by Thoufands and Plums.
" The Prifoner, *my Lords*, has been put to his fhifts,
" With refpect to concealing thefe prefents and gifts,
" Of FORGERY I would accufe him *with pleafure,*
" *Were I fure that the* COMMONS *would fanction the mea-*
    " *fure*;
" But they are fo *fcrupulous, nice,* and *exact,*
" That they want to confine me to MATTER of FACT—
" But I truft, I fhall not be, as formerly treated,
" If I only affert that the *Criminal* CHEATED;
" Gave in falfe accounts, and his Letters mifdated.
" His accounts and his Letters were form'd to beguile,
" His accounts are *Pindaric* in matter and ftile;
" His Letters are *Oyxmel* (nafty) of *Squills,*
" They are purges, emetics, and boxes of Pills.
Thefe Letters were highly offenfive indeed,
For EDMUND himfelf was unable to read;
So TAYLOR, whofe ftomach is not foon affected,
Read over thefe Letters, as EDMUND directed.

The

The Orator now *Virgin-modesty* shocks,

By imputing to HASTINGS *the Tail of a Fox*;

Then the Company turns to a LION *rapacious*,

And HASTINGS a *Jackall* of stomach voracious.

In this way he proceeded, comparing and railing,

Till at length he perceiv'd that his spirits were failing;

Then he begg'd that the LORDS would appoint him a
   day,

To hear something more it behov'd him to say,

Indeed, *my dear Brother*, we have to lament

The restriction on BURKE as a cruel event:

For though he is equally keen on accusing,

He is not, as formerly, half so amusing.

I heard many Ladies the MINISTER blame,

Who is jealous, they say, of the Orator's fame:

They think it is strange and absurd, that a Youth

Should fall so in love with the *Goddess of Truth*;

And indeed it would puzzle the statesman to tell,

Why a Galley Goddess may'nt serve him as well.

The say it is an *odd, unaccountable Passion*,

Unknown to *fine Speakers* of merit and fashion;

But I take it, the principal cause of their dread,

Is danger, if such an example should spread;

If the *Beauties of Speech* men are taught to condemn,

Deception may soon be disrelished in them.

But

But now, *my dear Brother*, this Letter I end,
As remarks of this kind might the Ladies offend;
And perchance I might get myself into the clutches
Of a *Woman of wit*—and that Woman—a Duchess.

May 9th, 1789.

LETTER XXV.

SIMON IN WALES,

TO HIS

BROTHER SIMKIN IN TOWN.

THE letters, *dear* SIM. you obligingly write us,
Never fail to inftruct, to amufe and delight us;
But though we've no caufe to arraign your neglect,
We have reafon to think you not always correct.
We do not complain of your making additions,
Of perverting the fenfe, but of fundry omiffions.
Mr. LLILLY LLANSTUFFIN, who often frequents
ST. STEPHEN's, is here for his *Michaelmas rents:*
And yefterday, fitting at table with him,
A fervant announc'd *an epiftle from* SIM.
He had heard of your name, and declar'd he'd be proud,
If I did him the favour to read it aloud;
So I read it all over as well as I cou'd;
He thank'd me, and faid, " that your verfes were good;
" But that many things pafs'd at that very debate,
" Which he wonder'd that *you* fhould forget to relate."

A nar-

A narrative Mr. LLANSTUFFIN began,

Which I'll verfify now as exact as I can.

He faid, that CHARLES Fox difplay'd infinite cunning

In perplexing the bufinefs; whofe fhifting and fhun-
    ning

He compar'd to a cock that fights *wheeling* and *running.*

He faid, one might travel a feven days' journey,

Before one might find fuch a *fogging Attorney :*

One moment a MANAGER's *rights* he maintain'd,

That his character facred could not be arraign'd :

The next, *he with fubtlety ftrove to revoke*

The words which the ORATOR *granted,* HE SPOKE :

And what EDMUND himfelf was fo free to confefs,

Fox *doubted,* and queftion'd it never-the-lefs.

The writers might well be fufpected of leaning,

Or of taking the words, and omitting the meaning :

Befides, 'twere *a fhame* to refer to a note,

Which a *man,* not a MEMBER *of* PARLIAMENT, wrote.

And the Members who heard *their* CHIEF MANAGER
    fpeak,

Were either afleep, or their memories weak ;

And as to confeffion, *'twas highly unfit,*

Advantage to draw from *what* BURKE *might admit.*

Now CHARLEY contends that it only belong'd

To the LORDS, to redrefs any man that is wrong'd;

Then

Then he hints, that fhould cenfure excite his difguft,
It might drive him, perhaps, to relinquifh his truft.
'Tis obfervable, this *tautological Speaker*
Is *louder* as much as his *argument's weaker* :
By bawling and noife, he creates a *diverfion*,
To cover the fallacy of each affertion :
By experience he knows, he can always engage
Attention, by *feeming to be in a rage.*
He often affects fuch a puffing and blowing,
That his words, for a time, are prevented from flowing.
The Senators now, from long habit and fafhion,
Own his right by prefcription, to be in a paffion.

   Here LLILLY digrefs'd, and the characters drew,
Of all the *rhetorical fpeakers* he knew.
He faid, it was vain and abfurd to expect,
The papers could give us their fpeeches correct :
And fince I prefer Mr. LLILLY LLANSTUFFIN
To YOU, *Brother* SIM. or a partifan's puffing,
As he fpoke, in fhort hand, MEMORANDUMS I took,
Which I've enter'd at large in my red cover'd book ;
And if till next winter in leifure I live,
Their characters all to the public I'll give :
For indeed I muft own, though I do it with fhame,
I envy your praife and poetical fame.

As Mr. LLANSTUFFIN thefe characters drew',
He faid fomething of EDMUND, *which if it be true,*
I'm furpris'd that it was not related by you.
The *critical part,* which it feems you forgot,
Was EDMUND's *reply to the* CHARGES *of* SCOTT ;
Who declar'd that the former was fully acquainted,
At the time he that picture fo horrible painted,
(At which female tendernefs *water'd* and *fainted.)*
That to HASTINGS no blame could be juftly imputed,
And that fince, *the whole calumny had been refuted.*
To this EDMUND anfwer'd, altho' I agree,
I have but *one witnefs* to weigh *againft* THREE,
What fignifies that, when I prudently chofe,
To give credit to *this,* and to *difbelieve* THOSE ?
I ftated as much as *my purpofes* FITTED ;
The reft I deem'd falfe, *and 'twas therefore omitted.*
This method of acting may poffibly do,
As a fubject of animadverfion for you :
You may fay with a laugh, that this mode of proceeding
Is owing to BURKE's *jefuitical breeding* ;
That Orators, when they engage in difputes,
Mention only as much as their purpofes fuits.
But you know, that the *innocent natives of* WALES
Are extremely averfe to *the garbling of tales;*
And we think that this BURKE, whom you feem to admire,
Is not half fo good as *a Taffyland fquire :*

And

And rather than I would fuch company keep,

I would live on the HILLS *with the* GROUSE *and the*

SHEEP.

But though I have given free fcope to my pen,

Don't let it prevent you from writing again.

'Tis true, that myfelf and fome others have noted,

To the Intereft of BURKE *you are too much devoted*;

And it has been fufpected you are in his pay,

In verfe to record all he chufes to fay.

But this, *Brother* SIMKIN, I know is untrue,

We are no PARTIZANS, fo I bid you adieu !

May 14th, 1789.

LET

LETTER XXVI.

ALAS ! *my dear* BROTHER, ill omens portend,
That our long correspondence draws near to its end :
I conjure all my friends, not to conftrue the effect
Of mifconduct in PITT, into SIMKIN's *neglect.*

> Oh ! may that STATESMAN ever hated be
> By all the Mufes in the fame degree,
> Curs'd by APOLLO, as by BURKE and ME !

The *buds of* FANCY in luxuriance blowing,
    Like Eaftern Wind, *his breath* peftif'rous blighted ;
The ftream of Oratory fweetly flowing—
    That ftream it dry'd, which you and me delighted.

The fragrant flowers in ELOCUTION's *fpring,*
    Like morning froft, HIS *breath* congealing nipp'd ;
In plumage gay, IMAGINATION's wing
    Soaring aloft his hand unhallow'd clipp'd.

In ELEGY folemn no more to complain,
As curfes and pray'rs are both equally vain ;

I muft

I muſt tell you, but not without horror and dread,

That the rage of reſtriction ſeems likely to ſpread ;

But I ſhould not break in at the midſt of a ſtory,

So I'll lay the proceedings in order before you.

Many PAPERS laſt Tueſday were read by the CLERKS,

Whoſe dryneſs was moiſten'd by EDMUND's remarks :

" By reading theſe documents, 'tis my intent,

" Of the *foot of* CORRUPTIONS to give you *the ſcent.*

" The ſcent of CORRUPTION is laſting and ſtrong ;

" If we follow our noſes, we cannot go wrong."

Then ſniffing and ſnuffing BURKE follow'd the track

Of corruption, like BRAWLER, *the head of the pack* ;

But in ſpite of this hunt and the muſical cry

Of BRAWLER, the ſport grew inſipid and dry.

By the Ladies the Court was but thinly attended,

And *the* CLERKS ſeem'd aſleep ere the buſineſs was
      ended.

For the *uſe of* LOGICIANS, I beg leave to add,

Where *preſumption affirmative* cannot be had,

A NEGATIVE one may be put in its place,

As a ſubſtitute good in a *criminal caſe.*

This doctrine to ſome appear'd dang'rous and new,

But in HASTINGS's caſe, EDMUND ſays it will do.—

Laſt THURSDAY again I attended the COURT,

Without any reaſon to boaſt of the ſport.

K 2

Oh !

Oh ! how I admire this moſt wonderful man,

For contriving a new œconomical plan !

As the COMMONS, you know, have refus'd him per-
    miſſion

To indent at his pleaſure for new ammunition ;

The balls which lay ſcatter'd and ſpread on the plain,

Are collected by GREY, *and fir'd over again.*

In this cannonade ſo terrific and hot,

NUNDCOMAR and his charge were unlawfully ſhot.

But to ſpeak in plain language, as GREY was proceed-
    ing,

The Counſel objected to what he was reading :

They ſaid that no credit was due to the tongue

Of a ſlanderous fellow, for *forgery* HUNG !

Now CHARLES, to keep HASTINGS's *Counſel* in awe,

In argument roſe againſt PLOMER, and LAW.

You have heard it by many repeatedly ſaid,

Like CHARLES's there never exiſted a head.

His head is a rich *inexhauſtible mine,*

Of arguments plauſible, ſubtle, and fine :

'Tis a BANK, where the *orders* of SOPHISTRY paſs,

And are paid on demand in *lead, copper,* or *braſs.*

This man, whoſe acuteneſs diſcover'd a fault

In every ſpecies of evidence brought,

To convict BURKE of—having ſaid, more than he
    ought ;

Tho'

Tho' EDMUND was twice heard to own and deare it ;
Tho' the writers took notes, and were ready to fwear it ;
Tho' CHARLES *was twice prefent, and happen'd to hear*
  it ;

Tho' the *Members* themfelves heard the ORATOR fpeak ;
All this was incompetent, futile, and weak.
This man, who contended againft the admitting
Proofs ftrong as all thefe, becaufe light and unfitting,
Now proves to the COURT, *in this* CASE to difpenfe
With an OATH, is confiftent with JUSTICE and SENSE.
" But in *lieu of an* OATH, or the Pris'ner's admiffion,
" We have NUNDCOMAR's *word,* and a *load of* SUSPI-
  " CION.
" And tho' he on a *gibbet* for FORGERY died,
" Does it follow from thence, that he conftantly lied ?
" I fay, (and 'twas feemingly faid with REGRET)
" We have brought the beft proof WE *could poffibly get.*
" 'Tis the cuftom of all the LAW COURTS of *our* KING,
" To *accept the beft proofs* that the Plaintiffs can bring ;
" And when there is doubt of what people advance,
" To *caft up the odds,* and be GUIDED *by* CHANCE.
" When you think of the charafter now at your Bar,
" And of HIS, who *accus'd him*—the faid NUNDCOMAR—
" Can any one harbour a doubt in his breaft,
" But the *word* of the LATTER is *fafeft* and *beft* ?"
This reas'ning of CHARLES, though *exceedingly good,*
Was either not relifh'd, or mifunderftood ;

K 3

For the LORDS to their chamber agreed to withdraw,
To confult with their Oracles, *men of the* LAW.
This determin'd the COURT for that day to adjourn,
And I hear that next Wedn'sday they mean to return;
The *genius* of CHARLES no eulogium can raife—
It is *proof againft* SHAME; and *fuperior to* PRAISE;
He turns like a *gig*, and you'd wonder thereat,
In a perfon like his, fo *unwieldly* and *fat*.
All his friends and his enemies freely confefs
His verfatile powers, his art, and addrefs.
There is nothing fo white, there is nothing fo black,
But CHARLEY *can either defend, or attack.*
Before, *my dear* SIMON, I lay down my pen—
(As I may not find matter to write you again),
I muft tell you, that HASTINGS's *counfel* objected,
To BURKE in a manner I never expected:
For HE, who had been fo extremely profufe,
Who had fcarcely omitted *one term of abufe*;
Who when his own language could furnifh no more, ⎫
Lamented its being fo barren and poor— ⎬
So *repeated* the fame he *had utter'd before.* ⎭
In the field of an argument ample and fpacious,
He gave to fome action the name of " *audacious.*"
The COUNSEL of this to *their* LORDSHIPS complain'd,
And BURKE for indelicate terms was arraign'd.

You

You will judge from this trifling, this fimple event,

What reafon I have to complain and lament;

If Burke is confin'd to *decorum* and *order*,

I'll relinquifh my Pen, and the *Poft of* Recorder.

20th May, 1789,

LET-

LETTER XXVII.

LAST Wednefday, *dear Brother*, their LORDSHIPS
    decreed,
That NUNDCOMAR's *Charge* 'twere unlawful to read;
That is, as their CONSCIENCES *could not believe it*—
They thought that in Juftice they could not receive it.
When the CHANCELLOR faid, " that *their* LORDSHIPS
    " were come
" To this refolution," *poor* EDMUND was dumb.
He ftood like a fpectre, aghaft and affrighted,
Then pray'd that the words might again be recited.
The words were repeated—The MANAGERS pray'd
For time to confult :—So the TRIAL was ftay'd.
You remember how MILTON has finely related,
That when the *dark* PRINCE was in battle defeated,
He to council conven'd all his LEADERS in *black*,
To confult about making another attack.
So EDMUND, extremely diftrefs'd and perplext,
Confults with his friends upon Battle *the next*.
Awhile they fat fullen ; then JOSEPH arofe,
And thus fpoke to the Chief in *poetical profe :*

" Th'

" Th' ADVICE I offer'd at the laſt debate,
" Was then rejected, and I now repeat,
" You will repent it, and repent too late.
" Why do we thus encounter *endleſs ſhame,*
" Like deſperate gamblers, *play the loſing game?*
" The very ſufferers, whoſe cauſe we try,
" DISOWN *it,* and *their advocates* DENY.
" The HOUSE which ſent us here to plead this cauſe,
" Diſguſted too, *its confidence withdraws:*
" *The* LORDS, who ought to favour and protect us
" On all occaſions, ſlightingly neglect us.
" Oh! that it had never been undertaken,
" *Would that the cauſe laſt week had been forſaken."*
Here MONTAGUE put in to ſave the name
Of his *dear* BURKE, from everlaſting ſhame.
" Fatal, ALAS! the conſequence muſt be
" To this great cauſe, if LEADERS *diſagree:*
" Shame and defeat attend deſponding fear,
" Whilſt FORTUNE yields to thoſe, who PERSEVERE.
" New ammunition let the Chiefs provide,
" To cannonade the fort on every ſide.
" *You,* CHARLES, a thund'ring battery muſt erect,
" To bear upon the *baſtion* INTELLECT.
" And JOSEPH—you, behind the curtain ſtealing,
" Muſt undermine *the* COURT on *fudge,* and *feeling,*

" Let

" Let Edmund's cannon on their *patience* play;

" To beat down *that, already giving way.*

" Pleas'd with th' advice, the Chiefs with ardor

  " burn'd;

" Dissolv'd the Council, and to Court Re-

  " turn'd."

Now Edmund begins to lament and complain,

That the *foot of corruption* is fcented in vain :

That if probable evidence cannot be taken,

The caufe to its very foundation is fhaken ;

And Charles alfo thunder'd againft the decifion,

Till *their* Lordships confented at length to revifion.

To determine, if what they rejected before,

As it loudly demanded admiffion *once more,*

Might not be let in at the *kitchen back-door ?*

A while they withdrew—to their Room to debate ;

But refus'd on returning, *to open the gate.*

Now Edmund pathetic, begins to implore

They would kindly conduct him to fome *other door :*

" Ah ! why will your Lordships permit us to ftray ?

" We are *ignorant travellers* lofing our way."

Then Edmund in paffionate language began

To prove that *himfelf* was an *ignorant man,*

That a *large ftock of ignorance* fell to the fhare

Of himfelf and the herd that was under his care.

That

That *they* could no solid advantages draw,

From confulting with DOUGLAS and DICK *of the law*.

Juft here a thought fuddenly enter'd my head,

Which *in private*, to you, may with fafety be faid;

If they want either will, or the power to affift,

Their civilians and counfellors might be *difmift*;

For why fhould the NATION incur an expence,

In the hire of *profound legal knowledge*, and *fenfe*,

From THOSE, to themfelves who fo clofely have kept it,

Or if BURKE did not think it worth while to accept it?

To RETURN to the fubjeƈt of EDMUND's oration;—

He faid, "that CORRUPTION and bafe PECULATION;"

From their LORDSHIPS' refolve would extenfively fpread;

That they aided in raifing INIQUITY's *head*.

Fox thinking that he could be *louder* and *ftronger*,

Would not fuffer his LEADER, to fpeak any longer;

Awhile there appear'd a *confufion of tongues*,

But CHARLEY *prevail'd by the ftrength of his lungs*.

He prov'd to the LORDS, 'twas exceedingly wrong,

To expeƈt from the MANAGERS evidence ftrong:

That they fhould not be fqueamifh, but joyfully take

The proofs that are offer'd, *for juftice's* fake,

And fince *all the doors* below ftairs were fhut,

To the *window*, a *ladder* CHARLES artfully put.

(For

(For tho' by the late unexpected conclusion,

The doors were close barr'd against daring intrusion,

That does not amount to a *total exclusion.)*

Again to their chamber their LORDSHIPS withdraw

To put this new question to men of the law :

There is *one* Dr. PARR, it behoves you to know,

Who won all the MANAGERS' hearts long ago,

By a *cramp Latin preface of broken quotations,*

In praise of their politics, parts, and orations ;

This *parsonage* often attends in their box,

To *glean hints for his* SERMONS, *from* EDMUND, *and* FOX ;

And perhaps as a *Casuist* deep, to suggest

Some subtle *new quirk,* when the cause is hard prest,

Or to furnish *dry scraps from* OLD AUTHORS : at least,

He can never be requisite *there,* as a PRIEST—

For *intentions so pure,* and such MEEKNESS OF SPIRIT,

Must of course, and of right, HEAVEN'S *kingdom in-*
  herit :

Unless as a *chaplain,* they'd have him say grace,

For *success on their arms,* ere the battle takes place,

This same MANAGER'S Box, I've observ'd to be lin'd,

With *hungry expectants* of every kind.

And PARR, as a *Regency* BISHOP ELECT,

Has a claim to a seat *among those who expect.*

For finding his LATIN, his WIG, and his BIRCH,

All too weak to secure *his ascent in the* CHURCH,

He

He dashingly join'd OPPOSITION in form,

Determin'd to *carry a Mitre by* STORM !

I have much more to say, but this moment a friend

Is come in, and of course, *my epiftle* muft end.

Howe'er of *remiffnefs* you fhall not complain,

I mean by next poft to addrefs you again.

May 25th, 1789.

LETTER XXVIII.

I TOLD you, *dear* BROTHER, their LORDSHIPS retir'd
To confider of that which the LEADERS requir'd :
On THURSDAY, the day to which they had adjourn'd,
They met, and Lord THURLOW their anfwer return'd ;
Which was, " that *their* LORDSHIPS not being *afleep*,
" 'Twas impoffible *now* through the window to creep !"
Here EDMUND brought in a poetic quotation,
Which attributes to NOW, *an eternal duration :*
He faid the word *now*, was a cruel obftruction,
A difficult *problem*, too *hard* for reduction ;
That the MANAGERS meant to return to their College,
For phyfical, and metaphyfical knowledge ;
Or *fome fort of knowledge*, informing them how
To purge from the caufe, *fuch obftructions* as " now."
After thefe obfervations, BURKE finifh'd his pleading,
And the clerk for awhile was engag'd with his reading ;
Then EDMUND that evidence offer'd once more,
Which the LORDS had rejected fo often before ;
And by way of fupporting his prefent pretenfion,
Of " NOW" and of " THEN," he defcrib'd the *dimenfion*,
The period of " NOW," with exactnefs he reckon'd,
And faid, " THEN" was the *firft*, and that " NOW" *was*
    the fecond.

I   Here

Here the CHANCELLOR wish'd that the LEADERS would
    say,
What motives they had for thus forcing their way?
Then CHARLES, in his vehement manner of storming,
The QUESTION *evades*, and objects to informing:
He said, 'twas *the* MANAGER's duty to try
(As HASTINGS would neither confefs nor deny)
To conftrue his filence, his want of expreffion,
Into *probable guilt*, and *prefumptive confeffion*.
He added, had HASTINGS's confcience been cleaner,
He had fhewn no omiffory fullen *demeanour*:
" Suppofe that I heard any perfon complain
" Of its being my fault, that fo many were flain,
" Of the WESTMINSTER PEOPLE that voted for HOOD,
" I would furely deny it *as long-as I could*—
" And if *I* this moment were put on my trial,
" I would *not* be found guilty, *for want of* DENIAL."
Now EDMUND put in, and with ardour befought
Their LORDSHIPS would kindly pafs over a fault;
He hoped, and he trufted, they would not reject
The proof he could bring for a trifling defect—
That fo high a tribunal ought not to be ty'd
To the forms, and the rules whereby LAWYERS decide,
But CONVENIENCY take, a lefs fallible guide;
" And if pains and penalties are not inflicted
" On *Eaftern delinquents, till fairly convicted,*

                    " The

" The MANAGERS here may a long time harangue
" Before they may see any one of them hang;
" And if *probable evidence* is not admitted,
" The Prisoner's in danger of being acquitted.
" *Living* WITNESSES into this country to bring
" From INDIA, *my* LORDS, is a difficult thing:
" There was but *one* BRAMIN who ventur'd to crofs }
" The fea, and he felt irretrievable lofs, }
" Nothing lefs than the *family title of* Doss." }
This allufion juft then I did not comprehend,
Till 'twas clear'd up by EDMUND's particular friend;
And as he detail'd an agreeable ftory,
I'll digrefs for a moment, to lay it before you ·—

―――――――

A STORY.

BURKE——*The* BRAMIN——*and the* HOT-HOUSE.

One GOONISHAM, my Authors fay,
Was bred a *Joiner* * at BOMBAY;
Where, by fome damnable tranfgreffion,
He loft *his caft* and his profeffion.
He gave his jailor too, the flip,
And got on board an Englifh fhip;

* The Carpenter Caft is extremely low in India.

There

There hiding underneath the deck,
From *halter* fav'd his forfeit neck.
When GOONISHAM to *England* came,
He heard of EDMUND's founding fame,
And adding Doss to his furname,
With that *enthufiaftic*, paft
For *Bramin* * of the higheft caft.
Now BURKE, with exultation big,
Like him who got *the learned pig*,
Grafps at this fund of information,
To furnifh many a long oration.
At home invites him to refide;
An offer which the SAINT deny'd.
EDMUND provided next a treat—
The fcrup'lous FATHER would not eat;
A *Jefuit's table* would not fuit him,
A *Cath'lic dwelling* would pollute him.
Now BURKE fits up, at vaft expence,
A HOT-HOUSE for his refidence;
The *old exotics out he threw*,
To make provifion for *the new*,
Pines and *et cæteras* out of number,
Were thrown away as ufelefs lumber:

* The Bramin Caft is the higheft in India, being of the Order of
Melchifedeck.

L

The

The Houfe was warm'd with conftant fire,

And all things done to his defire ;

Then EDMUND begg'd his Rev'rend Mafter,

T' inftruct him in his *Holy Shafter.**

No fooner does the Scholar afk,

Than GOONISHAM begins the tafk.

Without a Book he glibly reads

Four of his *own invented Bedes* ;†

Ordaining ceremonies fafter

Than *Mofes,* or than *Zoroafter.*‡

As far as BURKE could comprehend

The broken Englifh of his friend,

He thought the doctrine vaftly fine,

Angelic, heavenly, and divine :

And left the fragment fhould be mifs'd,

He got a learned man t' affift—

—'Twas JONES, the *Orientalift.*

You've read the ftory of the *Pigeon,*

That brought *Mahomed* his Religion ;

Juft fo this *fable, humming Bird,*

From *Ram* § to EDMUND brought the word :

* Hindoo Bible.

† Four Books of Hindoo Scripture, or Four Gofpels.

‡ Zoroafter, the Perfian Mofes.

§ Ram, a Hindoo Dewtah.

The two Difciples now prepare
A *Shafter* with uncommon care,
Which BURKE keeps ready to produce,
As often as it is of ufe.
But now the fhip departed hence,
And BURKE by way of Recompence,
At parting made a long Oration,
For this fad Joiner's Revelation :
Bound for BENGAL, the *Renegade*,
On board the Ship refum'd his trade;
So to CALCUTTA made his way,
(Not daring to approach BOMBAY :)
There known too well he laid afide,
The *name of* Doss, the BRAMIN's pride.

––––––––––

To return to the HALL, BURKE proceeded to fhow,
That all the Law Courts were *too vulgar,* and *low;*
That their practice was *pitiful, paltry,* and *mean,*
Not fit to be followed, fcarce fit to be feen.
That this *high* TRIBUNAL fhould conftantly act,
By *general opinion,* not *matter of fact.*
Here EDMUND was making a monftrous ado,
About fome bloody Letter, and † *Conta-Bah-Booh;*

* Mr. Burke's method of pronouncing it.

When

When CAMDEN obferv'd, that the leaders had try'd
To fhove themfelves in upon every fide.
But tho' they had fail'd, yet the COURT did not venture,
To fay there was *no place*, at which they might enter;
One conclufion, however, he wifh'd them to draw,—
If they enter, it muft be, *according to* LAW.
He therefore, requefted them, *now* to decide,
How many more *apertures* were to be try'd;
But the LEADERS perceiv'd his intent was to fix,
And, perhaps, guard againft their *Old Harlequin tricks*;
So requefted the COURT would excufe them from faying,
What cards they *now* hold, and keep ready for playing.
Then CHARLEY, with arguments fubtle, contended,
The *firft Period* of NOW, muft be perfectly ended:
That himfelf and the MANAGERS hop'd and expected,
In *Period* the *fecond*, they'll not be rejected.
He ended—their LORDSHIPS adjourn'd to decide—
If the hole they attempt, be *now* open and wide.—
As CHARLEY thus play'd his diverfify'd game,
It put me in mind of that beaft of his name,
Whofe paws are fo noted for ftealing and picking,
Who one night carry'd off, my *old Hen, and her Chicken*,
My guns and my houfe-dogs, my bolts and my locks,
Were too weak to refift the attempts of *that Fox*,
And into the Manfion, I'll venture a bet,
By *Hook* or by *Crook* that *this Biped* will get.*

* Simkin was miftaken.

This day by an accurate meafure 'twas found,

The MANAGERS gain'd not an inch of new ground;

And PROVIDENCE feems in no hurry to blefs,

Their Pious attempts with entreated fuccefs,

Notwithftanding the Pray'r of that brave *Devil-fighter*,*

Who I yefterday told you, was *ftorming a* MITRE.

Adieu—if next Wednefday fends food for my pen,

Be affur'd, *my lov'd* SIMON, I'll write you again.

May 27th, 1789.

* Doctor Parr.

LET-

LETTER XXIX.

LAST WEDNESDAY, DEAR BROTHER, the *Weſt-*
    minſter COURT
Was expected to furniſh much matter of ſport;
And as GWYNNY and WYNNY had never gone thither,
We call'd for a coach and proceeded together;
Not all the fine words of thoſe *eloquent Sparks,*
Not the ſtill finer documents read by the CLERKS,
Were half ſo diverting as GWYNNY's remarks :—
She ſaid, " that the LEADER, the *Captain Impeacher,*
Reſembled her Aunt's Methodiſtical teacher :
She was pleas'd to the life with his praying and canting,
And offended as much by his raving and ranting;
She thought that ſo much of the *Iriſhman's howl,*
Made the ſtream of his eloquence muddy and foul.
Her anxiety now, the dear creature expreſſes,
For the wear of the *Bayes* of the Manager's dreſſes,—
Who might, if they had œconomical ſenſe,
In *Monmouth-Street* change them at little expence."
I took down what ſhe ſaid, and perhaps I may ſpin ye,
A Letter or two from the ſaying of GWYNNY;
And if that's not enough for diverſion and laughter,
One or two from the ſayings of WYNNY hereafter.

For

For the girls on the *Mountains* of *Taffyland* bred,
Have ideas as ftrange, as can enter a head.
The remarks which they made, were fo new and amufing,
That I loft a great portion of EDMUND's accufing ;
Howe'er to continue my narrative plan,
I'll report all that happen'd as well as I can :——

When the CHANCELLOR faid that the Lords had
    agreed,
That NUNDCOMAR's Charge was improper to read,
Poor EDMUND appear'd to be fadly confounded,
Not knowing on what this decifion was grounded :
He faid, " PECULATION, however notorious,
" Would now be triumphantly great and *uproarious,*
" And HASTINGS, he fear'd, would at laft be victo-
    " rious."
He faid, " that this look'd like a *holy contrivance,*
" Of *clerical Men,* for the fake of connivance—
" My LORDS, I do fay, a Nabob's peculation
" Is wrapp'd up as clofe as a PRIEST's *fornication :*
" If a *Parfon* that damnable crime fhould commit,
" The Judges who try'd him were bound to acquit,
" According to ancient canonical law,
" Unlefs 'twas an act *thirty-two People* faw ;
" And to guard againft falfehood and flanderous lies,
" They muft fee the fact, openly done with their eyes :

L 4

" But

" But to prove that a BISHOP convers'd with a Miſs,

" Requir'd *forty witneſſes* added to this."

An agreeable doctrine to *Prelates* and *Graces,*

Whoſe feelings appear'd in their riſible faces;

And the Ladies, by ſympathy, ſeem'd to diſcover

The advantage of having a *ſpiritual Lover.*

Now I'm ſadly afraid that *Wives, Widows,* and *Miſſes,*

Will confine to the CHURCH all their favours and kiſſes;

And ſhould all the girls to this doctrine accede,

The State of the *Clergy* were envy'd indeed!

Here EDMUND a Letter proceeded to quote,

Which he ſtrongly ſuſpects the *old dancing Girl* wrote;

'Twas to prove the ſum total of HASTINGS's *fees*

Amounted to more than *three Lacks of Rupees.*

He ſaid, that as Ladies of that injur'd nation

Were excluded from view, by their cuſtom and ſtation,

They muſt have *ſome method of communication.*

" And 'tis not in nature, your LORDSHIPS may ſay,

" To block up a Lady, or *ſtop up her way;*

" And as Ladies can never be *falſe* or *abſurd,*

" Inſtead of an oath we may credit their word.

" Tho' *Eccleſiaſtical, Civil,* and *Common,*

" Tho' no law admits the bare word of a Woman,—

" Tho' EQUITY, CHANCERY, always reject it,

" The *High-Court of* PARLIAMENT *ought to reſpect it.*

" If

" If no rule can be found, we can't poffibly take one,

" 'Tis therefore the MANAGERS' duty to *make one*.

" And fince we've no evidence ftronger and better,

" Be pleas'd to accept of the *dancing Girl's Letter*."—

Now EDMUND affected to treat as a joke

The doctrine of Evidence, written by COKE ;

And of all the abfurdities he ever faw,

The greateft abfurdities were in the LAW.

Tho' their LORDSHIPS' decifion was certainly good,

As the principle of it was not underftood—

He admitted, however, for fear he fhould wrong 'em,

There was *great underftanding, and learning among 'em.*

But as they retir'd to their room to debate,

Where *himfelf* and his *friends* have no claim to a feat,

He could not divine, on what bafis they built

Their *mortal averfion* to *probable guilt.*

As the MANAGERS daily grow keener and keener,

To eftablifh *omiffory rules of* DEMEANOR ;

And to fave fuch a number of *mufic-lefs dances,*

They at laft had recourfe to *immaculate* FRANCIS.

This gentleman, when he appeared at the bar,

To give fome account of the *faid* NUNDCOMAR,

By the Counfel of HASTINGS was fuddenly ftopp'd,

And I cannot tell why, but the *bufinefs was* DROPP'D.

GWYNNY

Gwynny afk'd me to tell her the MANAGERS *meaning*
In trying to fettle new modes of demeaning ?
But WYNNY conceiv'd the intent of thefe rules,
Was *improvement of youth* in the MANAGERS' *Schools.*
By repeated defeat BURKE grew peevifh and fretful,
And LAWRENCE * fuppofing him rather *forgetful,*
Was correcting fome technical *error in trade,*
(Which he muft underftand *being recently made* ;)
When BURKE his kind offer morofely rejected,
And the *young* CIVIL LAWYER ftood juftly corrected.

As the *Poft bell* is ringing, this Letter I end,
But another, next week, I fhall certainly fend ;
For as long as *the* LEADER goes on with his pleading,
I can furnifh you always with plenty of reading ;
That the ORATOR's arguments merit renown,
Is th' opinion of all the *News Writers* in Town.

 May 30th, 1789.

 * The fuppofed author of the ROLLIAD, and with *peculiar propriety* therefore felected by Mr. BURKE *as one of the Council for the
Commons.*

LETTER XXX.

" YOURSELF and *my cousins* are frighted," you say,
" At my silence last week, and unlook'd-for delay;"
I promis'd another epistle should follow,
But I promis'd without the consent of APOLLO:
Oh, BROTHER ! a cruel disorder invades,
And ELYSIUM invites me to dwell with the shades.
As I lie on my bed in a state of dejection,
I am griev'd to the soul by this dismal reflection,
That if SIMKIN should sink underneath his disorder,
The LEADER of *Leaders* may want a RECORDER.

Before *great* EDMUND spoke, in strains sublime,
   Liv'd Orators who rav'd as long and loud;
Whose names have perish'd in the stream of time,
   Sunk in oblivion with the silent crowd !
In the cold earth, if he forgotten lie,
   What is the *indefatigable tongue ?*
The eloquent and mute alike must die,
   If ORATORY's praise be left unsung.

But

But if the aſſiſtançe of WARREN, and BAKER,
Diſappoint for the preſent the ſad Undertaker ;
I truſt that the CHIEFS will illumine my piece,
In fame will ſurvive like the *Worthies* of GREECE.

You aſk me, *dear* SIMON, if EDMUND the nice,
Who, like Jack, roſe to combat the GIANT of VICE ;
Who declar'd that *corruption* and baſe *peculation*,
Taints every good Chriſtian who viſits that nation :
That all are corrupt in the higheſt degree,
Except his *oft-mention'd immaculate* THREE.
You aſk me, if EDMUND, *theſe dangers foreknowing*,
Conſented to WILL, his *dear Relative's*, going ?
Oh ! SIMON ! I often reflect on thoſe days,
We have ſpent on the Mountains in innocent plays ;
Where from morning till night, 'twas our cuſtom to keep,
So our father commanded, the runts and the ſheep :
How often with GWYNNY, ſweet PHYLLIS, and CHLOE,
In the evening we danç'd, on the Banks of the TOWEY,
In thoſe innocent days, but, alas ! they are fled !
I never ſuſpected what any one ſaid :
In NATURE's plain words, in SIMPLICITY's ſtile,
We ſpoke what we thought, we were ſtrangers to guile ;
But in this *great* METROPOLIS, *few are ſo weak*
As to SAY *what they* THINK, *or to* THINK *what they* SPEAK.

Here

Here daily-repeated experience teaches,

How the *actions* of Men difagree with *their fpeeches*;

Their language and ftile, men adapt to their cafes,

As ladies, their colours, adapt to their faces :

And an Orator's fpeech ftands in need of adorning,

As a *City* DAME's face, does of paint in the morning.

Yes, *Brother*, the faƈt is undoubtedly true,

And I fafely may venture, to tell it to you,

To INDIA, his Coufin, great EDMUND fent o'er,

As *Agent* to TUL-JA-JEE, *Chief of Tanjore*;

But when into *Office, our Orator* got,

Coufin WILL * he remov'd, from *Tanjore*, to *Arcot*;

For BURKE and his family, *moft people fay*,

Are anxious at all times, *to finger the Pay*.

Tho' they look upon Gold, *as peftifirous Trafh*,

They are partial, it feems, to the *counting of cafh*.

'Tis written, offenders we fhould not condemn,

As perhaps fome excufe may be pleaded for them;

It may be, that BURKE's *coufin* was fent to that nation,

To fet an example of ftrange moderation.

So EDMUND and Fox, once *were* willing to take

ALL THE EAST to THEMSELVES, for HUMANITY'S SAKE!

* Mr. WILLIAM BURKE, Agent to the Rajah of Tranjore from 1777 to 1782, when Lord ROCKINGHAM appointed him, (at the recommendation of Mr. EDMUND BURKE,) Paymafter of the King's Forces in India, which office he ftill retains.

And

And left fouls fhould be damn'd for attachment to
    pelf,
Burke confented to take, *half the fin to himfelf*;
In hopes of affecting the purification
Of morals, by " *leading men out of temptation.*"

    But now, *my dear Brother*, 'tis time I recal
My attention to that which occurr'd at *the* Hall;
I expect in your next, I fhall find you complaining,
That the bufinefs of Thurfday was not entertaining;
It chiefly confifted of document reading,
And Grey and Anstruther alternately pleading;
Of whom in *one couplet* enough may be faid,
The one *was* Quicksilver, the other was Lead.'
With Hastings's *Counfel* they warmly debated,
What evidence fhould, and what fhould not be ftated?
It feems, the whole ftrength of their evidence lies,
In *queftions*, and *old* Munny Begum's replies,
But, it ftrikes me with wonder, I needs muft confefs,
When I think of the Managers' laying fuch ftrefs,
On the *word of a woman*, a pitiful creature—
As Edmund defcrib'd her, " the *outcaft of nature.*"
Some letters Grey faid, " appear'd very unfit,
To be read, as their tendency was to acquit;
And here, like *their Chief*, the *fubordinates try'd*,
To fhove in accufations on every fide;

For the MANAGING BODY, 'tis fit you should know,
With zeal, and with ardour, all equally glow,
From EDMUND *the head, to* SIR GILBERT *the toe.*

All equally eager and keen on accusing,
Tho' unequal to Fox in the style of abusing,
And unequal to JOSEPH, and BURKE, in amusing.

But the CHANCELLOR tir'd of their pleasant digressions,
Made use of some very unfriendly expressions.
Lord THURLOW is very precise and exact,
And relishes nothing but *matter of fact*;
To EQUITY *bred*, and inur'd from his youth
To *elaborate investigation of truth*;
He thinks oratorical flights and allusions,
In *criminal cases*, improper intrusions.
He says, that no charges are fit to be quoted,
Except *those alone* which the COMMONERS voted :
That the Managers should not be suffer'd to stray,
But *prove*, and *establish*, whatever they say.
Notwithstanding, *dear* BROTHER, this rigid decree,
Is destructive at once to *my* HERO and ME ;
Notwithstanding its consequence I may deplore,
The CHANCELLOR'S CHARACTER, *all men adore !*
'Twas HE who of late, on a trying occasion,
Was proof against *threats*, and the *arts of persuasion* ;
Who *his* MAKER invok'd, if HE *ever forsook*
His *sick Master*, to blot his own name from the book;

When BURKE, in his phrenzy, announc'd to the world,
" *That the king, by Omnipotence smitten, was hu-l'd*
" *From his Throne !*" He stood forth in that critical hour,
To secure to his KING, *the resumption of* POWER;
Like CATO, in *Virtue*, inflexibly strong,
No *passion can urge him, to* THAT *which is wrong.*

This day, tho' the reason I cannot yet find,
BURKE, like *insignificance*, rested behind;
And by way of amusement, Fox *went to a race*,
Leaving *well-belov'd* JOSEPH to act in his place;
Who, if GREY and ANSTRUTHER were forc'd to give
      back,
Like a *corps de reserve*, might renew the attack.
FAREWELL, my *dear* SIMON ! and *Deo volente,*
Another epistle shall quickly be sent ye.

    June 9th, 1789.

LET-

LETTER XXXI.

PREPARING laſt Wedneſday to viſit the HALL,
My *maiden Aunt* BRIDGET, juſt gave a call;
You know ſhe was frighted away from the *bar*,
By the ſtory BURKE told about PRINCE CANTEMAR,
I could never prevail on my *delicate Aunt*
Till Wedneſday, to think of repeating her jaunt :
And I firmly believe ſhe would not have gone then,
If I had not aſſur'd her, that modeſt young men,
Like GREY, and ſome others, who being beginners,
Wou'd not talk ſo looſely, as harden'd old Sinners.
So when the time fix'd by adjournment drew nigh,
Away went together *Aunt* BRIDGET and I;
It chanc'd that the LORDS, long engag'd in Debate,
This day did not make their appearance till late.
We ſat in the GALLERY more than an hour,
Whilſt my *Aunt* grew exceedingly peeviſh and ſour;
She abus'd without mercy, delays of the law,
And in gen'ral found fault with whatever ſhe ſaw :
She was not, however, averſe to allowing
That their LORDSHIPS *were highly improv'd in their*
　　　bowing;

M

This

This could not, fhe thought, be imputed to chance,

But that EDMUND, turn'd *Mafter*, had taught them to

dance.

And if BRIDGET, this fummer, fhou'd come down to

Wales,

You'll not be furpris'd, if, among other tales,

You hear her in Company boldly advancing,

That EDMUND has open'd a *College for dancing*.

Now the LORDS are affembled, and BURKE begins

boring,

The COURT, with fome papers collected by GORING;

And the COUNSEL, as ufual, repeat their objections

To receiving as *Evidence*, GORING's *Collections:*

Here EDMUND infifting, their LORDSHIPS withdraw,

To communicate queftions to *Men of the Law;*

They return, and the anfwer comes out as expected,

And GORING's *Collection* is alfo REJECTED.

Now querulous EDMUND proceeds to remark,

That himfelf and the MANAGERS were in the dark:

" I have fuffer'd no method, no mode to efcape,

" I have try'd, and will try it in every fhape;

" It may be that your LORDSHIPS are not well contented

" With the manner, in which our addrefs is prefented.

" If we fail in punctilio, or etiquette,

" The MANAGERS right, it behoves you to fet."—

Now

Now BURKE, like a fly that has tasted of honey,

Returns in great haste, to his *favorite* MUNNY :

With vehemence urges, " 'tis vastly absurd,

" To question or doubt of *her* HIGHNESS's *word* ;

" That where Ladies of rank cannot *decently swear,*

" We ought to believe what they choose to declare;"

And he mention'd some dames of such delicate pride,

Who *swore before men,* and in consequence *dy'd.*

He said, that in INDIA, great men had a pleasure,

In making fine Ladies, *deposits of treasure ;*

That the principal part of their riches were kept

By those Ladies, with whom they most frequeutly slept :

You'll remember, perhaps, that when HASTINGS af-
  serted

That custom *—by EDMUND 'twas much controverted ;

This, however, is *nothing*—for BURKE when he tries,

With equal *facility proves and denies.*

Now EDMUND impassion'd persists in declaring,

His indifference as to her Ladyship's swearing ;

That as long as life lasted, he never would fail

To *stick to the Lady,* and *stand by her tale.*

Here my *Aunt's virgin modesty* suffer'd a *shock,*

By supposing that BURKE meant the *tail* of her *smock ;*

And away from the HALL the *prim virgin* had fled,

If I had not explain'd what the MANAGER said :

* See Mr. Burke's Speeches last year, and Mr. Sheridan's.

  But

But as foon as his meaning was *well underſtood*;

She acknowledg'd that BURKE was *exceedingly good.*

And obferv'd that 'twas fomething uncommon to find,

In political men fuch a liberal mind;

And to women in years fo attentive and kind.

To proceed—BURKE declares, that the MANAGERS

            mean,

To keep their own confciences eafy and clean ;

" We offer good proof—if your LORDSHIPS rejeƈt it,

" All the fin is your own, and I'd have you expeƈt it.

" 'Tis owing to you, and 'twill ne'er be forgotten,

" That the firmament pillars are perifh'd and rotten."

At thefe words, my *Aunt's vifage* difcover'd her fears,

Left the firmament tumbling, fhou'd fall on her ears.

But EDMUND, involv'd in a mift of dark vapours,

At *this univerfal rejeƈtion of papers,*

Conceiv'd in his mind a moft intricate plot,

To make out his proof from the *conduƈt* of SCOTT :

Eftablifhing firmly a *new orthodoxy,*

That a man may confefs HIMSELF *guilty by proxy* ;

And indeed, I muft own, 'tis an excellent way,

Of making *the Agent* his MASTER betray.

This fail'd—and by way of retrieving his lofs,

BURKE adverts to the faying of RAJAH GOURDOSS ?

But this, like the reft, by the COUNSEL difputed,

Is repell'd as unworthy of being refuted.

Then EDMUND, to beat legal arguments down,

Made curious remarks on a COUNSELLOR's *gown*:

Whence I learnt that as *scarlet* makes OFFICERS brave,

A COUNSELLOR's *gown* makes a *Counsellor* grave:

And I think from their making their *perukes* so big,

Legal knowledge is chiefly *contain'd in the wig*;

For very wise people are free to confess,

Human character chiefly depends upon *dress.*

Just here, 'twas discover'd, that EDMUND the arch,

Upon HASTINGS's army was stealing a march;

But as rather too soon his intention was found,

The vigilant foe drove him back to his ground.

You must know, near the close of this tedious debate,

Where *my* HERO so frequently suffer'd *defeat,*

The term of " *Preposterous*" EDMUND apply'd,

In a way to the LORDS as affected their pride—

But whilst they consulted and talk'd of adjourning,

My HERO bethought him of *twisting and turning:*

He loudly demanded their LORDSHIPS wou'd stay,

Just to hear him adroitly explain it away;

He said, what he deem'd a *preposterous part,*

Was putting the *cart-horses* after the *cart.*

And as BURKE seem'd to speak with some marks of

      submission,

Their LORDSHIPS accepted of *this definition :*

Con-

Concluding, perhaps, that he beſt could define,

The true meaning of ſayings, ſo much *in his line.*

I obſerv'd in one part of my HERO's *Oration,*

He was ſuddenly ſtruck with profound veneration,

For the COMPANY's *Books :*—and I heard with ſurprize,

Theſe veridical Records can never tell lies :

And where he could get nothing fairer or better,

He would even put up with *a ſketch for a letter,*

I obſerv'd before EDMUND had clos'd the debate,

There was ſcarcely *a Manager left in his ſeat.*

Some reaſons induc'd all the CHIEFS to withdraw,

And they left BURKE to fight DALLAS, PLOMER, and
   LAW :

So when HECTOR compell'd all *the Grecians* to yield,

Old NESTOR alone ſtood diſputing the field.

At length, BURKE with pleading was deeply oppreſt,

So he begg'd to adjourn that *his tongue might have reſt.*

But as I'm in the humour for ſcribbling away,

I'll now give a ſketch of what paſs'd *the next day.*

 You muſt know, that BURKE wanted to ſee the In-
  ſtruction,

From HASTINGS to SCOTT, ſo he mov'd its *production :*

When the COURT was aſſembled, he ſpoke for two
  Hours,

About Major SCOTT, and his *general powers :*

3

He

He defcrib'd them as having *unbounded dimenfion*,

Whilft the COUNSEL deny'd this *uncommon extenfion* :

A whifper, mean time, round the GALLERY ran,

" *Which is he ?*" and " Where is this *powerful man ?*"

Now EDMUND proceeds with examining SCOTT,

Concerning what *powers*, he *had*, and *had not :*

But SCOTT, who is fond of beginning *de novo*,

And tracing the growth of *his Chicken ab ovo*,

Began a long fpeech, and went on to relate,

Some things which my CHIEF *did not want him to ftate;*

And unable to judge what he farther might fay,

BURKE *feem'd in a hurry to fend him away*,

So he left unfulfill'd THAT *repeated prediction*,

That HASTINGS, *to* SCOTT, *fhould owe certain conviction.**

In the courfe of this day, *an immortal commander*,

Difputed with LAW, on the meaning of *flander*.

You remember the COMMONERS once difavow'd,

Some things which the Orator utter'd aloud.

LAW thinks an *accufer*, that cannot fupport

His Charges, with *evidence given in* COURT,

Is *guilty of* SLANDER—but EDMUND and FOX,

In concert with all the *loud tongues in the box*,

Say, *falfe accufation* deferves no fuch name,

Till the HOUSE *of St. Stephen pronounce it the fame.*

* See Mr. Burke's Letter to Mr. Montague.

Here

Here this letter ends :—but expect, my dear Brother,
As soon as I've matter, I'll send you another :
But my AUNT BRIDGET says, left her nephew forget
    . her,
She too has some thoughts of transmitting a Letter.

June 17th, 1789.

LETTER XXXII.

OH, BROTHER! Oh, BROTHER! I'm deeply diftreft,
My mind is a *blifter*, a ftranger to reft :
I have fad news to give you, but when you receive it,
'Tis impoffible, SIMON, *that you fhould believe it.*
At St. STEPHEN's, laft Tuefday, BURKE fpoke of an
        order,
To turn SIMKIN out of *his poft* of RECORDER :
Oh ! where is that promife, made many months fince,
That I fhould be *Laureat*, one day, to *the* PRINCE ?
Alas ! all my hopes from HIS HIGHNESS are fled !
Ah ! why did I truft what *an* ORATOR faid ?
The praifes of EMUND, ah ! why did I fing,
And offend, for *his* fake, both *the* QUEEN and *the* KING ?
But what adds to my forrow, beyond all expreffion,
(I am cover'd with fhame while I make this confeffion)
Is, that EDMUND, becoming *my critical foe*,
Has declar'd that my ftile " *is exceedingly low* ;"
That *facts are miftated, affertions untrue,*
That I gave him not HALF *of the praife, which is due.*
He's afraid that good people, who live at a diftance,
Who read not *the* HERALD, and draw no affiftance,

From

From *such kind of prints*, which diurnally paint,
Burke's *party* as *cherubs*, and Burke as a *Saint*,
From reading *my letters*, may look on the Heroes,
As *Thrasonical Blocks*, or *tyrannical* Neroes.
And this, notwithstanding, I vow and protest,
I have always endeavour'd at doing my best.
If *the* Managers' speeches seem *not very good*,
I will swear, I detail'd them as well as I cou'd.
But he wishes the Press *to be under subjection*,
And publish no Speeches without his inspection,
And when they require it—*his learned correction*.
Burke says, that the *lying, iniquitous* World, *
For its manifold sins, should be " smitten and hurl'd."
He, who open'd a College for *bowing* and *capers*,
Would the Commons instruct in the hurling of *Pa-*
       pers :
He, who formerly thought it an innocent thing
In Junius and others, to libel *the* King,
Now holds it the greatest of scandalizations,
For *the* World to profane his *own sacred orations :*
He, who formerly held that a *Law Prosecution*
For a Libel, would ruin a *good* Constitution,
Is willing that Simkin should now undergo it,
For being a " low, an inelegant Poet."

---

* The daily Paper in which these Letters originally appeared.

Oh,

Oh, BROTHER ! we innocent *natives* of WALES
Are too often mifled by infidious tales ;
I have heard that a DUCHESS, remark'd for her tafte,
And, that ROYALTY alfo, fome minutes would wafte,
In reading my LETTERS, and us'd to admit,
That I wrote with fidelity, humour, and wit.
The DUCHESS afferted, that EDMUND's *fublime,*
Appearing in SIMKIN's fantaftical rhime,
Becomes fuch a happy, fortuitous texture,
That it ought to be chriften'd, *the* BEAUTIFUL MIXTURE.
But now, as the CHIEF has his Poet rejected,
A DUCHESS's *tafte* may be juftly fufpected :
But I've fomething to tell you, a hundred times worfe,
BURKE wants *to attach* both *my perfon,* and *purfe.*
Tho' he ne'er gave in money, fo much as *a penny,*
To his Poet, whofe verfes, you know, have been many.
It feems, if the HOUSE would concur in the plot,
He would take the *laft* FARTHING *poor* SIMKIN has
  got.
In all other cafes, *except this of mine,*
'Twere dang'rous, BURKE thinks, to proceed in that line :
Were an infolent fenator guilty of treafon,
An ATTACHMENT would not be confiftent with reafon ;
But becaufe his own Poet, in BURKE's eftimation,
Has not drefs'd to his liking, *for once,* an oration,

He

He would turn the DELINQUENT now out of employ-
    ment,
And ſtrip him of fortune, and ev'ry enjoyment.
Oh, BROTHER ! how cruel, how hard is the fate
Of thoſe who rely on *the words of the* GREAT !

But now your attention, 'tis fit I recall
To the bus'neſs of Wedn'ſday at WESTMINSTER
    HALL.
The HOUSE met :—and the CHANCELLOR ſaid, " 'twas
    " agreed
" That the MANAGERS be not permitted to read
" MUNNY BEGUM's *epiſtle :*"—Then EDMUND declar'd,
Tho' their LORDSHIPS deciſion he always rever'd,
He muſt, notwithſtanding, beg leave to remark,
That *their* PRINCIPLES *hitherto were in the dark;*
" And unleſs for *new lights* we have reaſon to hope,
" In darkneſs it muſt be our fortune to grope."
Now EDMUND, with fervour, *their* LORDSHIPS ad-
    moniſh'd
Of the dangers attending *Men's being aſtoniſh'd,*
At the wond'rous deciſion, which reaſon confounds,
Being built, as BURKE thinks, upon *technical grounds.*
" Howe'er, I muſt yield to your determination,
" Tho' it humbles the MANAGERS, COMMONS, and
    " NATION.
" But

" But left *as I am*, without light to conduct me,

" While your LORDSHIPS feem not much inclin'd to in-

        " ftruct me,

" May I venture *to guefs*, that you would not allow it,

" Becaufe MAJOR SCOTT did not choofe to avow it ?

" DISAVOWALS, my LORDS, are form'd into a *fyftem*,

" And as far as we're able, we ought to refift 'em."

As my HERO was fpeaking, I could not help thinking,

That he rather was faving *that fyftem* from *finking*.

For the fpeeches my ORATOR utter'd aloud,

As recorded by me, HE has fince *difavow'd*.

Nay, the MANAGERS all difavow and deteft,

Their own children, becaufe they are fhabbily dreft.

To return—EDMUND failing in this laft attack,

To RAJAH GOURDOSS he precipitates back ;

And here a new queftion arofe to be ftated,

Which by Fox and the COUNSEL was warmly debated :

The fubject, I cannot precifely fay what,

But 'twas whether fome action was *kindnefs*, or *not ?*

Some Office, conferr'd to oblige the NABOB,

Which EDMUND fufpects was *corruption* and *job*.

After ARGUMENTATION, at *half after two*,

To confider the queftion, their LORDSHIPS *withdrew.*

And while the *grave Peers* BURKE is driving about,

'Tis pleafant to fee them—*go in*—and *go out :*

But

But before, *my dear* SIMON, I bid you adieu,
I muſt tell you that nothing that EDMUND can do,
Shall ever prevent me from writing to you.
Not HOMER, who ſung of ACHILLES and *fighting*,
Had more pleaſure than me in heroical writing ;
A *ſubjeﬆ*, like BURKE, I can't think of forſaking,
But muſt keep him in mind, whether *ſleeping* or *waking* ;
Howe'er, for the preſent, my writing I'll end,
And to-morrow AUNT BRIDGET a letter will ſend.

June 24th, 1789.

LET

LETTER XXXIII.

AUNT BRIDGET TO HER SISTER MARGARET,

MOTHER OF

SIMKIN AND SIMON.

MY dear Sister MAGGY, this latter I write,
To remind you of *one* that is *out of your* sight;
But having no pleasanter tales to relate,
Like SIMKIN, I'll write about *matters of state.*
You must know, that as SIMKIN would take no de-
      nial,
I lately went with him to HASTINGS's *Trial;*
And indeed, I must own, I was highly delighted,
Without, as before, being dreadfully frighted:
You have oft heard me say, I should never forgive,
The ORATOR, EDMUND, as long as I live:
I thought him a wretch, of *ideas unclean,*
Of libidinous fancy, and language obscene;
If I heard any person but mention his name,
The remembaance of *Cantemir*, fill'd me with shame:
That *wicked young fellow*, whose Mother's delight
Was to lead to his chamber a Virgin each night.

How-

Howe'er, *my dear* MAGGY, the laſt day I went,
Great part of the time was agreeably ſpent;
But what above all did my wonder engage,
Is EDMUND's attention *to Ladies in* AGE.
Ev'ry man that you meet with, makes uſe of his *tongue,*
In praiſe and behalf of a LADY *that's young;*
But EDMUND, than others more *generous* and *bold,*
Is fond of protecting, *the* DAMES *that are old.*
Oh! when EDMUND dies, how the Ladies will miſs
   him,
And I think, while he lives, *the old women ſhould kiſs him!*
He has made an impreſſion ſo deep on my breaſt,
That if his OLD WOMAN were ſettled at reſt,
And BURKE were to offer, I could not withſtand,
The temptation of taking him *faſt by the hand.*
And as his finances are not very great,
He might like to partake of *his* BRIDGET's *eſtate.*
How often together we'd walk on the mountains,
Sit down on the rocks, and drink out of the fountains!
There EDMUND would make a moſt elegant farmer,
And at times make ORATIONS to me, *as his charmer:*
Oh! how the *Welch Squires* after dinner would ſit,
And admire, like the bottle, the ORATOR's *wit.*

 When EDMUND is ſpeaking, my ſoul ſo rejoices,
In the accent attending that ſweeteſt of voices;

It

It puts me in mind of that *good natur'd Paddy,*
Who liv'd as a footman, you know, with our Daddy,
And us'd to divert us with comical scenes,
When you and I, MARGARET, were in our teens.

When the LORD's were affembled, and BURKE began
 fpeaking,
I obferv'd *many* NOBLES with laughter were fhaking;
For fo pleafant is he, that he cannot " *fateague 'em,*"
Tho' he fpoke for a twelvemonth *concerning* " *the* BHEA-
 " GUM."*
But I am not lefs charm'd with *the* ORATOR's *figure,*
Whofe fize and appearance make promife of vigour.
Tho' fome people fay, that this is not a truth,
For his power, like a *ferpent's,* all lies in his mouth;
But be this as it may, all the cafh in my purfe,
I would give to poffefs him, " for better and worfe."

I now have to add, when their LORDSHIPS adjourn'd,
To LILLY LLANSTUFFIN's your fifter return'd;
There I found Mrs. WELLS, who, for *new imitations,*
Might challenge with fafety *all* COUNTRIES, and NA-
 TIONS.

* We fuppofe AUNT BRIDGET is in love with BURKE's method of
pronouncing the word Begum.

N

With

With refemblance furprifing, fhe imitates all   .
The Speakers that figure in Westminster Hall.
When like Fox I obferve her with vehemence fpeak,
She has got to the life—his *rat-tat* and his *fqueak.*
When fhe imitates Edmund, *the Irifhman's* tone,
Is fo like, that you'd fwear 'twas *the* Orator's *own*;
To his mode of pronouncing furprifingly true,
When fhe fpeaks of *the* Bheagum, and Canta-bah
      Bhoo;
And when fhe's repeating what Anstruther faid,
You have Saturn before you, *the father of lead.*
Then all of a fudden fhe changes the play,
And fhews her white teeth as politely as Grey.
When reading, like Erskine, fhe rifes and drops,
And is equally careful in minding her ftops:
There is not one fpeaker, as far as I find,
Save only the Clerk, who can leave her behind :
But what will furprife you ftill more than the reft,
—And I folemnly tell you it is not a jeft—
She wrote *twenty lines,* and I ftood by the while,
Exactly in Simkin's own manner and ftyle :
And as Simkin acknowledg'd he could not write better,
He ftole them to fill up a fpace in his Letter.
The people who heard her, are led to fuppofe,
That as foon as the Trial fhall draw to a clofe,

She'll .

She'll *exhibit her* CHARACTERS all on the ftage—
Where fhe never can fail to *amufe*, and *engage*.
One proof of her merit muft all people ftrike,
Which is, *vulgar papers exprefs their diflike.*
Till CHARACTER rifes in *fame* and *renown*,
ENVY's *never employ'd in the pulling it down.*—
And now, *my Dear* MAGGY, no more will I write,
As I'm going to RANELAGH this very night.

BRIDGET.

June 19th, 1789.

LET-

LETTER XXXIV.

LAST WEDNESDAY, *dear* BROTHER, I went to the
    HALL,
But as matters turn'd out, for juft nothing at all.
For indeed, you muft know, in the fcriptural way,
" The beginning and end made the whole of the day."
But fome *metaphyfical People* pretend,
That it had no beginning, and yet had an END.
This point I muft leave to your EDMUNDS, and FOXES,
Who can eafily make, and expound paradoxes.
To fpeak in plain terms, it came out as expected,
That the evidence offer'd was alfo rejected.
Then a motion was made by a *dignify'd* PEER,
That the JUDGES of ENGLAND be afk'd to declare,
From what *principle* or what *conftruction* of LAW,
This decided opinion they learnedly draw?
That moment the CHANCELLOR mov'd to adjourn,
And back to their CHAMBER, their LORDSHIPS return.
'Twas expected that BURKE would have made an attack,
But the LORDS, for fome caufe, did not choofe to come
    back :
Perhaps being weary of bowing and fcraping,
They feiz'd the occafion at once of efcaping;

z

But

But Burke means it well—as a Cure for the Gout,

And makes them—as *Physic*—go in and go out.

But those Lords, who like Burke, are ambitious of

      soaring,

And of heights unattain'd have a zeal for exploring,

Or wish for a ride in Lunardi's *Balloon*,

To visit the man who inhabits the Moon :

Those Lords to whose lot such high qualities fall,

Like me, have their Bonum, in Westminster Hall.

But to shew you, *dear* Simon, in what estimation

All classes of people hold Edmund's oration ;

To what Countries far distant, his glory is spread,

Wherever the World and *my Letters* are read—

From Dublin, *dear* Dublin, ten Citizens came,

From Waterford six, Carrickfergus the same,

From Limerick seven, and nearly as many

From the town and the country surrounding Kilkenny ;

From the *Highlands* of Scotland the *Lairds* and the

      Thanes,

From Sky the M'Donalds, from Mull the M'Leans,

Are expected in town in the course of the week—

For once in their lives to hear eloquence speak.

The *Gallery tickets* so rise in demand,

And promises given so long beforehand,

That Wednesday, Miss Bridget, our delicate Aunt,

For want of a ticket, was stopt in her jaunt :

                           She,

She, who long was accuftom'd to *purr* like a CAT,
To find fault with this—to be angry with that,
Is now fo affected, fo fmitten with love,
That *fhe cooes to herfelf,* like a mate-feeking dove.
Whether waking or fleeping, or fitting or walking,
Of BURKE and IMPEACHMENTS, fhe's conftantly talk-
     ing.
And it is my opinion, I give you my honor—
She will die, unlefs EDMUND has pity upon her.

   The *Gallery Strangers,* who came from afar,
Who had never heard EDMUND declaim at the BAR;
Whofe minds were inflated with high expectation,
Of hearing the ORATOR make an oration;
With faces extended, with grief, and with fhame,
All went to their lodgings, as wife as they came.
I confol'd them by faying, they need not be vex'd,
For BURKE would harangue us at *Meeting the next.*
And after by accident refting fo long,
His fancy and tongue, would be lively and ftrong;
And CHARLES, who has ftudy'd each *Species* and
     Genus,
Of Laws in the *Courts,* and the *Temple of* VENUS;
And SHERIDAN too, it is thought will unbridle,
Or they'll lofe all their fame by remaining fo idle.

                And

And 'tis alfo expected, that ERSKINE and GREY,
As *Readers*, or *Speakers*, will figure away;
For great is the tafk they have taken in hand,
To throw on its back all the LAW *of the* LAND.

And now, my *dear* SIMON, I hope you'll excufe,
My dullnefs this time, if I fail to amufe;
The LADY who formerly us'd to affift,
To recal to my mind, any point that I mifs'd;
To whofe good underftanding, found judgement, and
      tafte,
I fubmitted the lines which I fcribbled in hafte;
Who expung'd all the parts fhe confider'd unfit,
And the places fupply'd from the ftores of her wit,
To CHELTENHAM has fled!—

And farther, ftill farther—I am told fhe is going,
Impell'd, I fufpect, by th' ambition of fhowing
To MAJESTY, which from the height of its ftation,
From EDMUND and Fox never heard an oration,
Their *mode of declaiming*—in her IMITATION;
For the MONARCH himfelf, 'tis on all fides allow'd,
Of fubjects like them, may with reafon be proud;
ROME boafted of TULLY—DEMOSTHENES, GREECE;
But which of thofe Orators left us a piece
Of eloquence equal to EDMUND, or Fox,
When they fport their *dark brows* in the MANAGERS'
    Box?   N 4   As

As of coming to town it may anfwer the end—
From your mountain fublime I would have you defcend,
And fee Mrs. WELLS, who will give you your Brother,
So like, that you fcarce will know *one*, from the OTHER.

And now, my *dear* SIMON, I bid you adieu,
Till EDMUND finds matter for writing to you!

July 6th, 1789.

LETTER XXXV.*

FROM SHENKIN IN WALES,

TO HIS

COUSIN SIMKIN IN LONDON.

MY DEAR COUSIN SIMKIN, your kindred in
    WALES
Are quite overcome with your excellent tales;
Which have work'd like a charm on *your family* here,
And we meet twice a week, who scarce met twice a year.
All the toils, all the pleasures of life at a stand,
  Till SIMKIN's *expected address* comes to hand;
And proud to partake your poetical flame,
We strive to exhibit a spark of the same.
There's SIMON sits rhyming from morning till night,
Who in *shooting*, and *coursing*, once plac'd his delight;
Nay, even *your* AUNT, has her share of your vein,
And has teem'd with a *sweet little brat of the brain.*
So this must account and atone for my scrawl;
Since your friends are grown *Poets, Aunt* BRIDGET, and
    all.

* This Letter was by another hand, as were some few others.

Dear

Dear Coz, now I've once broke the ice in my way,
I hope you'll excufe what I'm going to fay :
I, who never faw London, nor London's *ftrange folks,*
May well be fuppofed, *a fit dupe for your jokes;*
But the devil fhall take me, if e'er I could credit,
One half what you write, *tho' an angel had faid it.*
Forgive me, *dear* Simkin, altho' at this diftance,
I prefume not to queftion *the* Trial's *exiftence :*
(The trial of *one* Warren Hastings, *I* mean,
Said to come back from India, *with hands not too clean.*)
Yet the *out-line* is all I conceive to be true ;
It's fantaftical fhade I attribute to you.
I applaud both your parts and your courage, *dear*
      Cousin,
Thus to *ftand by a man,* when attack'd by two Dozen.
But furely you write for the Pill'ry or Stocks,
When you handle fuch names, as Burke, Adam, and
      Fox ;
And venture erecting your batt'ry, *point blank,*
At Chiefs of fuch *high,* Senatorial *rank.*
Our choiceft, beft patriots, you fhrink not to paint,
Like Devils combin'd to demolifh a Saint ;
And *their leader* for Satan's *own picture* might fit,
If he had but less *malice,* and *ten times* more *wit.*

Laft

Laſt year, when you told us the ORATOR took,
That beaſtly quotation from CANTEMAR's *book*,
Your fancy, I thought, like a high-mettled horſe,
Had joſtled your judgement quite out of the courſe:
For a *brute*, ill-condition'd enough, to make ſport
On ſuch a *grave cauſe*, in ſo *ſolemn a court*,
With groſſeſt obſcenities tainting the ears,
Of LADIES, and JUDGES, and BISHOPS, and PEERS,
Muſt deſerve from *all human abodes to be hurl'd*,
Scoff'd, huſtl'd, hiſs'd, thump'd, and kick'd out of the WORLD·
This ſtory I therefore conclude is a creature,
Merely hatch'd in your brain, to embelliſh your metre.

All your letters have lately been fill'd with freſh croſſes,
Attending this *Antediluvian Proceſs*:
How often the MANAGERS play the ſtale game,
Of *diſmiſſing the* AUDIENCE *as wiſe as it came*; *
While their LORDSHIPS *come in—then go out—then come in,*
Like puppits, ere PUNCH *is·prepar'd to begin.*
From BURKE *the ſublime*, to ANSTRUTHER and GREY,
You give ev'ry one a ſmart laſh in you way,
That they'd readily palm, *any papers they found,*
For evidence legal, ſubſtantial, and found;

* Mr. BURKP ſent the LORDS *ſix times*, from Weſtminſter Hall, to the Chamber of Parliament, *upon the ſame queſtion.*

And

And proteſt in a huff, if a doubt croſs their words,

As if any traſh might ſuffice for the LORDS.

'Tis but lately you broach'd, with miſchievous intention,

A ſcandalous tale of your own vile invention;

That your HERO, of looſe and incontinent tongue,

Had *been ſnubb'd* by the COMMONS for language too

    ſtrong.

If a MANAGER thus ſhould be *ſnubb'd by the* HOUSE,

His word is no more worth " three ſkips of a louſe;" *

And I ne'er can believe that ſuch infatuation,

Could ſeize all the wiſeſt, beſt heads in the nation,

As to liſten with pleaſure, or liſten at all,

To what a *ſnubb'd* MANAGER *ſays in the* HALL.

In ſhort, *my dear* SIMKIN, I can but admit,

Your letters moſt choice, both in metre and wit,

But beware, leſt that ſad inclination to lye,

Bring you living to *jail,* and to HELL when you die.

Retreat then in time from the path you have choſen,

Is th' advice of your *friend* and affectionate COUSIN.

SHENKIN.

July 2d, 1789.

* See Mr. BURKE's ſpeech on the Regency Bill, in January.

LETTER XXXVI.

YOU REMEMBER, *dear Brother*, my ſtating to you,
The queſtion on which the *Tribunal* withdrew;
They on ſomething reſolv'd, tho' I cannot ſay what,
As when *the Court* met, they diſcover'd it not;
But 'twas hinted to me, *they ſuſpected a* PLOT.
For knowing that EDMUND is arch and deſigning,
A *good pioneer*, and converſant in *mining*,
'Twas concluded, that if they diſclos'd the foundation,
He would blow up at once, *all the* LAW *in the nation.*
When *the* LORDS were aſſembled, Fox roſe up to
   plague 'em
With GORING's *Epiſtle*, and one from " BURKE's
   " *Bheagum* ;"
Which, as they were publicly printed, he ſaid,
For their LORDSHIPS' *Appendix*, they ought to be read;
But HASTINGS's *Counſel*, an argument drew,
To prove *printing a paper*, can't render *it* TRUE.
Fox anſwer'd—" *The* COUNSEL muſt yield to their fate,
" For indeed they have made their objections too late;
" And as they had read the ſaid Paper *before*,
" There could be no harm if they read it *once more.*"

That

That it ever was read, the *learn'd* Counsel deny'd,—

It was enter'd *as* read, their Opponent reply'd;

Who rested his case on this argument sole,

That *reading a part*, must be *reading the* whole;

And of error the Managers try'd to convict 'em,

By praising and quoting the Chancellor's *dictum*.

Then Edmund, who constantly loves to regale

The ears of *the* Court, with a *ludicrous tale*,

Inform'd us, at length of the perils and dangers,

Which may happen at Venice, to *ignorant strangers*.

He told us of *one*, who the State reprehended,

And another who highly extoll'd, and defended;

" Both *of whom*, by the Senate *of* Venice were hung,

" For *unjustifiable licence of tongue*.

" One was hang'd for making a *verbal attack*,

" The other for *whitening*, what *never was black*.

" To the Chancellor only then let it belong,

" To disprove that his doctrine deliver'd was wrong."

After many disputes, and long trials to state,

The questions the Lords were about to debate;

And Fox had exprefs'd his pathetical fears,

That *simplicity* might be dislik'd by the Peers;

Their Lordships again had the honour of showing,

Their graceful deportment, in Coming *and* Going.

They return'd with an answer we did not expect,

" *That the* Managers *had* not *been very correct*;

" That

" *That the Orator* CHARLES *had improperly faid,*

" *That the* LETTER *of* GORING *was* ENTER'D *as* READ !"

Then CHARLES, who is feldom or ne'er at a lofs

When the *dice run againft him,* or FORTUNE *is crofs,*

Another expedient immediately found,

And offer'd the letter on *quite a new ground.*

He faid, as *their* LORDSHIPS before had confented

" This letter fhou'd in the *Appendix* be printed :

" THEY, at any time after, were bound to receive it,

" And, *being in print,* they of courfe MUST *believe it.*"

In anfwer to CHARLEY, LORD CAMDEN remarks,

That the *printing* was merely an *aƈt of the* CLERKS ;

To the printing the MANAGERS fhould not refort,

Unlefs they could PROVE it, an *aƈt of the* COURT.

Then CHARLEY lamented, with tears in his eyes,

That he, a poor Commoner, was not fo wife,—

That he could not difcover, whilft left in the dark,

The *aƈt of the* HOUSE from the *aƈt of the* CLERK :

The *Doƈtrine of Evidence,* then he diffeƈted,

Shewing what fhou'd be taken, and what be rejeƈted.

Here EDMUND broke forth, in his violent way,

Like a *mountain parturient,* he *labour'd* to fay,

" That an *Epilogue is the beft part of a play* ;"

That the Epilogue fhow'd, (which *their* LORDSHIPS had

       made)

That as *writers of Plays,* they were *young in the trade* :

I fym-

I sympathiz'd with him, when Burke was complaining,
That the epilogue was not at all entertaining.
" If it will not, says he, serve the end of *accusing,*
" I'm sure there is nothing in't very amusing ;
" It has neither the *beautiful* nor the *sublime*
" And the reading thereof is profusion of time,"
Here Burke *œconomical,* sadly regrets
The enormous increase of our National Debts ;
And frightened to death, left the *empire* should sink,
By *their* Lordships *profusion of paper and ink.*
'Tis expected hereafter, in some of his bills,
 He will limit the Peers, in their *paper* and *quills.*
Nor will this be thought such a comical thing,
When we think of his conduct *respecting the* King ;
The man whom œconomy urged to withstand,
The *grant of a lemon,* for Majesty's *hand,*
With justice and reason may move for the stinting,
Their Lordship's expence in superfluous printing.
Now Edmund observes to the Lords, he has done,
Excepting a word, and it should be *but* one ;
But, alas ! *taciturnity's* not in his pow'r,
For his tongue like a larum, ran more than an hour.
In printing, he humbly conceiv'd the prevention,
Of reading the paper, was not their intention ;
And he hop'd that the Court, in its gravity, never,
Printed that which could answer *no purpose whatever.*

That

That it was not like timber, which can't be employ'd,

In a ſhip, or a houſe, and ſo may be deſtroy'd.

The timber, he ſaid, which no artiſt can turn

To ſome kind of building, 'twere proper to burn.

Here one of the NOBLES ſeem'd not to admire,

The compound idea, *appendix,* and *fire,*

Then CHARLEY came forth, and his Leader defended,

By whom it appears no offence was intended.

This ſettled—their LORDSHIPS as uſual withdrew,

To debate on a queſtion, that's perfectly new :

They return'd, and the CHANCELLOR ſaid, 'twas agreed

That the MANAGERS, *are not permitted to read.*

Then EDMUND came forth, and began an oration,

With off'ring to Heav'n an ejaculation ;

Like a *chaplain* he pray'd, for that *ſpiritual light,*

Which leads all tribunals to that which is right.

He ſaid, that although they oblig'd him to yield,

He very reluctantly quitted the field ;

That during the courſe of the preſent long trial,

He had never been mortify'd ſo by denial.

Now EDMUND, although much depreſs'd by the vapours,

In evidence offer'd additional papers :

Then HASTINGS's *Counſel* aroſe, as expected,

Saying ſimilar proofs, *have been often rejected.*

But CHARLEY contended the MANAGERS ſhou'd,

Try *all,* and ſtick faſt to the thing which *is good* ;

O

That

That as the *said* MANAGERS could not learn why
Their LORDSHIPS so often are pleas'd to deny,
'Twas a duty incumbent to *offer* and *try*.—
And now, *my dear Brother*, I lay down my pen,
And when I have matter, I'll write you again.

July 7th, 1789.

LET-

LETTER XXXVII.*

SHENKIN IN WALES,

TO HIS

COUSIN SIMKIN in LONDON.

ENOUGH—enough—Dear SIMKIN ! fpare a while
Thy reader's laughter, and thy hero's bile !
Yet, yet avert the threat'ning ftorm that lowers,
Nor brave too rafhly Tribunitian powers !
Shall he, whofe fame thy antifeptic rhymes,
Have fous'd and pickled for remoteft times,
All alkaline antipathy fupprefs,
And gulp with patience all the pungent mefs ?
What, are there no officious prompters near,
To whifper vengeance in his fmarting ear ?
No Managerial Brothers of the pack,
To bark and bounce, *and bellow at his back ?*

O ! then, in time direct thy wayward way,
Where panegyric's foft'ring breezes play ;

* By another hand.

O 2

Low

Low at IMPEACHMENT's crimſon altar bow,
Where PEERS obſequious bend—*and well may'ſt thou.—*
That PRINCE, whom common tranſports could but cloy,
Who proffer'd millions for a new-found joy,
Now might at laſt his unclaim'd gifts beſtow
At conj'ring BURKE's *judicial raree-ſhow.*
O ! could I hear him as he raves and foams,
To tempt deluded idlers from their homes ;
And ſhews his *living* LORDS in robes ſo fine,
While Salmon's Peers of wax unheeded pine !
Could I partake for once the magic ſport,
To wait ecſtatic in an empty court,
While jaded nobles keep whole hours aloof,
And wince, and ſtartle at illegal proof !

If, then, fate urge thee headlong on to write,
Explain the myſtery of this new delight :
Say, by what *hocus pocus,* SIMKIN, ſay,
IMPEACHMENT reigns the faſhion of the day ?
Why on one objeƈt all its ſtores employ ;
Has BURKE a patent for this new-found joy ?
Sole *Arbiter Deliciarum* he,
And Britain's juggler with excluſive plea ?

Nought but the Trial's wonders now prevail ;
The Trial's Records load our lagging mail.

Aſk

Aſk a pert LONDONER, " What news of late ?"

" —BURKE, Sir, laſt Thurſday was *prodigious great.*

" A ſlender phial's drippings now anoint

" His tongue, which erſt was delug'd with a pint :

" To give the laſt perfection to his note,

" 'Tis thought a thumb bottle muſt wet his throat.

" With lemon too, he calms th'intruſive wheezing ;

" His mouth all parch'd—now ſpeaking, and now
      " ſqueezing,

" 'Tis he amuſes now alone the town ;

" GUIMARD is ſtill—the Op'ra-Houſe burnt down.

" No puffs of profit buoy the lank balloon :

" No BLANCHARD ſpies Impeachment in the Moon.

" In vain, with painted effigy on high,

" A new Goliah courts each gazer's eye :

" The Tower's fierce Lions unattended roar ;

" The ſtarv'd Stone-muncher dines on flints no more.

" Huſh'd are the gruntings of the Sapient ſwine,

" Which throng'd Saloons once hail'd almoſt divine :

" Poor PIG !—he dy'd, they ſay, of mere deſpair,

" His rival's triumphs were too much to bear."

—SIMKIN, I burſt, impatient to be taught,

What ſums this grand diſcovery has brought.

By all thy paſt and preſent well-earn'd bays,

By all thy hopes of *fifty more ſuch days,*

O 3

O ſay

O fay (nor think I mean thy fhare to rob)
Are thine the only profits of the job ?
For thine is doubtlefs no mean niggard penfion,
Recording Laureat to this bleft invention.
Do *purchas'd* tickets, belles and beaux admit
At diff'rent price, to Gall'ry, Box, and Pit ?
Or is all debt-reducing fyftem crofs'd,
To treat fpectators at the nation's coft.

Stands each Performer penfion'd by the week,
Puppets and all—or only thofe that fqueak ?
Who fhare the fplendid pickings of the fhow ?—
It's joint-exhibitors—viz. BURKE and Co. ?
Or ferve the whole, *as one prodigious fee,*
A *bonus* for the *grafping patentee ?*

If thou *muft* write—be, SIMKIN, this thy toil,
Thou great Apollo of our Cambrian foil !
So may adjournments, welcome fweets, prolong
Thy hero's blifs, thy ftipend, and thy fong !
So BURKE and SIMKIN's mutual aid fupport,
The pall'd attention of th' infulted Court !
So thy new FABIUS crufh (as well he may)
His much-enduring victim *by delay !*

July 9th, 1789.

LET-

LETTER XXXVIII.

SIMKIN IN LONDON,

TO HIS

Cousin SHENKIN IN WALES

DEAR SHENKIN, 'tis time you should now under-
    stand
That your letters, in order, came safely to hand:
That if to *the former* I made no reply,
'Twas because, indirectly, you *gave me the lye.*
You, by way of a compliment, chose to admit
That my letters were good as to *humour* and *wit*;
But whilst you allow'd that my verse was amusing,
My credulous readers you thought me abusing.
The TRIAL's *existence* you grant, to be sure,
But the *picture*, you said, was a CARICATURE.
There's nothing, believe me, that SHENKIN can say—
No compliment fine, he can possibly pay,
That can ever atone with a *Native of Wales,*
When his honour is wounded, by *doubting his tales.*
There is not at WESTMINSTER, even *one* PEER,
Among those to whom BURKE, and *his party* are dear—

        Who

Who join him in other political acts,
But freely subscribes, to *my statement of facts.*
And though it is true, that the facts I rehearse,
Have a farcical mien, when reported to verse,
You would say, *if you once heard my eloquent speaker,*
The *original*'s strong, *but the picture is weaker.**

You're ignorant, you say, and I'm glad you avow it,
'Tis your only excuse, and I therefore allow it;
You foolishly balance in Justice's scales
A POLITICAL CHIEF, with *your neighbours* in WALES;
But since from the mountain *your* HIGHNESS came down,
And heard it confirm'd by the dwellers in town,
It seems, though you question'd *your cousin's relation,*
You implicitly credit a *stranger's* narration.
In your Second Epistle, you pleasantly mention
A supposal that SIMKIN *possesses a pension*;
My Letter to SIMON, you've surely forgot,
I said—and now say it, " *Indeed I have* NOT."
To whom could I possibly make the request,
The PRIS'NER's *half ruin'd,* and deeply distrest:
My *Heroes themselves are in general needy,*
And PITT, *as a Statesman,* is shockingly greedy:

* To the truth of this Observation, we are sure every Man,
Woman and Child who has attended the Trial, will subscribe.

HE

He would tell me, perhaps, all the cash that he gets,
Will scarcely suffice for the *national debts*.
Nay, *the counsel*, if Edmund could do well without 'em,
Such a miser is Pitt, *he'd be happy to rout 'em.*
I grant, that I *once*, did indulge such a hope,
But my Hero now thinks me *deserving a rope*;
The speeches he makes, *in the moment of madness*,
In his intervals lucid, affect him with sadness.
And when he is told they will injure his fame,
His *Recorder* is sure to come in for the blame.

Believe me, *dear* Shenkin, I've no other ends
To answer, than barely amusement of Friends;
And when from engagements I'm free and at leisure,
I visit the Hall as a matter of pleasure:
But, from your last letter, I cannot help thinking,
That prejudic'd men have impos'd upon Shenkin;
For you write, *my dear Friend*, as if touch'd with com-
        passion,   .
A weakness (not Virtue) *that's much out of fashion*.
'Twas nothing but prejudice caus'd you to say
That Hastings a victim must fall to *delay*.
You are wrong——and if now it were not out of season,
On the subject before me to argue and reason,
I could prove that a Man, who his youth has expended
In *serving his country*, who bravely defended,

All

All *India* in times of moft imminent dangers,
From *ill-judging Colleagues*, and *quarrelfome ftrangers*,
Should, when he can ferve us in no other way,
Amufe and divert us—*inftead of a play*.
The *high-polifh'd* ATHENS, whene'er fhe beheld
A fubject, whofe zeal in her fervice excell'd
His equals,—with juftice that fubject EXPELL'D.
And that mode of treatment was certainly wife,
Howe'er it might feem in HUMANITY's *Eyes*.

Yes, yes, my *dear* SHENKIN, there once was a time,
I ingratitude held a deteftable crime;
When I faw the diftrefs of a poor fellow-creature,
I us'd to give way to *the feelings of nature*.
But fince I've convers'd with *political* HEROES,
Who are TITUSES often, *more frequently* NEROES,
I am fully convinc'd that in ev'ry condition,
We fhould ftudy *that only* which ferves our AMBITION,
Or adds to our pleafure; and hence I confefs,
I look on the whole as a *conteft at* CHESS.
When BURKE his game forward endeavours to bring,
LAW advances a *pawn*, and gives *check to his King*;
BURKE covers *his King*, PLOMER inftantly fees
An advantage—and, lo! EDMUND's *Queen* is *en prife*.
BURKE rallies his men, and prepares for the fight,
DALLAS whifpers a *move*, and BURKE lofes a *Knight*.

BURKE

Burke fpeaks in a circle, it proves of no ufe,
It fuggefts the idea of *playing at goofe*.
And hence inexhauftible pleafure I find,
Whilft a thoufand comparifons rife in my mind.

    You fpeak of *my chief*, as of Breslaw and Jonas,
Or a *ftrange Patentee*, and his grafping a *Bonus*.
You talk of expences, whereby it appears
The report of *new taxes*, has work'd on your fears:
But tell me what room there can be for complaining,
When the caufe of expences is fo entertaining;
And tho' *my dear* Shenkin fhould never partake,
He ne'er fhould begrudge, for his *relative's fake*.

    To conclude—With your numbers I'm really fmitten,
But like not the fpirit in which they were written.
In *Letter the Firft*, you accufe me of trying,
To impofe on the weak with fantaftical lying;
In *the Second*, your feelings, for Hastings diftreft,
And your dread with *new taxes* of being oppreft,
Have giv'n too ferious a turn to your letter,
So write not again till your humour is better.

    July 13th, 1789.

LET-

LETTER XXXIX.

SO LITTLE, *dear Brother*, of late has been done,
That I'm forc'd to confolidate, *three days in one*;
For *their* LORDSHIPS whenever BURKE fends them away
To their Chamber of Parliament, commonly ftay,
And put off the trial to fome other day.
The refpect due to place, the fpectator forgets,
And *the* HALL is a room for *the laying of bets.*
BURKE rifes to fpeak—and they cry—" *The* SUBLIME
" Shall run for ten guineas, a race againft time."
BURKE offers fome papers with arguments long,
They propofe, " ten to one that the orator's wrong."
To confider a queftion *their* LORDSHIPS adjourn,
They lay " five to three that they do not return."
To proceed—On laft Thurfday *their* LORDSHIPS agreed,
That GORING's *Epiftle* the Clerk muft not read.
Great EDMUND arofe—but what's fomewhat furprifing,
He did not burft forth in a paffion at rifing;
He requefted the Clerk might read over fome papers,
Which are always fo dull that they give me the vapours.
At laft to fome readings *the* COUNSEL objected,
And off went *the* LORDS, as the audience expected,

And

And did, as they frequently have done before,

Remain in their hole, for we faw them no more.

When EDMUND propofes, and the COUNSEL object,

On the Court it produces, *the felf-jame effect*,

As the bark of a dog, that fome dwelling inhabits,

Or happens to ftray, *near a* WARREN *of rabbits.*

On Tuefday they met, and *the* CHANCELLOR faid,

That the papers difputed, might fitly be read :

The papers were read, and they went to evince,

That there is a diftinction, *'twixt Nabob and Prince.*

Now EDMUND fearch'd into the caufe, and inquir'd,

Why HASTINGS " the Begum" fo vaftly admir'd;

" *My* LORDS, with the *Bheagum* the criminal had

" A connection corrupt, and I beg leave to add,

" That FRANCIS, my friend, did much benefit mean 'em,

" When he labor'd to break the connection between 'em.

" But in vain he exerted his pious endeavour,

" The connection continued as wicked as ever."

Some Ladies who heard of this fhocking connection,

Were unable to fmother the figns of affection ;

A connection of fexes they thought was a crime,

Dependent on *place*, *fituation*, and *time* ;

And they faid BURKE was dead to the feelings of fhame,

When he gave to connection, fo *filthy a name.*

BURKE continued—There's nothing can ever perfuade ⎫

Any perfon to think " he would ftick to the jade, ⎬

" Were it not for their wicked corruptible trade :" ⎭

" For,

" For, *my* LORDS, he not only fupported her ftation,

" In fpite of her tricks and mal-adminiftration,"

But without any grounds, or the fmalleft pretenfion,

He advifed the Directors to grant her a penfion.

Of a penfion, my LORDS, fhe was never in need,

And if it's difputed, I'll prove it indeed !

Here the COUNSEL put in—BURKE proceeded to ftate,

That the Begum's refources were many and great.

With caution *their* LORDSHIPS, he kindly admonifh'd,

That they muft unavoidably all be aftonifh'd,

Whenever he ftated the Lady's recourfes,

From which fhe obtain'd never-failing refources.

Hefaid—" She, whom HASTINGS has publicly painted,

" As a Lady whofe character never was tainted,

" And whofe manifold virtues deferv'd to be fainted,

" Permit me to mention, my LORDS, is the fame

" Who I told you from *dancing* deriv'd all her fame,

" Whom *the* NABOB maintain'd, as a *Lafs of the game.*

" If you hear of this woman and fome occupation,

" You wou'd think it were fomething becoming her

  " ftation;

" Not fo:—for this dame fo untainted with fin,

" *My* LORDS, kept a fhop for the felling of *gin:*

" There was not in ASIA, I boldly aver,

" Any dealer in fpirits fuperior to her :

" Perhaps by the doctrine which Mahomet taught,

" *That women want fouls*—fhe moft happily thought,

" The

" The best way to compensate for Nature's defects,

" Was with *plenty of spirits* to furnish the sex"

This *double entendre* created some fun,

But *your* CRITICS declar'd, 'twas a pitiful pun;

And some who had read the Alcoran explain'd,

That the *Musselman faith*, no such doctrine contain'd.

But whether my Hero's assertion be true,

Or not, matters little to ME or to YOU.

Now EDMUND determines again upon boring

The COURT with his questions, intended for GORING,

And by way of encomium, or character puffing,

He adds the appellative—HASTINGS's *Ruffian !*

Which is, that on HASTINGS he was not dependant

And thence a good witness against the defendant.

In a few minutes after, *their* LORDSHIPS adjourn'd,

The COURT was dissolv'd, and the audience return'd.

But before I proceed to describe the last day,

There was something escap'd me which now I will say :

It seems that *the* CHANCELLOR made some remark,

On the keen, eager grasp of my eloquent spark,

(Who was urging his papers on some slight pretence)

And created a laugh at *great* EDMUND's expence;

His feelings long callous, now sensibly stung,

At once put a stop to his garrulous tongue.

Aghast

Aghaft EDMUND ftood, *o'erwhelm'd with confufion*,
Whilft away went *antithefis, trope,* and *allufion.*
Then wither'd the flowers, the figures all fled,
Nor was there a metaphor left in his head.
To return—On laft Wednefday I went to *the* COURT,
Tho' I can't fay with much expectation of fport;
For ANSTRUTHER intended to fpeak, it was faid,
Whofe fpeech is as dull, tho' lefs weighty than *lead.*
But whether *their* LORDSHIPS had reafon to fear him,
Or, like me, had no great inclination to hear him;
Or whether they acted from fome other reafon,
They ended *the* TRIAL, at leaft for this feafon.

But now, *dear* SIMON, let me reft awhile,
Collect my thoughts, and *drop the loofer ftile.*
He, who in public never fpoke before,
Who with *abufe* has been INSULTED more
For years, than ever human patience bore—
Arofe, and thus began——

Mr. HASTINGS's SPEECH *in Weftminfter·Hall,*
Wednefday, 9*th July.*

" Illuftrious Peers !—*tho' ftrongeft words be faint,*
" At once *the torture of whole years to paint,*
" *Aw'd (as whom wou'd not fo much State o'erwhelm?)*
" *By all the* worth *and* wifdom *of the* REALM,

" *Your*

" *Your much-wrong'd Suppliant—O indulge the pause !*
" *Craves* one attentive moment *to his cause.*
—" Already *wire-drawn forms of fram'd delay,*
" *Have wasted* two sad suff'ring years *away :*
" *Faults* yet unprov'd—scarce outlin'd—e'er I plead—
" *Have reap'd* already *guilt's severest meed.*
" Unclos'd *yet lingers—swoln with comments large,*
" The twentieth item of the twentieth charge.
" TWENTY WHOLE CHARGES *stretch'd in endless line,*
" *No life can reach—much less a life like* mine :
" *While judgement's rod,* usurping hands *assume,*
" Fore-stall *conviction, and* pre-act the doom.

    " *Oh ! had the varied annals of mankind,*
    " *Brought* one eternal TRIAL *to my mind,*
    " That case, *terrific omen of suspense,*
    " *Had quash'd all plea ! defeated all defence !*
    " *Bade me my hopes on* instant sentence *place,*
    " *And grasp at* condemnation, as a GRACE.

" *O yet, nor arrogant be deem'd the pray'r,*
" Yet *a few parting, precious minutes spare :*
" *By* one short Session *years of anguish save,*
" Nor fix IMPEACHMENT on me to the grave !
" *Clear but my fame,* than dearest life more dear,
" (—*And* that *triumphant* TRUTH *at length* must *clear*)
" Clear but my fame, *and close the process here !*

P

—" *Yes*

—" *Yes*—clofe it here !—*its* prefent *merits try !*

" I wave all PROOF—all witnefs—all reply.

" Sure in my fame, *whate'er accufers fay,*

" Be their's all elfe to give, or take away !"

Here HASTINGS ended, and a *general figh,*

Difclos'd the feelings of the ftanders by,

The drooping head, the downcaft look, exprefs'd

The ftrong emotions felt in ev'ry breaft,

Through the *whole audience* foft compaffion ran,

All pray'd deliv'rance, to the *fuff'ring man.*

E'en BURKE himfelf, with heart more hard than fteel,

Was ftruck—was over-aw'd—was *forc'd to feel.*

Here then, *my* SIMON, and my *Cambrian friends,*

For fome few months our correfpondence ends.

But if (which HEAVEN forbid !) the LORDS prolong

The TRIAL—BURKE again fhall fhine in a fong.

July 10th, 1789.

LETTER XL.

SIMON IN WALES,

TO HIS

BROTHER SIMKIN IN LONDON.

DEAR SIMKIN, with forrow, with heartfelt con-
    cern,
Your friends—your acquaintance—your relatives learn,
That the mirth of their meetings muft now be diminifh'd,
As HASTINGS's caufe for this Seffion is finifh'd :
But whilft this misfortune your friends were condoling,
Came a letter from SCOTT that was rather confoling ;
He fays, that when BURKE's *allegations were counted,*
By one of his Friends, the fum total amounted
To more than two thoufand, by which it appears,
That the trial might laft, for *at leaft fifty years.*
This pleafing intelligence fill'd us with hope,
That your hero will long have, *unlimited fcope,*
From whofe fancy more rich than the Taffyland *Moun*
    tains,
Shall iffue forth fweet, inexhauftible fountains:

P 2

So

So Whilſt EDMUND in town the ſpectator regales,
SIM. ſhall ſing to his dear principality, *Wales.*

You may tell Major SCOTT, he excites our diſpleaſure,
By his ſtingy remarks on BURKE's *ſpending the treaſure* :
We are highly offended to hear him *complaining*
Of *expence,* when the ſubject is ſo *entertaining* ;
And ſooner than narrow the Orator's bounds,
We would yield to a tax, upon *Pointers and Hounds* ;
Nay, though it confine us to *Bachelor's lives,*
We had rather ſee PITT *lay a tax upon wives* :
But ſuppoſing, indeed, the ſolicitors' bills
Should exceed all the reſt of our national ills,
If the public ſhou'd deem it a hardſhip to pay 'em !
Let the tickets be ſold, that wou'd help to defray 'em !
Their privilege ancient, the LORDS might forego,
And the audience might pay, for their *ſeats at the ſhow.*
Their LORDSHIPS ſo many advantages get,
They may part with this one, without any regret.

I hope I may ſay, without giving offence,
That whenever SCOTT talks of *impeachment expence,*
He ſhows himſelf wanting in *judgement* and *ſenſe.*
In one of his letters, this gentleman hinted,
An idea of having BURKE's *Counſellors ſtinted* :

For

For Counfellors he no neceffity faw,

As *three of the Managers are of the Law.*

But to EDMUND's fuccefs, had the MAJOR adverted,

A thought fo abfurd, he had never afferted :

For though BURKE's *legal Phalanx*, in number is ftrong,

Their attempts and opinions were *conftantly wrong,*

And in whatever quarter they made their attack,

They were always *repuls'd, and beat fhamefully back.*

After what I have faid, need I farther infift,

On the folly of *catting the Counfellor's Lift ;*

Nay, I think that the COMMONS fhou'd *ftrengthen the corps,*

By adding at leaft *twenty Counfellors more.*

And this is th' opinion of JOHNSTONE *(Sir* JAMES)

Who in national caufes, *œconomy blames.*

The generous BARONET gave his confent,

That a *million or two* fhou'd on HASTINGS *be fpeut.*

A queftion occurs, which permit me to afk,

Have not HASTINGS's counfel a difficult tafk ?

But tell me how is it, three SPARTANS contrive,

To *fight Managers twenty,* and *Counfellors five.*

Befides all their friends in the *rear of the lines,*

Such as *Painters, Hiftorians,* and *able Divines.*

There is one thing, my SIMKIN, which if it be
      true,

I am forry to fay, *it reflects upon you,*

The

The remarks you once made on the conduct of PARR,
That *Pedagogue dròve, from the Wesminster Bar*;
And the MANAGERS robb'd of that *spiritual light*,
Which illumin'd their darkness, and guided them right.
Sir JOSHUA REYNOLDS was also perplext,
Lest he shou'd appear, in *Epistle the next*;
And GIBBON, their worthy *historical friend*,
Thought it *rather unsafe*, in *their box to attend*;
Historians, and *Painters*, *Divines* are afraid,
To put in their *mite*, to the MANAGER's *aid*:
All this we have heard, and to you they impute it,
But I trust that my Brother with ease can refute it.
There is something remaining I almost forgot,
Which I have to alledge 'gainst the *conduct of* SCOTT.
In a passion that Gentleman seems to be flying,
At EDMUND's attempt to *convict him of lying*.
His opponent what right has the MAJOR to blame,
When himself *vice versâ*, did lately the same?
In print and in speech, he is always advancing,
That EDMUND is *guilty of wilful romancing*,
And tho' before BURKE, this and more was asserted,
His politeness was such, *that he ne'er controverted*:
'Tis therefore ingratitude boorish in SCOTT,
When BURKE says, YOU LYE, to declare I DO NOT.

But

But before this Epiftle fo querulous ends,

I requeft in the name of *your Taffyland friends*,

You will now and then take up the pen to amufe us,

As occafions occur; nay, you muft not refufe us;

But if obligation ftill greater you mean us,

Let us have your remarks upon PARR's BELLENDENUS.

Aug. 1ft, 1789.

LFT.

LETTER XLI.

SIMKIN to SIMON in WALES.

BE affur'd, *my dear* BROTHER, whene'er I have lei-
    fure,
I fhall always be happy to add to your pleafure;
And fince you folicit them, fuch as they are,
I will give you my own obfervations on P—R.
You know, for two feafons, I've try'd every art
To conciliate and foften the ORATOR's heart;
But, alas ! I have long unfuccefsfully toil'd,
And in all my endeavours been conftantly foil'd;
I refolv'd to examine the caufe of my failing,
And the fecret find out of the DOCTOR's prevailing:
To my BOOKSELLER then I directed a note,
To fend me the Book which the PEDAGOGUE wrote:
The moment I turn'd to the PREFACE, furprize
Forc'd its way to my brain thro' the pores of my eyes.
It prefented an object uncommonly fine,
A moft beautiful Picture, and almoft divine !
Believe me, *dear* SIMON, no landfcape in WALES,
Full of rivers and rocks, full of mountains and vales,

A more

A more ftriking diverfity offers to fight,

Than the Preface which P—r was fo good as to write;

I'm convinc'd that DIVINITY only could fpeak

Such an *elegant jargon* of Latin and Greek ;

Not a page but exhibits unnumber'd quotations,

From hiftories poems, and ancient orations ;

QUINTILIAN and HOMER, DEMOSTHENES, HUME,

Are work'd up in one *panegyrical loom* ;

The texture difplays the vaft fkill of the *Weaver*,

And gives him ftrong claim to the ORATOR's favour,

I have heard that P—r's Scholars, fix days in the week,

Were tranflating the HERALD to Latin and Greek,

Whofe paragraphs choiceft the Doctor felected

For his preface—the reft, he as *lumber* rejected.

'Tis a Work, which the ftrangeft of *Chequers* furpaffes,

Whilft the diff'rence of ftyle fhews the diff'rence of
    claffes.

But what you muft think more miraculous ftill,

Is the depth of the PEDAGOGUE's magical fkill;

A hundred dead Authors, he readily raifes,

Who all fing altogether the MANAGERS' praifes.

After all thefe exploits, is it longer furprifing,

That SIMKIN fhould fink, whilft the DOCTOR is rifing?

But as matter feems wanting to fill up this letter,

·Perhaps, *my dear* BROTHER may relifh it better,

If,

If, instead of relating my own observations,

I give some examples of P—r's *Commendations*.

You will find in *page six*, of the *Second Edition*,

P—r speaking of Burke with the deepest contrition,

Laments, that *his friend* is a specimen sad,

" *Of* Fortune *once good, now deplorably bad.*"

The days he remembers, when Edmund was young,
Those agreeable days, when the Senators hung
On the *long-twisted rope* of the Orator's tongue ;

But in danger of choaking, and weary of hanging,

They are now quite regardless of Edmund's haran-
      guing ;

And there's scarcely one Member who listens, altho'

His Orations partake of the nature of *Snow*.*

In the following page, P—r is certain and sure,

That Burke leads the life of the *True* Simon Pure,

And that all other men (as 'tis proper they shou'd,)

Must account for their conduct to Edmund *the good* ;

But among the best traits he has noted in Burke,

Is this—that in spite of the rascally work

Of Fortune, his dignity never can yield,

But tho' *beaten* and thump'd, still remains in the field ;

And in all undertakings, tho' hooted and hiss'd,

His conscience approving has made him persist.

---

* *Cujus enim dicentis ex ore Senatus quondam pendebat, illius jam oratio etsi nivibus hybernis similima sit, sibi tamen audentiam vel ullum facit.*

But

There is one thing, perhaps, I hereafter may do;
Which, by way of a fecret, I mention to you,
As my heroes efteem what is crabbed and cramp,
My writing next feafon fhall be of that ftamp;
Our *Welch* and their *Englifh* I'll happily mingle,
Which, like P—R's Greek and Latin, may prettily jingle;
And to render the found ftill more ftriking and full,
From Burke's *native Irifh* fome phrafes I'll cull;
With thefe I will now and then fpangle my line,
And I queftion, if P—R's will look better than mine.
It is not, however, for me to expect,
Like him, to excite univerfal refpect;
Greek, *Englifh*, and *Latin* in gratitude join,
To the Doctor obliged, for his plentiful coin.
With *Burkius* and *Foxius*, and fuch pretty founds,
As ὁι Γαλλίζοντες the preface abounds;
There is one thing indeed, which I cannot yet find,
Why Pitt by ὁ δεῖνα is always defign'd;
Nor do I fuppofe that the Doctor could tell,
Why *Pittius* for Pitt, would not read juft as well.
But the reafon of this, ere I come to the end,
'Tis likely enough I may well comprehend;
For indeed, *my dear* Simon, 'tis fit you fhould know,
That I have not, as yet, read the Preface half through;
In *Lexicons* oft, difappointed, I feek
For the Doctor's *new coinage* of Latin and Greek.

I muft

I muſt not forget to inform you, the ſtyle
Is a recipe good for the cure of the bile ;
So, like *Convaleſcents*, who ſtore up their pills,
I reſerve it for bilious and ſplenetic ills.

Here this Letter ends, but in caſe *my dear* BROTHER
Should the ſubjeċt approve, I can ſend him another;
For P—r's Preface reſembles a pantomime diſh,
Made of all ſorts of meat, of fowls, puddings, and
    fiſh.

Aug. 13th, 1789.

LETTER XLII.

YOU tell me, *dear* SIMON, you relish the feaſt
I procur'd you from P—R, the *political Prieſt* ;
Now, ſince my Remarks correſpond with your liking,
Let me add a few more, that are equally ſtriking.

P—R tells us, *the deluging language of Fox*
Runs down from the mountain and tears up the rocks !
(And among other mad, unaccountable pranks)
It blows up the bridge and runs over the banks—
And whene'er, in this manner, FOX *chuſes to ſpeak,*
The minds are aſtoniſh'd of thoſe that are weak !
In the very next page, the *meek Doctor* is ſtruck
With the horrors, at CHARLEY's long run of ill luck ;
The *paſt* he conſiders a terrible curſe,
But the *future*, he fears, will be fifty times worſe ;
He ſees, at a diſtance, ſome ſtorm that is brewing,
And likely t'involve the *whole* PARTY in ruin ;
But what ſtill increaſes the DOCTOR's regret,
Is, that all *honeſt men* were with CHARLEY upſet.—
At length he obſerves, in the way of condoling,
The *good Conſcience* of CHARLES muſt be very *conſoling—*

And

And tho' at *O' deina* P—r conftantly fnarls,

He's indulgent enought to the foibles of CHARLES,

Who fpent a great part of his youth in the ftews,

Yet found himfelf MORE *than a* MATCH *for the* JEWS;

Peccadilloes, like thefe, P—r is pleas'd to infift,

Cannot place his dear friend on the *criminal lift*—

And the truth of that adage he ftrongly enforces,

That the *wildeft* of *colts* make the *fineft* of *horfes*—

And the converfe of this propofition the fame,

Your *horfe* proves a *flug*, if your *colt* was too *tame*;

And thence, as *O' deina*'s not fond of a wench,

P—r thinks him unfit for the Treafury Bench.

In *page* the *fifteenth*, the *fad* DOCTOR laments

That the PARTY funk under the worft of events;

For, whilft they were ufing their utmoft endeavour

To make themfelves firm in their places *for ever*—

And when Fortune feem'd willing to grant all their
       wifhes,

The PHILISTINES rufh'd in, and laid hold of their
       fifhes—

But tho' filenc'd juft then, by regard for his bones,

He now may, with fafety, give vent to his groans.

When the DOCTOR had ftorm'd and expended his
       rage,

By fighing and groaning for more than a page,

With

With profusion of logic, and deep erudition,
He began a defence of a *late* COALITION !
All those who condemn, says the learned Divine,
Wrap in high-sounding words *elocution canine* ;
That is, they are *house-dogs* that watchfully bark,
When they smell out a *thief, that would steal in the dark.*
After all these hyperboles, laughably odd,
P—r should be created, a *Father in God* ;
And CHARLES, *when he can*, must reward with a mitre
The merit of this panegyrical writer.—

DOCTOR JOHNSON, I've heard, with no stronger pre-
tension,
Got from Administration the grant of a pension :
Of *pedantry*, HE, late *egregious professor*,
To P—r left the chair, as his *rightful successor*.
The first a COLOSSUS, of straddle so wide,
As to spread o'er this globe, and *whole systems* beside—
The next a COLOSSULUS, standing on pegs,
With all the *dead languages under his legs*—
The *former* knew more than will ever be known—
The *latter* makes Latin and Greek *of his own.*

'Tis diverting to see how the DOCTOR can scold,
At *nescio quis* WILBERFORCE,* who was so bold

* Page 42.

As

As to say, " that Burke's *judgement* had loft *all its*
    " *powers,*
" And that time had *deftroy'd* his *rhetorical flowers.*"
Then *O'deina* comes in for his fhare of the blame,
For rafhly prefuming to *echo* the fame,
Without being mov'd by confufion or fhame;
But P—r's of opinion, the moft they can fay
Is, that Burke's *elocution* begins to grow *grey.**
But now, my dear Simon, 'tis proper and fit
I fhould give P—r's remark on O'deina or Pitt.
His *political* courfe, when O'deina began,
P—r thought him a *promifing, decent young man;*
But when, unexpected, he *alter'd* his tack,
From *charmingly white,* he grew *frightfully black.*
Now 1 think that the Herald, or fome other print,
Should give this forgetful young Statefman a hint,
That, *black* as he is, he might foon become *whiter,*
By giving the Doctor the next vacant mitre.
How ufeful 'twould be in *political war,*
To have fuch a *militant* Bifhop as P—r,
Who, if Opposition fhould venture to fpeak,
Would well cannonade them with *Latin* and *Greek.*

* The Preface, which is the fubject of Simkin's pleafantry, is full
of fuch incongruities; nothing but the genius of pedantry could
have formed fuch an union of ideas.

As PITT has not many years quitted the *College*,
P—R thinks he muſt needs want political knowledge;
Tho' this is a failing I ſhould not ſuſpect
In PITT, were it not for his *ſhameful neglect*
Of the *merit* of P—R, but this conduct at once
Proclaims him to be a political dunce.

But 'tis time I ſhould think of concluding this Letter;
And, perhaps, you would tell me, The ſooner the
     better—
For the preſent I therefore will ſtay all proceeding,
Being heartily weary of writing and reading.
For tho', like our *Welch Mountains*, it catches the eye,
P—R's preface, like *them*, is *hard, barren, and dry.*
When I take up the book, I can't poſſibly keep
My eyes for five minutes, from yielding to ſleep.

But if no other ſubject occurs, MY DEAR BROTHER,
Upon *this*, I hereafter muſt *ſend you* ANOTHER.

Aug. 19th, 1789.

Q

LETTER XLIII.

NO fubject occurring as food for my pen,
On P——R I reluctantly comment again.
There is *one* thing, indeed, I omitted to mention,
Well worthy of your's, and all writers' attention ·
As the *principal object* of all *Dedications*
Is attainment of friends by *well-tim'd Adulations* ;
And as he who is eager to ferve his own ends,
Can ne'er have too many well-wifhers and friends,
When he brings out a work, 'tis an excellent plan
Into *Books* to *divide* it, as much as he can.
For *each Book* a *Patron* he thought to felect,
And to praife him much more than he well can expect,
The fafhion the DOCTOR led up in his work,
Beftowing a Book on NORTH, CHARLEY, and BURKE,
And having *fome* firkins of Butter to fpare,
And fuppofing his Patrons more DRY than a *Hare*,
Their fkins with his greafe he dripp'd, larded, and
  bafted,
'Till in ftreams it ran down, and he fear'd 'twould be
  wafted.

Yet

Yet profuse as he was, 'twill hereafter be found,
His Butter will bring a good price by the pound.
My stomach was turn'd, I grew rather unwell,
So affected was I by the sight and the smell ;
'Tis so loathsome that no English taste could abide it,
Had not P—R had in *Latin* the prudence to hide it.
So Lovers, who practise the arts of deceiving,
Finding those who are flatter'd, too fond of believing,
Take care, when they *season* their *compliments high*.
That none but the person they flatter, be nigh.
On this principle, P—R, who in nature is learn'd,
Conceal'd it from all but the parties concern'd.

In the 45th page, it is sadly lamented,
That the *Gentry* of *England* are much *discontented*,
To find themselves forc'd in the House to sit down
With men of no *family, rank,* or *renown.*
Great part of the Senate is made up of *Jobbers,*
According to P—R, and of *Callico Robbers.*
And he thinks, at the entrance a porter should stay,
To tell the new Senators which is the way.

As P—R could to SHERRY give no dedication
For want of a book—he made full compensation,
By declaring, that *numberless* QUALITIES join,
Essential to make that *great Orator* shine ;

Q 2

And

And the firſt proof thereof which the Pedagogue brings
Is, that SHERRY has very great knowledge of THINGS;
He has alſo a *knack* at *ſatirical joking,*
At making *ſhort anſwers,* and *very provoking;*
With *learning* (alluding perhaps to the STAGE)
Such as *Gentlemen* have in this *elegant age.*
But the DOCTOR has candour enough to admit,
That among all the ARMY which *fight* under PITT,
WithS HERRY to match not a *Soldier* is fit.
Nay, tho' PITT talks apace, without tripping or halt-
    ing,
SHERRY beats him to nothing, at *cutting* and *ſalting.*
SHERRY ſoon *tripp'd* up GRENVILLE, whoſe glory and
    pride
Is, in having a *fall* unſuccesfully *try'd.*
All the talents, which NORTH, FOX, and EDMUND
    have got,
According to P—R, fall to SHERIDAN'S lot:
Like Fox he is *ſubtle, ingenious,* and *bold—*
Like BURKE he can ſpout forth a FOUNTAIN of *Gold,*
And like NORTH *with urbanity, rattle* and *ſcold.*

When the DOCTOR had got no more *Butter* to *ſpare,*
'Twas divertingly curious to hear him declare,
That without the leaſt view to his *dignity* raiſing,
'Twas *truth,* and *truth only,* that ſet him a praiſing;

To

To *truth* you muſt think him *extremely devoted,*

As he has not a *wiſh* for the being *promoted:*

And to ſhow himſelf truly impartial and right,

In PITT he diſcovers one ſpot that is white.

For when on the CHURCH an *attack* was *intended,*

And her rights by LORD NORTH were as bravely defended—

PITT's eloquence alſo came in to her aid,

Which ſerv'd as NORTH's *Lacquey,* or young *Chamber-
  maid.**

And now, my *Dear* BROTHER, with P——R I have done,

And, perhaps, 'twere as well, had I never begun;

For I find, on inquiry, among learned men,

His Book was ne'er heard of by *nine* out of *ten;*

And among the *few* people that heard of its *name,*

Not one part in ten has look'd into the ſame;

And I firmly believe, in this *light-reading age,*

Not a *man* in *ten thouſand* could *drag* through a *page.*

 Sept. 3, 1789.

 * All the bombaſt quoted by Simkin is to be found in the Preface
to Bellendinus, and infinitely more.

Q 3

LETTER XLIV.

SINCE the day that I animadverted on P—r,
That bright theologo-political Star,
No fubject for writing has fall'n in my way;
So I refted—becaufe I had nothing to fay.
But now, *my dear Boy*, by the blefling of Fate,
I have got an occurrence or two to relate.
You muft know thro' the City a rumour was fpread,
That the Parliament foon would be legally dead;
The WHIGS, hearing this, in a ftate of dejection,
Affembled to fettle th' enfuing Election!
And whilft they were ftating and folving their doubts,
As to who'll be the IN's, and who muft be the OUT's,
The veteran Orator was not forgot—
That is—whether BURKE be re-chofen or not?

Then JOSEPH rofe, and thus a fpeech began:
" We've had fufficient of this prating man:
" The juftly-hated name of EDMUND draws
" A gen'ral odium on the faireft caufe.

" The

" The Nation once, by pompous found mifled,
" Implicitly believ'd whate'er he faid,
" And thought his *heart* much better than his *head*.

" But now the WORLD his head and heart attack,
" And fay the one is *weak*—the other *black*;

" With all his actions men are now acquainted,
" His private character is alfo tainted,
" St. Omar's Jefuit is at length unfainted:

" His friend, the MARQUIS, long before he dy'd,
" Repentant, cut the knot, [illegible] blindnefs ty'd:
" LORD V———Y too, found [illegible] to regret
" That *patience* which ill[illegible] DEITY;
" His *pious zeal* againft a great NABOB,
" Is now confider'd as a pilf'ring JOB;
" A difh of gravy-meat of EDMUND's carving,
" To feaft himfelf, and keep poor DICK from ftarving,
" His foolifh triumph,·fhamefully expreft,
" Refentment kindled in each royal breaft;
" The caufe, the fole detefted caufe, was he,
" That we were lately burnt in effigy:
" In deteftation, we have long been held,
" And muft remain, 'till EDMUND is expell'd.
" The ficken'd Senators, when EDMUND prates,
" Some ftay to hifs, while others quit their feats.
" From him a ftream of pompous nonfenfe flows,
" And *ferves* the caufe he labours to *oppofe*:

                                    " His

" His numerous blunders in a recent cafe,
" Have fixed on us indelible difgrace :
" A motion now I make, (let none refift)
" To blot his name from the difhonour'd lift."

 He ceafed—and MONTAGUE arofe to fpeak :—
" I grant his heart is black, his head is weak. :
" But ftill I think a reafon might be giv'n,
" Why from the Party BURKE fhould not be driv'n ;
" He is, you muft allow, an ufeful *Butt*,
" For Wits to fire upon, to flafh and cut ;
[illegible]
[illegible]
" Should BURKE a patriotic life forego,
" The fhaft of Ridicule might fall on JOE ;
" 'Tis hard to fay, fhould men their conduct fcan,
" If BURKE or SURFACE be the faireft man."
Here ended MONTAGUE—and COURTNEY rofe,
With ever welcome wit, to interpofe :

" The Chief who fpoke firft, and the Chief that did
" follow,
" Are ORACLES equal to thofe of APOLLO ;
" With SURFACE, indeed, I am free to admit,
" That EDMUND is worth twenty Members to PITT ;

That

" That the name of St. EDMUND's fufficient to tarnifh

" All the *colours* of Fox, and all SURFACE's *varnifh* :

" Notwithftanding all this, I'm unwilling to fcout him,

" Becaufe we may probably fare worfe without him ;

" 'Tis prudent to facrifice *wrinkle-horn'd Rams,*

" To fave from the *Altar* fweet *innocent Lambs.*

" Should BURKE be difcarded, as MONTAGUE noted,

" Some victim or other muft foon be devoted ;

" The well-meaning CHARLES, or the innocent JOE,

" Muft feel the fharp lafh of fome libellous foe ;

" The writer of news muft have food for his pen,

" To raife entertainment for fcandalous men :

" The follies of BURKE are fo many and glaring, ⎫
" His actions fo wild, and his fpeeches fo daring, ⎬
" As to yield conftant matter for wonder and ftaring." ⎭

Here CHARLIE, whofe words are more weighty
    than lead,
Obferv'd on both fides a great deal might be faid ;
That he had not as yet fully made up his mind,
If to *drag him along,* or to *leave* him *behind.*
Here this Letter ends, but whenever thefe men
Shall agree on this point, I will write you again ;
In the mean time, I fear, if BURKE is not re-chofen,
My *Pen* will be *pointlefs,* my *Ink* will be *frozen.*

    Oct. 20, 1789.

LET-

LETTER LXV.

YOU remember, *Dear* SIMON, my formerly ftating,
That BURKE was difpleas'd with my ftile of narrating.
Alas ! now I find, I'm for ever rejected,
As a new Poet Laureat is lately elected :
This intelligence cruel, I draw from a hint,
Convey'd thro' a *late publiſh'd, ludicrous* Print.
Left this fhould be thought not explicit enough,
I muft tell you, the *Party,* that wears *Blue* and *Buff,*
Have *fubfcrib'd* for an *Artiſt,* a *liberal Fee,*
(Tho' they never once thought of *fubfcribing for me)*
Who, with great Ingenuity, Labour, and Pain,
Has pourtray'd the defign of fome Partizan's Brain;
'Tis infcrib'd, by confent, to a * DUCHESS DIVINE,
The *Pride,* and the *Hope,* of the CAVENDISH line.

Firft, LIBERTY'S GODDESS, affuming the *Face,*
The *Perfon,* the *Air,* and the *Shape* of HER GRACE,

* If Simkin is in error—the Artift, Mr. POLLARD, muft be re-
fponfible.—The words are " To HER GRACE the DUCHESS of
" DEVONSHIRE, *this Print* of INDIA VINDICATED, is, *by* HER
" PERMISSION, muft HUMBLY DEDICATED."

Holds

Holds out her *Fore-finger*, intending to fhow

Her Apoftles—BURKE, FOX, PHILIP FRANCIS, and
    JOE.

With her *Cap* and her *Staff*, fhe feems ready to *holloa*,

Lo! thefe are the lads, which the DUCHESSES *follow*.

BURKE, drefs'd like the great *Roman Orator* GRAC-
    CHUS,

Wants only a mob at command, to attack us;

And the vifage of CHARLES, full of fpirit and fire,

Seems as if he would lay *Ten* to *One on* HIGH-FLYER;

And the *modern drefs'd* JOSEPH, with Rouge in his face,

Looks as if he could *collar* a *Juftice* of *Peace*;

Whilft thefe heads all feem in an attitude fpeaking,

PHILIP, drawn at *full length*, appears creeping and
    fneaking.

Mean time fee the GODDESS her left hand direct

To a beautiful figure—RECORDER ELECT!

Whofe likenefs expreffive, decidedly fhews

Her Sifter renown'd, is " *th' Hiftorical Mufe.*"

The Lady, I've heard, is preparing a Work,

The ACTS of the PATRIOTS—FOX, JOSEPH, and
    BURKE.

As

As a proof of her ſkill, an incloſure I ſend,
'Tis a Copy I luckily got from a friend,
Of a ſweet pretty ODE, which her Ladyſhip penn'd.

T H E

GREAT ANNIVERSARY ODE,

BY THE

HISTORIC MUSE.

GENTLE BUTCHERS! ring your cleavers——
ROYAL COBLERS! Barbers! Weavers!
CHIMNEY-SWEEPERS! and COAL-HEAVERS!
    Leave your work, and come away!
COOPERS, down with adze and wimble!
TAYLORS, drop the yard and thimble!
LINK-BOYS and LAMP-LIGHTERS nimble,
    Come and keep this HOLIDAY!

Drink and drive away the vapours——
When the night comes, light your tapers;
Dance and ſing, and cut high capers,
    Dedicate this day to mirth.
Let this day be ne'er neglected!
But, like CHRISTMAS, be reſpected——
FOX this day was firſt elected——
    FOX *the greateſt man on earth!*

Not

Not the glorious REVOLUTION,
Checking lawlefs perfecution,
Which fecur'd our CONSTITUTION
    Free, for overturning fhocks—
Not the BRUNSWICK *Coronation*,
Chafing POP'RY from the nation,
E'er deferv'd commemoration,
    Like th' ELECTION *of* CHARLES FOX !

When the HERO tells his ftory,
Acts of fplendor, deeds of glory,
Will diffufe their light before ye—
    Then beftow your loud applaufe !
WALTER TYLER, clad in armour !
MASTER CADE, the great Reformer !
CROMWELL's *felf* was never warmer,
    Than CHARLES FOX in Virtue's caufe !

C****** and B*****, by joint endeavour,
Thirteen Provinces did fever
From the BRITISH CROWN for ever !
    Noble CHARLES, *and loyal* BURKE !
Irifh Independence rearing,
Kingdoms two afunder tearing,
Make the CROWN not worth the wearing—
    This, indeed, is glorious work !

Gallant

Gallant CHARLES, the Nation's blessing;
Eas'd your SHOPS of tax distressing,
Laid thereon by PITT, oppressing—
    Hail, for ever, BLUE and BUFF!
Still there's something more provoking,
PITT has laid a tax on *smoaking*,
Whilst your wives and mothers, croaking—
    Dread another tax on *Snuff*.

TOAST the PRINCE and ROYAL BROTHER,
Whilst some folk, in places other
Toast his Father and his MOTHER—
    Drink the PEOPLE's MAJESTY!
Drink about, ye *thirsty fishes!*
Toasting with sincerest wishes,
RUSSELS, BENTINCKS, CAVENDISHES,
    With FITZWILLIAM, ever free!

Godlike CHARLES, the World's *Eighth Wonder!*
In St. STEPHEN's squeaking thunder,
Keeps the frighted Members under:
    Oh! let FOX be ne'er cast out!
Rise, ye gallant sons of freedom!
Damn the laws, and never heed 'em!
Wealthy villains only need 'em—
    Honest poor can live without.

I   See

See the SIRE, by SON forſaken—
F— perſuades the *Heir miſtaken,*
The Prerogative to weaken—
    Thanks to CHARLES's ſoothing tongue.
When he ſpeaks—Huzza !—encore him !
Tumble down, and kneel before him !
Kiſs his *ſhoe-ſtring,* and adore him—
    CHARLES from *Freedom's Goddeſs* ſprung !

At next WESTMINSTER ELECTION,
Guard with care againſt defection ;
Give delinquents juſt correction—
    Bring a *Hundred Thouſand Votes.*
Collar MAGISTRATES and fright 'em—
Meet your foes, and boldly fight 'em—
SAMSON like, with jaw-bone ſmite 'em,
    Make clean work, and cut their throats.

———————

This model of eloquence, ſtyle, and expreſſion,
Was preſented the Day of KING CHARLES's ACCES-
    SION ;
I mean on that great ANNIVERSARY DAY,
When the WESTMINSTER MOB firſt acknowledg'd his
    ſway ;
And that this bleſſed day may be never forgot,
'Twill hereafter be *kept* like the *Gun-Powder Plot.*

Next

Next year we expect all the Bells in the Steeple
Will ring the whole day, for this *Man* of the *People*;
And if I were KING GEORGE, while the Hero is
    living,
I would make it an Annual Day of Thankſgiving.
And the *Almanack Makers*, in future, 'tis ſaid,
Will diſtinguiſh the *Tenth* of *October* with red.

Should JOSEPH, *Dear Brother*, his promiſe fulfil,
(Tho' on *caſting* the *Odds*, I much doubt if he will)
I'll give you the *cream*, when he lets me peruſe
The *Acts* of the *Patriots*, by Liberty's Muſe.

To return to the Print—where the *Goddeſs of Free-*
    dom
Deals Her Oracles out, to ſuch people as need 'em,
'Tis delightful to ſee this DIVINITY *trample*
On *chains*, ſetting ſubjects an uſeful example;
And ſhe who has *forc'd* ſuch a number to *wear 'em*,
With eaſe can inſtruct her own *Captives* to *tear 'em*.
Her Vot'ries, however, would gladly pull down
The *Enſigns* of *Government*, *Scepter*, and *Crown*.
At the *Foot* of the *Column*, black people are kneeling,
To raiſe in the *Patriots, compaſſionate feeling*;
Or to gratefully thank them for having procur'd
Relief from *Diſtreſſes they never endur'd*;

For

For perfuading the *Commons*, that man to condemn,
Who *preferv'd* to the *Crown* its moft *brilliant Gem*;
Or, perhaps, for preventing all farther abufe,
By turning THEIR WEALTH *to the* NATIONAL USE.
MUNNY BEGUM, whofe *Fame* BURKE fo *wickedly*
> > *painted*,
Is drawn like the LADY, who formerly fainted
At a Tale of Diftrefs,* with which you are acquainted.

This BEGUM, BURKE faid, was a *Proftitute common*,
A *difgrace* to *her Sex*, a *vile profligate Woman*;
And though from the dregs of the people fhe fprung,
Made a BEGUM, *becaufe fhe enchantingly fung*:
But, in juftice to BURKE, I muft own *he recanted*,
When his Evidence *fail'd*, and the BEGUM'S was
> > wanted;
Then her *Credit* arofe *unimpeach'd* and *unfhaken*,
And a hearfay from *her* was a proof to be taken.

But 'tis furely affronting CECILIA, to place her
In a ftation like this—nay, it needs muft difgrace her;
And, indeed, at *firft fight*, I fufpected a plot,
That the ARTIST was *brib'd*, and *corrupted* by SCOTT,

* The Story of DEBY SING.

R

To

To exhibit this BEGUM, *whom* EDMUND *accus'd*
Of crimes, as an *Angel*, by HASTINGS *abus'd*—
To shew *Inconsistency* and *Variation*,
Thus fixing discredit on EDMUND's Narration;
But the MAJOR, if wise, of his cash might be sparing,
For the changes of BURKE *are sufficiently glaring.*
But sure inconsistency is not alarming,
On the contrary, I think variety charming;
And now I am reading a book of that name,
Whose *pleasantries varied*, demonstrate the *same*.

The Artist display'd some satirical fun,
By putting forth GREY and ANSTRUTHER for *one.*
Wherein, I presume, he adopted the plan,
Of their putting *nine Talors* to make up a *Man*;
And concluded that RAJAH CHEYT SING to pourtray,
Would take two such men as ANSTRUTHER and
   GREY.
But perhaps into error the Artist was led,
By reading what ANSTRUTHER *formerly said*;
For who would conceive that CHEYT SING *was the*
   same,
The *identical Person*, as well as *the Name,*
Whom ANSTRUTHER said, *in his conscience he held*
To be *legally fin'd*, and *with justice expell'd.*

But

But now, as this *verfatile Hero contends,*
Was punifh'd unjuftly, *for villainous ends.*

Farewell, I fhall write you again when I glean
The Acts of the Apostles—(the Patriots I mean).

Nov. 18, 1789.

LET-

LETTER XLVI.

Sent by a MANAGER *to* Mr. BURKE.

DEAR BURKE, with deepeſt tribulation,
I have to give you information
Of an untoward thing that paſt
At Weſtminſter, on Wedneſday laſt.
Charles Fox, you know, who loves his KING
Far beyond ev'ry earthly thing;
Who cannot brook the ſlighteſt hint
In ſpeech, in writing, or in print,
That tends to caſt the leaſt reflection
On MAJESTY, or its connection.
(And by the bye, I can't but wonder
How he forgave your *Iriſh Blunder*,
When to the wind your ſail unfurling,
You ſpliced together KING and *Hurling*.
'Twas once, I heard, his reſolution
To move againſt you proſecution,
Till *Grey*, your able, kind phyſician,
Made known your ſtate and mind's condition;

And

And therefore tender Charles forgave you,
And join'd with other friends to save you).

But with digreſſion to have done,
At leaſt till I've my Tale begun—
You know that CHARLES was diſcontented
With ſomething Mr. STOCKDALE printed;
I mean that Pamphlet, the *Review*
Of *Charges* mov'd and pen'd by you :
He, with the deepeſt penetration
Therein diſcover'd *Defamation*
Both of the COMMONS and the KING,
Which was, indeed, a ſhocking thing.

Some Members, who were rather blind,
No harm could in the Pamphlet find,
Although to us of optics keen,
'Twas plain as Noſes to be ſeen.
Howe'er, as CHARLES ſo clearly ſaw,
The HOUSE gave *Stockdale* up to Law ;
And *Wedneſday* laſt the *Cauſe was try'd*—
And how d'ye think they did decide ?
Not all th'ATTORNEY GEN'RAL's learning,
Not all that he could urge concerning
The dangers *Libels* may produce,
By coming too much into uſe,

Could

Could make a *purblind Jury* fee
What was fo clear to CHARLES and ME.
Th' ATTORNEY GENERAL once, 'tis true,
(One ought to give the Devil his due)
Exprefs'd a doubt, that *'twou'd not do*.
He faid it was in vain to try
To give a microfcopic eye,
Or make a Jury magnify.

ERSKINE (I wifh the devil had him,
Or that to fpeak he had forbade him)
Did with his ufual vehemence,
And rapid ftream of eloquence,
Prove, that a fingle loofe expreffion
Could conftitute no vaft tranfgreffion ;
He pray'd the *Jurymen* to look
Into the Contents of the Book,
And for themfelves judge, if the writing
Was matter proper for indicting.
They took his counfel, and withdrew,
And read fome pages through and through.
Pretext and Context they compar'd,
And after all their fearch, declar'd
If any thing amifs there be,
'Tis more than Jurymen can fee.

But that which moſt afflicted me,
Was ſeeing Scott ſo full of glee,
After the legal battle winning,
Depart from Court in triumph grinning.

But oh, my Friend, my heart is ſad—
I think this omen very bad :
Hastings was thought a great oppreſſor,
And Burke of wrongs the juſt redreſſor;
Of work divine the nobleſt creature,
The gen'rous friend of human nature :
But now, alas! all ſee the trick—
Curſe on employing Brother Dick—
Curſe on his vain Procraſtinations,
Curſe on all *over-ſpun Orations*,
Curs'd be the cauſes of delaying—
Forgive me, Burke, for what I'm ſaying ;
I'll make amends by future praying.
Pieces of timber *very* long
Are *very* ſeldom *very* ſtrong,
So fine Orations loſe their ſtrength,
When they exceed a proper length.

'Tis written by our Shakspere's pen,
" There is, in the affairs of men,

" A tide,

" A tide, which taken at the flood,
" Leads on to fortune fair and good;
" But if they flothfully neglect
" The tide, alas! the veffel's wreck'd."

There was a time, when thy Oration
Produc'd, by virtue of inflation,
A public mental inflammation,
That for decifion was the feafon,
When paffions warm'd extinguifh'd reafon.

Oh, EDMUND! once o'er the opinion
Of men, thou hadft fupreme dominion;
But now, alas! thou'rt fallen fo low
As to force pity from a foe.
HASTINGS himfelf, fhould he outlive thee,
And fee thy exit, muft forgive thee.
Oh, EDMUND, EDMUND, I could weep!
But firft I'll try to get a fleep.

Dec. 15th, 1789.

LETTER XLVII.

MR. BURKE's ANSWER.

GOOD God! the Letter you have fent,
Has fill'd me full of difcontent.
Can you fuppofe that I require
More fuel heap'd upon the fire?
You know how long and hard I toil,
How much my fpirits fume and boil,
While all my flefh and entrails broil.
What! did a JURY dare diffent
From Fox, the *Man* of *Parliament?*
What! did not KENYON fend 'em back,
Nor put them on a better track?
Nor MANSFIELD-like, diftinction draw,
Between the *Fact* and *point of Law?*
Fox faid, it was a *Libel* ftrong,
And his opinion can't be wrong.
I am, by G—d, in fuch a fury,
That were they mine, I do affure ye,
I'd give the Devil J—dg— and J—.

Mercy upon us ! Heaven defend !
God only knows where this will end.
The *Mob*, perhaps, at *next Election*
May hold *Fox* Worthy of *Rejection*.
The fickle dogs may change their plan,
And chufe fome other for their man.

This is, of all things moft provoking,
Except your curfed mode of joking ;
Don't talk to me of Brother Dick,
The bare remembrance makes me fick :
Don't fpeak about Procraftination,
For I have plann'd a new *Oration*,
Replete with *Recapitulation*
Of all that Warren Hastings did—
Both what he own'd, and what he hid :
Into *Synopfis* I have brought
What he did think, and fhould have thought :
I've pick'd up *Tales*, to make *Digreffions*,
Enough to laft for *Twenty Seffions*.

Anstruther tells me, he can fpeak
A day or two in ev'ry week ;
And Fox (unlefs in certain cafes,
Like being at *Newmarket Races)*

Will

Will lend his aid the scene to vary,
And make a speech, when I am weary;
And all the rest shall ready stand,
To lend in need an helping hand.

But, truly, 'tis confounded hard,
To always play a losing card;
For spite of mine and Party's skill,
Let's cut and shuffle how we will,
COURT CARDS and TRUMPS *we never get*,
But deeper still sink into debt.
FORTUNE! my Curses light upon her,
Lets none of us get any Honor:
Long have I study'd to cajole her,
But now *by force* I will control her.
I will not cease till I exhibit
HASTINGS's body on a *gibbet*,
And ev'ry Scribbler, Poetaster,
Shall share the fortune of his Master;
But above all, that *R—sc—l* SCOTT,
By me he'll never be forgot:
That *Dog*, whene'er I *colour high*,
Makes it appear a *horrid Lye*;
Pursuing me in all directions,
He makes, and glories in detections:

I

When I inveigh with language ſtrong,
He writes a book to prove me wrong,
And keeping with me trick and tye,
He writes and ſpeaks as much as I.
That curſed SCOTT, not only ſhows
My errors in ſarcaſtic Proſe,
But gets ſome half-ſtarv'd *Grub-ſtreet Poet*,
In *doggrel Verſe* again to ſhew it.
ANSTIE (indeed I do ſuſpect him,
Let him beware how I detect him),
Author of SIM. THE FIRST, is reckon'd
The Author too, of SIM. THE SECOND.
When SCOTT informs him, *Stockdale*'s free,
He'll be as bold as bold can be.

 I've heard he is about a Work,
Th' ORATIONS (call'd) of EDMUND BURKE—
My Speeches made at ſundry times,
Are all t' appear in SIMKIN's *Rhymes.*
Another work, I've heard, beſide—
'Tis call'd the PATRIOTIC GUIDE;
Wherein he tears the maſk away,
And ſhews the tricks *we Patriots* play.
All this and more from SCOTT has ſprung—
Would I could ſee the Villain hung,

Into

Into the flames, would I could cram him !
Oh *vengeance, vengeance ! damn him, damn him !*

I'm nearly now to *madnefs* driven,
And almoft wifh myfelf in heaven ;
And here on earth I merely ftay,
Becaufe I'm fo much wifh'd away ;
Yes, I will ftay on earth to plague 'em,
With tales of Brow and Munny Begum.

Dec. 16th, 1789.

LET-

LETTER XLVIII.

SIMON in WALES,

TO HIS

BROTHER SIMKIN in TOWN.

THRO' TAFFY LAND, *Brother*, a rumour has
    fpread,
That SIMKIN, alas! muft be certainly dead;
From your filence unufual, the rumour arofe,
Or from fomething, 'tis likely, that nobody knows.
Some think you're difgufted at lofing the poft
Of RECORDER to BURKE, and his tongue-fighting
    Hoft:
But I hope that my SIMKIN, though B—— is unjuft,
Will not hold himfelf back, giving way to difguft;
Tho' Lady D—NC—N—N's RECORDER elect,
Your Verfes in Wales will be read with refpect.
Your Kindred and Friends all unite in befeeching,
That as ED——D and COLLEAGUES go on with *im-*
    peaching,

Not-

Notwithſtanding your preſent official diſmiſſion,
You will, in defiance of BURKE's prohibition,
In the Boxes, as formerly, take up your ſtation,
And give us the ſubſtance of every Oration.
From your Letters, when finiſh'd, I mean to compoſe
A curious collection of ED———D's *Bon Mots,*
Of ideas ſublime, dreſs'd in beautiful Proſe.
The work will be uſeful, as well as amuſing,
And inſtructive to Youth in the *arts of abuſing.*

There's STOCKDALE, who deals in political writing,
Who has ſuffer'd in pocket, I hear, from indicting;
And to make up the loſs, in the way of his trade,
Is ſelling the Speech that his Advocate made ;
That Speech muſt be able, concluſive, and ſtrong,
Which could prove to a JURY the COMMONS were
      wrong :
Through TAFFY LAND, ERSKINE has ſpread his re-
      nown,
By this Speech, ſo I beg you will ſend it us down.
This STOCKDALE, hereafter, ſhall publiſh my work,
I mean the *Bon Mots* of the Orator Burke :
And the ſayings of CHARLEY and JOSEPH are equal
In value, and are to appear in the ſequel.

We

We have children of four, who, in high imitation
Of the Weſtminſter Heroes, can make an Oration,
For an hour by the clock, againſt baſe peculation.

One thing I have heard, but I can't think it true,
If it were, it had ſurely been mention'd by you:
ANSTRUTHER, they ſay, was once HASTINGS's Friend,
And in *Leadenhall-ſtreet* did his conduct defend;
That conduct which now 'tis his pride to attack,
And to prove to the COURT is ſo frightfully black;
That very ſame conduct he prov'd to be right,
Without ſpot or blemiſh, and perfectly white.
Oh! tell me, *dear* SIM. can this poſſibly be,
Or are Travellers idle, impoſing on me?
If the ſtory were grounded, I'm certain the Court
Would think all he ſaid a mere matter of ſport:
All the BISHOPS would pray for new light to conduct
  'em,
And in ANSTRUTHER's *myſtical ways* to inſtruct 'em.
Lord TOWNSHEND would aſk him, if what he expreſs'd
That day, ſhould be conſtru'd in earneſt or jeſt?
Lord THURLOW would think it extremely provoking,
That his time ſhould be ſpent to hear ANSTRUTHER's
  joking;
Unleſs he loves Muſic, and therefore rejoices
In the harmony ſweet of the MANAGERS' Voices.

But,

But, pray, can a Sophist so able be found
As to prove the same Timber's both rotten and found?
I'm convinc'd, on reflection, it cannot be true;
For 'tis more than a fogging Attorney can do:
The man who confesses he once has deceiv'd,
Has no reason to hope he'll again be believ'd.

I shall finish this Letter with high expectation
Of your giving new proofs of your versification
In ANSTRUTHER's, FOX's, or EDMUND's Oration.
The Lungs of the latter, from resting so long,
Have recover'd, no doubt, and are active and strong;
From practising oft in the BENCH and the PLEAS,
ANSTRUTHER can speak with more freedom and ease:
The LORDS have recover'd, 'tis hop'd, from their
      fears,
And got well of the bruises they had in their ears;
Whilst HASTINGS, grown callous from habit and
      use,
Can bear, with more patience, reproach and abuse.
I have heard something else, which I almost forgot;
'Tis improbable, therefore I credit it not;
By his friends and his foes 'tis in general expected,
That BURKE, as a Candidate, will be rejected,
And never in PARLIAMENT be re-elected:

S

There

There was fomething he faid of a PERSONAGE ROYAL,
Which is highly refented by all that are Loyal;
Perhaps the fame ftory related by you,
'Tis the HURLING I mean, but I hope 'tis not true.

    Oh, SIMKIN! you foon muft want food for your
        pen,
If depriv'd of this beft of Political Men;
I will work double tides, and his character raife.
By my Verfe, and the HERALD, fhall publifh his
        praife;
Were I fuffer'd to whifper in MAJESTY's Ear,
I could arguments bring, irrefiftibly clear,
That if BURKE utter'd language that border'd on
        Treafon,
'Twas when difappointment had fmother'd his Reafon;
That His MAJESTY's Servants were chiefly in fault,
Who rewarded BURKE's merit much lefs than they.
        ought;
For where is the man who has ftrong pretenfion
To a PAYMASTER's *Place*, or a MINISTER's *Penfion?*
I have heard that he once was for ftarving the ——,
But you know that *revenge is a pitiful thing;*
Nor can we expect that fo generous a man,
Should follow his own œconomical plan.

2

Indeed,

Indeed, *my dear* BROTHER, I cannot help thinking,
'Tis our inter'ft conjointly to fave him from finking,
By hiding his faults, and his virtues revealing—
So forget his unkindnefs, and ftifle your feeling.

Jan. 21ft, 1790.

LET.

LETTER XLIX.

SIMKIN to SIMON in WALES.

OH, Brother! Oh, Brother! with deep tribu-
    lation,
I muft try to unfold an afflicting narration :
I'm tortur'd with grief, I'm alarm'd with my fears,
I blot all I write with a torrent of tears,
When the Mob of this City that building pull'd down,
Which let all the Vagabonds loofe on the Town,
It gave not the *Cits* fo much caufe to lament,
As the people now have for this *cruel event*.
Not even the Greeks, when the hot-brain'd Atrides
Took Briseis away from her Lover Pelides,
When they loft in the latter their ableft Protector,
And were frighted to fits at the coming of Hector—
Not all the diftrefs they endur'd in the fequel,
The *approaching diftreffes* of *England* can equal.
Oh, Brother ! thefe Heroes, whom commiferation
Rous'd up as your knights in defence of your Nation,
Whom zeal for Great Britain and her Conftitution,
Has furnifh'd with Rivers of fine Elocution—

Have

Have *quarell'd ! !*—And EDMUND's expected to fever,
In *Political Queftions*, from JOSEPH for *ever !*
Like wildfire, 'tis dreaded, Diffention will run,
And not ENGLAND alone, but *the* WORLD *be undone !*

The Conteft arofe from a clafh in Opinion,
With refpect to the properly placing Dominion :
For BURKE in the SENATE declar'd, he arofe
The *Doctrine* of JOSEPH and CHARLES to *oppofe*,
Whofe Principles growing ftill ftronger and ftronger,
Are fo fhocking and bad, he can bear them no longer.

" I difcover the fpirit of bold *Innovation*,
" Which muft in its confequence ruin this Nation;
" And here, in the prefence of all, I advance,
" That I never encourag'd the *Rebels in France*."

Then he hinted, as if he had reafon to fear
Some *diforder* or other would *vifit us here* ;
And feem'd to imagine that one of his friends
Some *change*, or fome *new Revolution* intends ;
And that, for his own part, he ne'er underftood
That the laft *Revolution* produc'd any good—
'Twas only the changing one Man for another,
Like putting by RICHARD for ROBERT his brother ;

S 3

He

He said, Though my feelings it horribly shocks,
To think I muſt leave ſuch a fellow as *Fox*,
Although I would ſooner be robb'd of a limb,
Than be parted one moment from JOSEPH or *him*,
Yet ſhould they proceed with a *wicked intention*,
I *myſelf will oppoſe them*, by way of prevention.
He of GOVERNMENT ſpoke, and at length he confeſt
Ariſtocracy was, in his judgement, the beſt.

Then CHARLEY aroſe, and began an Oration,
Diſclaiming th' idea of all *Innovation* ;
Lamenting in terms moſt pathetic and ſad
His conviction at length, that *his Leader was mad* :
" BURKE's friendſhip to me is exceedingly dear,
" As is very well known to all you that are here ;
" And I freely confeſs, my *Political Knowledge*
" Was chiefly deriv'd from that Jeſuit's College :
" Half the learning I have (I with confidence ſay it)
" Had I *Metaphyſical Scales*, and could weigh it,
" I obtain'd from attending to BURKE's *converſation*,
" And yet, notwithſtanding this vaſt obligation,
" Were he to engage in that criminal meaſure,
" I ſay he would greatly incur *my diſpleaſure*.
" And ſhould he rebel, I, on ſuch an occaſion,
" (If I could not prevail by the arts of Diſſuaſion),
" Would riſe up in arms to repel the Invaſion.

" But

" But ftill, with regard to the *two Revolutions*,

" With refpect to the beft and the worft Conftitutions,

" I think not with Burke, for I am of opinion,

" That fafety confifts in divided *dominion*;

" And tho' I admit 'tis a very good thing

" To have plenty of Nobles and even a King,

" And am willing that they fhould partake with the reft,

" Yet the fhare of the *Mob* fhould be *largeft* and *beft*.

" As to what I declar'd on a former debate,

" About *France*, and the things which befel her of late,

" If my pleafure and joy were too warmly expreft,

" 'Twas only humanity ftirr'd in my breaft."

Here Joseph broke in, and with ftrong agitation
Began to exclaim againft *Infinuation*;
He declar'd to the Houfe, that he could not tell what
Made Edmund fufpect he was laying a *Plot*;
That with fear and amazement he heard him advance
Hard *libellous words* on the *People* of *France*;
That he needs muft acknowledge, the laft *Revolution*
Had giv'n this Kingdom a *fine Conftitution*.

Here Burke's paroxyfm grew ftronger and ftronger,
And his violent tongue could be bridl'd no longer;
In a rage he arofe, and exclaim'd—Here I *fever*
In *Political Matters, from* Joseph *for ever!*

An

An honeſt and juſt indignation I feel
Againſt people who wiſh to diſplay *the Baſtile:*

Here ended the Conteſt, which ſome think a *Trick,*
And ſay that the Party of EDMUND are ſick;
That 'twas *artifice* made them their LEADER condemn,
To prevent his hereafter expoſing of them.
But howe'er it may be, this *deplorable ſtory,*
GREAT BRITAIN will rob of its honour and glory;
For, his aid and aſſiſtance if EDMUND withdraws,
Oh, who will ſtand forth in HUMANITY's CAUSE?
With grief I foreſee in this *horrid defeƈtion,*
All *Aſia* and *Britain* depriv'd of Proteƈtion.
But HASTINGS's *party,* I fear, will rejoice,
And already, methinks, their unanimous voice
Declares to the Public, the *quarrel of knaves,*
Is one of thoſe bleſſings, which innocence ſaves.
But here, my dear BROTHER, this Letter I end,
And as matter ariſes, another I'll ſend.

POSTSCRIPT,

Dear BROTHER, I ſcarcely had laid down my pen,
When I heard ſomething more of theſe *wonderful men :*

Lord

Lord DERBY, whofe table is almoft *divine*,

Whofe cellars are ftor'd with the richeft of wine,

Next morning invited the *Heroes* to dine.

A meafure he try'd, with the hope of *prevention*

Of the *evils* arifing from *civil diffention*.

They met—and agreed on his LORDSHIP's *fuggeftion*,

To make a *good meal* e'er they handled the *Queftion*.

And I fully concur with his LORDSHIP in thinking

Good *fellowfhip* fprings from good *eating* and *drinking*.

And the Modern Philofophers frequently tell ye,

That to *foften* the *heart*, you muft *harden* the *belly*.

At half after three, when they all were grown *mellow*,

And the *heart* of each MANAGER *yearn'd* on his *fellow*,

His LORDSHIP, th' advantage of *concord* to teach 'em,

Read part of that fcene between LOCKIT and PEACHUM,

Whofe arguments *folid*, *fubftantial*, and *ftrong*,

Made 'em cry, " BROTHER, BROTHER ! *we're both in*

  " *the wrong !*"

So they, who laft night were fo *hot* and *high-mettled*,

Like LOCKIT and PEACHUM, their quarrels have

  fettled.

Then the *Port* and the *Claret* went merrily round,

And *Difcord* itfelf in a bumper was drown'd.

 Feb. 11th, 1790.

LETTER L.

YOU say that my friends all unite in beseeching—
Thus SIMKIN, as EDMUND, goes on with impeaching,
To follow the track he has long been pursuing,
And to versify all BURKE is saying and doing :
Oh, SIMON! alas! though I cannot refuse ye,
I fear, 'twill be difficult now to amuse ye ;
PLUMBOSO, than whom ne'er existed a Speaker,
Of ideas more dull, or of argument weaker,
On the COURT is prepar'd to *inflict* an Oration,
Which may last twenty days, by his own calculation ;
But before *my new Hero* his Speech shall begin,
As you lately requested, I'll shew you wherein
He *dissents from* HIMSELF, in a mode so capricious,
That I'm sadly afraid you will hold it suspicious ;
Nor could aught but his own *ipse dixit*, prov'd clear,
Induce me to give you its history here.

You must know then, long since, on a *certain occasion*,
PLUMBOSO employ'd all the arts of persuasion,
To induce INDIA *Stockholders* not to recal
WARREN HASTINGS, the Governor then of Bengal ;

His

His Speech is too tedious for quoting at length,
So I'll juft give a tafte of its fpirit and ftrength;
But to do it fome juftice, I muft for the while,
Drawl on in the Gentleman's LEADENHALL *Stile.*

" There are, faid he, Directors here, who ftrive
" To taint the pureft character alive
" By loofe and general Charges, which I truft
" I foon fhall prove unfounded and unjuft.
" With unfuccefsful toil they've labour'd long,
" To find in HASTINGS' conduct fomething wrong,
" And having views finifter to promote,
" For his recal they've pafs'd a general vote;
" In general terms their Refolutions fay,
" That HASTINGS did our orders difobey;
" That his ambition did in broils engage,
" And complicated wars fuccefsful wage;
" Treaties repugnant made to common fenfe,
" And crufh'd *the* COMPANY with vaft expence:
" For thefe, and fuch like ills, we deem it meet,
" That HASTINGS fhould no longer hold his feat.
" But mark, my friends, in vain Direction fought.
" To fix on HASTINGS one fpecific fault;
" And here I call upon their boldeft Man,
" (The challenge let him anfwer if he can)

" To

" *To ſtate a* SINGLE INSTANCE, *or to name*
" ONE ACT *that* HASTINGS *did, deſerving* BLAME ! ! !
" In general terms they couch a cenſure ſtrong,
" T'obſtruct our proving, that their cenſure's wrong ;
" Thoſe only in ambiguous language ſpeak,
" Who feel their proofs and arguments are weak.

" Now ſtop awhile and turn your obſervation
" To men applauding their own moderation ;
" For Wiſdom they their reputations raiſe,
" By taking to themſelves another's praiſe.
" They tell us, the M'HRATTA *War* is due
" To HASTINGS—tho' they know the fact *untrue :*
" And can DIRECTORS, void of truth and ſhame,
" For *ſelf-committed* crimes their SERVANTS blame ?
" Bold truths I ſpeak, deny it if ye can,
" Our wiſe DIRECTORS laid the hoſtile plan ;
" 'Twas their command the peaceful Treaty broke,
" War's Trumpet blew, and gave th' aggreſſive ſtroke.

" One fact—you'll not believe, when I relate it,
" But let them contradict—if I mis-ſtate it—
" FLETCHER, whoſe voice his own encomium ſings,
" FLETCHER, who this falſe accuſation brings ;
" Who told you HASTINGS was the baneful ſource
" Of War, of Rapine, and of lawleſs Force ;

I   " *This*

" *This very* FLETCHER d—n'd the Treaty made,

" And bade them feek occafion to invade;

" In thefe mad acts the COMMITTEE join'd,

" He firft the war-provoking letter fign'd.

" It was not HASTINGS who the Treaty broke,

" FLETCHER was he that did the war provoke :

" In fcouting Peace, lay FLETCHER's moderation—

" His faith and wifdom in its violation;

" His juftice, in condemning HASTINGS, fhone,

" For Crimes his confcience tells him are his own :

" FLETCHER ftand forth ! and make thy own defence,

" Or clear from foul afperfion, INNOCENCE !

" On grounds like thefe, are all their charges built,

" They *fin themfelves, and* HASTINGS *bears the guilt.*

" Againft one man were e'er fuch fchemes devis'd ?

' Was ever character fo fcrutiniz'd ?

" By *two* COMMITTEES caft, without a hearing,

" Without a friend on his behalf appearing :

" But, after proving, by fevereft teft—

" Convinc'd, his foes reluctantly confeft,

" They had in all his public conduct found

" *Integrity of* HEART *and judgement found;*

" Experience, knowledge, qualities that muft

" Capacitate a man for PUBLIC TRUST.

" Shall talents fuch as thefe incur difgrace ?

" Shall ignorance and folly take their place ?

Shall

" Shall madnefs drive this PREFECT from his feat,

" The only Man that can preferve the State ?

" This our DIRECTORS do, in imitation

" *Of* Fox *and* BURKE, *and* THEIR ADMINISTRATION.

" To prove, howe'er abfurd CHARLES Fox may be,

" DIRECTORS *can be more abfurd than* HE :

" The RAJAH's Exile, and the BEGUM's Tales,

" Which General SMITH fo tenderly bewails,

" Are facts which ftand in need of no defence,

" Confiftent all with equity and fenfe :

" The RAJAH larger tribute juftly paid,

" The LORD with juftice claims the VASSAL's aid ;

" With juftice fines, for orders difobey'd.

" To all their pleadings on the BEGUM's fide,

" The COMMODORE has perfectly reply'd ;

" But grant, what I deny with reafon ftrong,

" In fome few cafes HASTINGS acted wrong :

" Yet, no felf-int'reft did his mind miflead,

" The Public Weal fuggefted ev'ry deed—

" Accufers, torture facts with all your fkill,

" *Then fhew me* ONE, INTENTIONALLY *ill."*

I think, after reading this *verfify'd Profe,*

Wich has nothing but truth to adorn it, God knows !

(A fac-

(A *fac-simile* sketch of the Gentleman's speech,)
You will ask with what face can PLUMBOSO IMPEACH?
Perhaps you'll exclaim, that he's doing the same,
As what fix'd upon FLETCHER indelible shame,
That for HASTINGS's conduct he ought to atone,
As by pleading excuses he made it his own.
Oh, SIMON! I've said, and now say it again,
You know nothing yet of political men!
PLUMBOSO once more would be HASTINGS's friend,
Leave BURKE and that party, and HASTINGS defend—
Could you make him believe it would answer his end.
This modest young man had his eye on the Chair
Of CALCUTTA's *Chief Judge*, with eight thousand a
    year;
From PARTY he strives that promotion to draw,
Which ought to be his, from the *study of Law*;
Could HASTINGS assist him that office to fill,
He would vote for him, plead for him, worship him
    still.

Dear BROTHER, it often has happen'd, no doubt,
That in crossing the Hills, you've mistaken your route;
When finding your error, you gladly came back,
And sought for some other more probable track:
So, as HASTINGS his views wanted means to promote,
PLUMBOSO gives BURKE his assistance and vote;

In

In Parliament, alſo, he joins Oppoſition,
As the probable means to improve his condition:
For if looks may be truſted, I'll venture to ſay,
He is in a mournful, deplorable way;
But for or againſt, he is free to harangue,
And with equal indifference—*ſave* HASTINGS, or *hang*.
I know, that to uninform'd beings like you,
Such characters muſt appear ſhocking and new;
For I've oft heard you ſay, that if B—KE were not void
Of ſhame, his own Brother had ne'er been employ'd :
Such remarks, *my Dear* SIMON, are quite out of ſeaſon,
You ſpeak from your feelings and not from your reaſon;
PLUMBOSO's ſweet infants, and Spouſe, muſt be fed,
BURKE's *family* too, muſt not languiſh for bread;
Nor muſt other wrinkled Diſciples of Famine,
Be depriv'd of their chance of good ſtuffing and cram-
  ming.
Your flocks and your herds in the Mountains you feed,
Induc'd by futurity's probable need;
In the final diſpoſal, conſulting the pay,
You fat them, you ſtarve them, you kill them or ſtay.
A moment's reflection proves this to be true,
One principle governs PLUMBOSO and you.
But now from your Mountains, I'd have you come
  down,
And mix with the folk that inhabit this town :
        Then

Then experience will quickly your fentiments change,
And nothing appear inconfiftent or ftrange;
GEORGE HARDINGE once faid WARREN HASTINGS's
    name,
Like CHATHAM's, would live in the annals of fame.
If from Infamy's record their foes are exempt,
There is nothing can fave them but fcorn and contempt;
And with HARRY DUNDAS, 'tis a frequent expreffion,
To HASTINGS we owe all our Eaftern Poffeffion.
Thefe two for IMPEACHING him, join'd in the vote,
And would hang him To-morrow, their ends to pro-
    mote;
For Ingratitude let not your tendernefs weep,
'Tis exactly the cafe with yourfelf and your fheep.

I have fomething to add, which perhaps may be new,
And I give you my word, 'tis undoubtedly true:
The *Genius* of BURKE, for the honour of trade,
Has a great *Linguá-factory* recently made—
'Tis a kind of a MINT made for Character-ftriking,
And coining anew to an Orator's liking;
BURKE's *Mint*, when you put a fair character in,
Impreffes upon it the *picture of Sin:*
But if it be black or deform'd to the view,
It can beautify alfo by coining anew.

T

And

And what is ſtill more, it can alter, with eaſe,
Appearances juſt as the Orators pleaſe ;
But JOSEPH, who thinks he has equal pretenſion,
Diſputes with his LEADER the right of invention :
Yet I hope they'll agree, and conjointly apply
For a PATENT, which MAJESTY cannot deny.
Not HERSCHELL, who found out the *Roads* in the *Moon*,
Not the Chymical Head which contriv'd a *Balloon* ;
Not the man who firſt gave us the notion of Print,
Is greater than BURKE in his *Character-Mint*.

    Oh, GEORGE ! ſhouldſt thou hold it in juſt eſtima-
        tion,
And think, like myſelf, that 'twill better thy nation,
To reward his deſert, and encourage invention,
As well as a *Patent*, oh ! grant BURKE a *Penſion* :
For not even thy Gold, ſhould his Currency paſs,
Will illumine thy name like his *Copper* and *Braſs*.
But now, my *Dear* BROTHER, this Letter I end,
And another new Speech I hereafter ſhall ſend—
When I fairly have heard what PLUMBOSO can ſay,
And have found him deny what he ſaid t'other day.

    Feb. 16th, 1790.

LET-

LETTER LI.

SIMKIN TO SIMON.

IF my Letter fhould give you lefs pleafure and fport
Than ANSTRUTHER laft *Tuefday* afforded the COURT,
I expect you will take up your Pen, to implore
That on fubjects like this I will write you no more.
But among all the virtues by POETS poffeft,
FIDELITY being the rareft, is beft;
I therefore fhall ftrictly adhere to my plan,
And give you the words of this *verfatile* man,
Who arofe in his place, and thus fpeaking began :

    " You remember, my LUDS, when the PARLIA-
       " MENT clos'd,
" I told you the tafk which my LEADER impos'd.
" *Some years have elapfed*, fince it fell to my lot,
" (I remind you thereof, as you may have forgot),
" To fum up what proof we were able to bring,
" As to HASTINGS's conduct to RAJAH CHEYT SING ;
" I proved to your *Ludfhips* by arguments ftrong,
" That HASTINGS was always *externally* wrong;

T 2

" And

" And *now* 'tis a *duty incumbent* to add,
" That his conduct was alfo *internally* bad ;
" For whether we view him without or within,
" We fee nothing elfe but the *Picture of Sin.*"

The HERO went on in this manner of pleading,
Whilft fome were his *former Antithefis* reading :
They afk'd, if the man whom he thus reprehended,
Was the fame whom he formerly prais'd and defended ?
And concluded at laft, that 'twas *only the name*
Which mifled them to fancy the perfon the fame.
They fuppofe the *Defender* was ANSTRUTHER's *Brother,*
Or inftead of this HASTINGS, it muft be *fome other :*
But whilft their *identity* was in debate,
PLUMBOSO announc'd—*he was going to ftate :*
Then he ftated—I cannot precifely tell what,
Or, if ever I knew, I remember it not—
'Twas fomething of HASTINGS's having deftroy'd
Six *Revenue Councils,* and having employ'd
Black Agents, who follow'd his orders and rules,
When they brought into ufe a *Committee of Tools.*
The *Committee of Tools,* he was free to admit,
For the *requifite ufe,* might be proper and fit ;
But becaufe they were qualify'd well for a poft,
They, of all people, fhould be avoided the moft.

He

He faid, that when HASTINGS had fully demolifh'd
All check and controul, by thus having abolifh'd
The *Revenue Councils,* he fear'd no detection,
And gave to the SINGS an extenfive collection.

Here the Hero, with gravity folemn, defcribes
The *places* and *times* of receiving the bribes;
And tho' HASTINGS carry'd the *total amount*
Of all he receiv'd to the *public account,*
Yet ANSTRUTHER thinks that he meant to have kept
     it—
Why elfe, in God's name, did he ever accept it?
Of this he declar'd he had perfect conviction
From his Minutes, containing a flat contradiction.

" My LUDS, I fhall fhew 'tis extremely abfurd
" To credit a man that departs from his word:
" When *a man with himfelf in diffention* we find,
" 'Tis evidence ftrong of a very *bad mind.*"

Here their Lordfhips to each other *laughingly* faid,
" *The blow which the Orator gave his own Head,*
" *Had fractur'd the fkull—if it had not been* LEAD."
Whilft the Ladies, *all tendernefs,* ftar'd, I fuppofe,
Expecting to fee the *blood run from his nofe.*

T 3

To

To demonſtrate his great *architeЄtural ſenſe*,
And *rhetorical ſkill*, he declar'd the *Defence*
Of HASTINGS was built of *materials unſound*,
The *foundation* of which he would *pull to the ground*.
Having ſhewn himſelf thus a *profound Rhetorician*,
He prov'd himſelf next a moſt able *Logician*.

    " My LUDS, to your *Ludſhips* I'm going to ſtate ;
" But firſt I muſt beg you'll attend to the *Date :*
" *January* the 20th, the year Eighty-two,
" This Letter was written——which cannot be true ;
" The ſhip ſail'd in *March* ; for which reaſon I ſay,
" 'Twas only *apparently* written that day."

    To prove himſelf very preciſe and exaЄt
In quotation, as well as in ſtatement of faЄt,
He firſt told the LORDS, that he meant to extraЄt
A paſſage from HASTINGS's Letter, and next,
He gave his own Comment inſtead of the Text.
" My LUDS, we have *no direЄt proof* to adduce,
" *That the Preſents were taken for* HASTINGS's *uſe* ;
" But yet, tho' the Evidence is not direЄt,
" *ConſtruЄtive* muſt ſerve to ſupply the defeЄt.
" On *proof* by *conſtruЄtion* did DONELLAN die,
" Then in HASTINGS's caſe let *conſtruЄtion* apply.

                             " My

" My Luds, to your *Ludſhips* I'm going to ſtate,

" That folk *without-door* are with triumph elate,

" Becauſe Deby Sing was on trial acquitted

" Of the cruelties Edmund declares he committed ;

" But, my Luds, notwithſtanding that Burke's alle-
      " gation

" Was made, I admit, *without proper foundation* ;

" And tho' Deby Sing was but ſlightly to blame,

" Yet Hastings's guilt is preciſely the ſame :

" For Hastings the Government held at the time—

" Reſponſible therefore for every crime ;

" Whence-ever crimes riſe, or wherever they fall,

" All the guilt is his own—*let him anſwer for all !*"

In this manner Anstruther expended three hours,

And aſtoniſh'd the Court by the length of his pow'rs ;

But ſtill all this *ſtating, re-ſtating,* and *ſhowing,*

Left me and moſt others extremely unknowing :

For we could not find out, in the *maſs* of *confuſion,*

One clear allegation, or proof, or concluſion ;

And as for my own part, with ſhame I confeſs ;

The more I attend, I remember the leſs ;

By the Judges, no doubt, he is well underſtood,

But to me he appear'd like a *fox in a wood,*

Where hounds inexperienc'd may wander about

All day, without finding the animal out.

T 4

At

At leaſt twenty times had the Hero repeated,
" My LUDS, *I have ſhewn, I have prov'd, I have ſtated,*"
When I aſk'd the By-ſtanders to tell what was ſhewn,
But their knowledge appear'd to be leſs than my own ;
If therefore my Letter's perplex'd and obſcure,
'Tis an evil that does not admit of a cure.

In the morning, the HALL was but thinly attended,
And deſerted almoſt e'er the ſtory was ended.
Tho' HASTINGS, as uſual, was often *abuſed*,
'Twas ſo *heavily* done, that we were not amuſed ;
Of courſe I reſolv'd on poſtponing my Letter,
In hopes the next day would produce ſomething better ;
But in this expectation again I was wrong,
We had only the *Clerk's monotonical ſong*.

Before I've quite finiſh'd this Letter, I'll mention
The reaſon of JOSEPH and EDMUND's *diſſention* ;
The *latter* maintains, it were ſafeſt and beſt,
That the Conſcience of Men ſhould be put to the teſt ;
Whilſt the *former*, a man of ideas enlarg'd,
Whoſe troubleſome conſcience has long been *diſcharg'd*,
To doctrines *reſtrictive* can never agree,
But would have, *like his own, ev'ry Conſcience go free*.

Feb. 23d, 1790.

L E T-

L E T T E R LII.

DEAR SIMON, it needs muſt afflict you to know,
That the MANAGERS' *Box* is deſerted by JOE;
But, by way of affording you ſome conſolation,
'Tis ſuppos'd that he means to compoſe an oration,
To deliver in perſon, not many months hence,
In the HOUSE of St. STEPHEN, in WARREN's Defence—
And to prove that the Party by BURKE was miſled—
He will contradict all that he formerly ſaid.
He'll affirm the DEFENDANT's of virtue a pattern,
And the BEGUM of OUDE a deteſtable ſlattern;
For on *this ſide* or *that* JOSEPH enters the liſt,
And partners are chang'd, like a *rubber of whiſt*.
But now your attention once more I recal,
To the MANAGER's *Battles* in WESTMINSTER HALL—
PLUMBOSO, alas! indeſcribably dull,
On Tueſday ſaid nothing for SIMKIN to cull;
And, indeed, 'tis a point of incertitude, whether
The COURT had not loſt all the Ladies together,
If EDMUND, *Great* EDMUND! who always attends,
Had not made us, on Thurſday, ſome little amends.

But

But now, in difcharge of my truft as RECORDER,
The Proceedings of Thurfday I'll give you in order.

PLUMBOSO addrefs'd himfelf thus to the Peers—
" My *Luds*, I fhall ftate, *in the courfe of three years*
" All the Revenues which in BENGAL were collected,
" Amounted to lefs than what HASTINGS expected :
" In the three former years, I fhall fhew an excefs,
" Whilft the following three were productive of lefs."
'Twere needlefs the Evidence here to rehearfe—
'Tis fufficient to fay—that it prov'd the *reverfe*.
PLUMBOSO next faid—He was ready and willing
To prove GOONGA GOVIND a terrible villain ;
And, this to effect, he proceeded to quote
A Letter, which LARKINS from INDIA wrote—
It ftated that GOONGA's detention of treafure,
In HASTINGS's mind had excited difpleafure ;
Then the Hero, from HASTINGS, a document brought,
To fhew GOONGA GOVIND was never in fault.
At the moment, it ftruck me, that this accufation
Was brought againft HASTINGS, in retaliation
For SCOTT's charging PLUMMY with like variation.
Perhaps, in your fnarling farcaftical way,
On the reading of this, you'll be tempted to fay—

That

That LARKINS and HASTINGS, like *Calvin* and *Luther*,
Are perfons diftinct, but that PLUMB and ANSTRU-
  THER
Are one and the fame—and 'tis thence more abfurd,
In PLUMMY to vary from ANSTRUTHER's word.

 Having thus prov'd, that GOONGA was vaftly to
  blame,
He would prove KELLORAM was precifely the fame—
An unprincipled fellow, (perhaps a *Diffenter*),
And therefore unfit for a Company's Renter.
This *Charaƈter-cutting* awaken'd the feeling
Of the foft-hearted LAW, who is clever at healing;
He mov'd—" That the MANAGERS might not enlarge
" On matter which could not be found in the Charge."
Here the bufinefs appear'd to be ill underftood,
For tho' LAW could not find it, the MANAGERS cou'd:
For *Charaƈter-cutting* PLUMBOSO contended,
And declar'd, upon *that* the whole Trial depended—
" For my *Luds*, to your *Ludſhips* unlefs we can ftate,
" That HASTINGS's Renters were villains complete,
" That his motives were bad beyond all contradiction,
" We fhall never be able to carry conviction."

 Here BURKE, fpringing up, a comparifon drew
From the *Merchant* of VENICE and SHYLOCK the *Jew*.

In

In language pathetic the Leader complain'd,

That in cutting of HASTINGS his hand is reſtrain'd :

" My LORDS, on reflection, it needs muſt be found

" That the Counſel have taken untenable ground—

" From the body of HASTINGS, ſuppoſe it be true,

" That but one pound of fleſh is the MANAGERS' due,

" Yet we hope that your LORDSHIPS will let us take

    " two.

" In criminal caſes, except only this—

" To act with preciſion may not be amiſs ;

" But the cutting of HASTINGS, and ſpilling his blood,

" For the cure of extortion's a recipe good :

" So we truſt that your LORDSHIPS will not bid us ſtop,

" But let us proceed till we ſpill the laſt drop.

" My LORDS, to the Proverb whoever attends,

" Muſt know that a chain has a *couple of ends* ;

" And that, by experience, 'tis conſtantly found,

" That the perſon who binds, is in *vinculo* bound :

" That is, whoſoever brings forth accuſation,

" Is bound to eſtabliſh his own allegation.

" My LORDS, in the cauſe we are hearty and ſteady,

" And to prove all we ſay are both willing and ready ;

" And do it we ſhall, by God's bleſſing and gift,

" If your Honour and Juſtice will lend us a lift :

" Your LORDSHIPS, I think, muſt undoubtedly know,

" How much we are hated above and below :

ı

" If

" If Hastings hereafter acquitted should be,

" *Pray what will become of my colleagues and me ?*

" Your Lordships should, therefore, in commisera-
  " tion

" Of *our* dangers, indulge us in strong aggravation."

And I think, my *dear* Brother, as most people must,

'Twere better that Hastings, by sentence unjust,

Shou'd suffer for crimes *that he never committed,*

Than Burke be disgrac'd *by his being acquitted :*

But Law, who, perhaps, never made this reflection,

Or weakly supposes a Lawyer's protection

Is due to the Client, renew'd his objection.

So the Lords were in consequence forc'd to retreat,

And on Kelloram's character held a debate.

They return'd—and the Managers then were acquainted,

That Kelloram's character must not be tainted ;

But Edmund, much hurt by their Lordships' decision,

Made a comment or two, in the way of revision :—

" The Commons, my Lords, do but ill under-
  " stand

" The technical forms of the Law of the land ;

" And

" And as few of us here are profeſſional men,

" We a latitude claim for the tongue and the pen;

" And not being bred in LEGALITY's *Schools*,

" We ſet at defiance all ſhackles and rules :

" We are privileg'd men, and the Guardians of Free-
    " dom,

" And liberties take whenſoever we need 'em.

" My LORDS, there muſt follow a conſequence bad,

" If the MANAGERS are not permitted to add

" New matter at pleaſure, without going back

" To St. STEPHEN's for licence to change the attack :

" From the Chapel new Charges, 'tis true, we may
    " bring,

" And give the old Story about DEBY SING :

" But I wiſh not, my LORDS, to put this to the proof,

" *Leſt the Commons ſhou'd ſay, we have voted enough.*

" My LORDS, your deciſion, tho' ill underſtood,

" Was made, without doubt, on a principle good :

" A PRISONER, you think, ſhou'd be tenderly us'd,

" And anſwer that only of which he's accus'd;

" But HASTINGS, my LORDS, has long ſince been ac-
    " quainted,

" That we thought KELLORAM deſerv'd not to be
    " ſainted—

" Beſides, ſhould the COMMONERS Articles draw

" According to rules, and the cuſtoms of Law,

                        " I main-

" I maintain it would be an iniquitous breach

" Of *Privilege*, granted to thofe who IMPEACH—

" But, my LORDS, it would make all the MANAGERS

      " glad,

" To prove KELLORAM bore a character bad."

All this notwithftanding, the COURT ne'er expreft

The leaft inclination to grant his requeft;

This failing, PLUMBOSO more artfully try'd

To bring in his proof on the oppofite fide :

But HASTINGS's Counfel the danger forefaw,

And the door was clofe barr'd by the *vigilant* LAW.

Then BURKE wou'd have prov'd, had the LORDS not

      refus'd him,

That HASTINGS's *Libellers daily abus'd him*;

And what he conceiv'd a more dangerous thing,

Was, their knowing the proof he intended to bring :

But LAW, who on EDMUND ftill fixes his eye,

Begg'd to know to what Article this could apply :

In a few minutes after their LORDSHIPS adjourn'd,

And the MANAGERS all to St. STEPHEN's return'd.

One thing, my dear BROTHER, I have to remark,

Upon fomething I lately was told by a CLERK :—

CHARLES faid to the CHANCELLOR, not a week back,

That in five or fix days they wou'd end the attack.

I was

I was frighten'd at this, and inclin'd to fuppofe,

That in lefs than a twelvemonth the Trial would clofe.

But now I'm convinc'd that my CHIEF will endeavour

To make the IMPEACHMENT *continue for* EVER ;

And I hope that the LORDS his endeavours will blefs,

And grant him, in all things, the wifh'd-for fuccefs.

March 2d, 1790.

An

An ALLEGORICAL TALE.

The CACKLING HEN, DUNGHILL COCK, *and* HAWK.

YOUR Students and great Scholars know,
That many thousand years ago,
The birds which in the forest sung,
Possess'd the powers of human tongue.
There liv'd at the aforesaid time,
A Cackling Hen of flight *sublime*,
Within whose walk was often picking
An ill-shap'd, half-starv'd, *Dunghill Chicken*;
This Dunghill Chicken got a seat
Among the Fowls which rul'd the State,
Where, hearing that a certain Hawk
Had done some mischief in his walk,
Either by aiding of his foes,
Or something else that no one knows;
He did resolve (his schemes to further)
To charge the Hawk with horrid murther:
The Hawk, as I have heard the story,
Flew to the Moon in quest of glory;

U   The

The feather'd Prince who rules the Moon,
In war employ'd this young Dragoon;
Where he fuccefsful honours fought,
And many a Battle bravely fought.

It happen'd, that fome years ago,
The Prince profcrib'd a plundering Crow;
But what induc'd him to profcribe
This Leader of a fable tribe,
Was this; the Crow both night and day,
Was looking out in queft of prey,
And carry'd all he found away.
At length, the Hawk by fudden fpring,
Fix'd on the Crow and broke his wing:
The Crow before the Prince was brought,
And juftly fentenc'd for his fault.
The news foon reach'd the black Banditti,
Who mov'd with anger and with pity,
Arofe in arms, refolv'd to fave
Their pilfering Leader from the grave.
The Hawk, who fcarce a morning fince,.
Receiv'd an order from his Prince,
To execute the rebel Crow,
Forefaw, and ftruck the timely blow.
The Dunghill Chicken, who had heard
This ftory by the Hawk averr'd,

Thought

'Thought by this means to over-reach him,
And mov'd the Affembly to impeach him.
He faid, the lunar feather'd King
Had done a moft unlawful thing,
In fentencing the Crow to die,
And then he told the Affembly why:
" It is—It is—It is, becaufe
" 'Twas not by Sublunary Laws:
" My fentiments I can't exprefs,
" You'll underftand me ne'er the lefs.
" This is my own, my fix'd opinion,
" The Lunar Prince had no dominion.
" How do we know the Crow was try'd
" By thofe who juftly might decide?
" And that they follow'd all the rules
" Prefcrib'd by Sublunary Schools?
" Our want of proof and knowledge fhow
" That this faid Hawk, who kill'd the Crow,
" Had murder done, and fhould exhibit
" His body on a lofty Gibbet."
He cackled much, but every Bird
Declar'd his cackling was abfurd;
At laft, as well might be expected,
The Chicken's ftory was rejected.

The

The Hawk, who heard himſelf accus'd,
And did not like to be abus'd,
Next morning went to give the Chicken
A Lecture upon quarrel-picking.
The Chicken, who foreſaw the Lecture,
Call'd to his aid his great Protector,
A cackling Hen, a lingual Hector.
The Hawk, impatient, did denounce
His aim, before he made the Pounce;
So that the Chicken would not walk
One ſtep alone, nor even talk
One word in private with the Hawk.
The cackling Hen then ſpread her wing,
And ſaid, " 'Twas an atrocious thing,
" When Birds of State are ſpeeches making,
" To hinder them from freedom taking:
" Hundreds and hundreds I've accus'd,
" And tho' ſome thouſands I've abus'd,
" I never was ſo roughly us'd.
" Sooner than I'll permit the Hawk
" To ſtop the Chicken in his talk,
" Or let them have a ſpar together,
" Indeed I'd part with every feather;
" Sooner than ſuffer ſuch a thing
" To happen, I would burn my wing.

" A Dung-

" A Dunghill Chicken's tittle tattle
" Should not provoke a Hawk to battle.
" Nor does it to myself appear,
" The Hawk had any right to hear :
" For whether it was good or ill,
" 'Twas said upon our own Dunghill;
" And ev'ry Dunghill Cock, you know,
" Of right may on his Dunghill crow."

Thus the Old Hen contriv'd to baulk
The vengeance of the pouncing Hawk;
Who, without either Judge or Jury,
Had slain the Chicken in his fury,
And verify'd the Chicken's saying,
That he (the Hawk) was fond of slaying;
But now the disappointed Hawk,
(Who though a fighter could not talk)
Finding he could not make a dart,
Nor get the Hen and Chick a-part,
Submitted to this hard condition—
That Dunghill Fowls should, by permission,
On their own Dunghills broach a lye,
Provided Hawks may make reply.

April 2d, 1790.

LETTER LIII.

SIMKIN to SIMON.

INDEED, *my dear* BROTHER, you'll feel yourself
    wrong,
In declaring that SIM. has been silent too long;
When you find that for want of some pleasanter stuff,
I am forc'd to put up with *Tobacco* and *Snuff*.
That HERO who gain'd reputation and fame,
By pleading the cause of a *Dowager Dame*,
Joe *Surface*, I mean, who was mightily proud
To be rank'd as the Knight of the BEGUMS of OUDE,
Is the champion of *Smoakers*, and *Snuffy-nos'd Beauties*,
To exonerate *Snuff* and *Tobacco* from duties.
Three Hours and a Half, by his voluble tongue,
On *Snuff* and *Tobacco* the changes were rung;
But first let me say, he commenc'd his Oration
By stoutly defending *his own reputation*.

" Mr. SPEAKER, (said JOE) ever since I arose,
" In defence of our *Noses*, this Tax to oppose,

           " My

" My fame *once so spotless*, with STAPLE *abuse*,

" All the MINISTER's *Prints* have combin'd to

  " traduce;

" They have faid, fince in favour I grew with HIS

  " HIGHNESS,

" The DUKE has look'd on with fufpicion and fhynefs;

" That I, Traitor-like, have been falfe to the *League*,

" And have fever'd two HOUSES by artful intrigue.

" It would be, Mr. SPEAKER, my glory and pride,

" If the COMMONS, the LORDS, and the PEOPLE

  " befide,

" Like his GRACE, would approve of my faying and

  " doing,

" And permit me to fave the whole Nation from ruin.

" Shou'd ANY my CHARACTER dare to attack,

" And to hint that both Private and Public are black;

" That in ANY ONE PART, my Efcutcheon is blotted,

" Or the fkin of my legs even fpeckled or fpotted;

" I fay, and I truft, it will ne'er be forgot,

" I defy *human Malice* to find out a fpot;

" And unlefs any Gentleman *rife in his place*,

" And will point out fome action, DISHONEST or BASE,

" Although from reproach I may not be exempt,

" All abufe *out of doors*, I fhall treat with contempt:

" To anonymous fcandal I ne'er fhall reply,

" And for *warfare* fo trifling, MY MIND *is too high*;

U 4" For

" For I live in a land where a man cuts a figure,
" In proportion to intellect, spirit, and vigour."

Whilst this was deliver'd by Joseph, in thunder,
I obferv'd all the Hearers were gaping with wonder;
All fmitten, perhaps, by *the force of conviction*,
For they could not fuppofe Joe was *dealing in fiction*,
And indeed, my *Dear Simon*, with grief and furprize,
I reflect on the many malevolent lies,
Which of late thro' the wicked Metropolis ran,
Concerning this *worthy, refpectable Man.*
But in cafe you've not heard them, the ftories *I mean*,
Are his urging the P— to difpute with the Q—;
That when he had rais'd himfelf up to the top
Of the ladder, he fpeedily kick'd down the prop;
That being too haughty, too great to be led,
Of the *Party*, his vanity made him the head;
Whilft the Duke growing jealous, declar'd him unfit
To impofe Loans and Taxes, in lieu of Young Pitt:
That the *entré* to Drury, to make up a fum,
Honeft Joseph had fold, for ten feafons to come;
And thus he efcap'd, at a critical pinch,
For you know 'tis unfafe—to drive *juft to an inch*:
That a worthy old man had his fortune invefted,
Where Joey's *beft hopes*, for the *prefent*, are refted,

I

But

But had lately been forc'd to abandon the realm,

Tho' JOSEPH ftood firm, with his eye *on the* HELM,

From Duns well fecur'd, by a feat in a place,

Where non-payment of debts was ne'er reckon'd difgrace.

Thefe, and other *deteftable, infamous* tales,

Through England are fpread, and, *perhaps,* have
 reach'd Wales.

And 'twas faid, that without fome *efpecial protection,*

Sir ELIJAH would *ouft* him at Stafford Election;

But after fo *bold,* and fo manly a Speech,

Who, in *future,* will *venture* his *fame* to impeach.

After much contemplation, I'm free to admit,

As a *Minifter,* I prefer JOSEPH to PITT;

Harfh *Laws* ev'ry Seffion, by PITT are *enacted,*

To pay off *the Debts* which *by* NORTH were contracted;

But were JOSEPH a Minifter, *he* could contrive

To make Debtor and Creditor *equally thrive* ;

That is, he would raife money fome other way,

Than by *taxing* the Public, the public *to pay* ;

For tho' they are *Debtor* and *Creditor* both,

To *receive* they are *prompt,* but to pay they are *loth.*

Now JOE, fo his *friends* and his *enemies* fay,

Has been us'd to *receive,* not accuftom'd to *pay* ;

For his genius inventive, has found out refources,

To fupply, without cafh, his extravagant courfes;

And

And were Joseph the Minister, doubtlefs, he would
His *fecret* difclofe *for the National good :*
Or would ftrike out a mode, for the Public to get
The Intereft, *at leaft,* on its great load of debt.

But, alas ! notwithftanding his eloquent pleading,
I fee little profpect of Joseph's fucceeding;
For Pitt, and *his friends,* feem'd to think he was *joking,*
Tho' he talk'd for three hours on fnuff-taking and
       fmoaking;
'Yet I cannot but own, 'tis exceedingly hard,
That virtue, like Joseph's, fhould fail of reward;
But the *Chapter of Accidents* ftill may befriend him,
And when next he burfts forth, *better luck may attend him.*

Farewell, my *Dear Brother,* this Letter I end,
But when Anstruther opens, I another will fend.

April 22d, 1790.

LETTER LIV.

LAST Thurſday, DEAR BROTHER, by half after
  one,
WARREN HASTINGS's Trial once more was begun;
PLUMBOSO ſet off, with expreſſing his wonder,
At diſcovering ſome *typographical blunder*;
Which having corrected, as well as he cou'd,
He requeſted their LORDSHIPS would then be ſo good
As to hear him go on with his ſtating, and ſhowing,
Some things, which he fancy'd were fit for their know-
  ing:
He ſaid—" I believe I can make it appear,
" That the COMPANY'S TENANTS were much in
  " arrear,
" And that HASTINGS had let them their Leaſes too
  " dear.
" *Forty Thouſand Pounds Sterling*, or near that amount,
" WARREN HASTINGS receiv'd on the public account,
" And I'm going to prove, the receipt of that ſum
" Dry'd up the reſources for ages to come:
" The Papers and Documents, now in my hands,
" Will prove KELLORAM's having rented ſome lands,
      " Which

" Which lands, upon terms fo injurious, were let,

" As to bring the poor Renter extremely in debt:

" This was HASTINGS's doing, and, in the event,

" The COMPANY fuffer'd, *by lofing fome Rent.*"

Here LAW, (who is fkill'd in defence and attack,

And who loves to fee ANSTRUTHER *fprawl on his back,*

Who always a pleafure malevolent feels,

Whenever he trips up a MANAGER's *heels,*)

Objected to ANSTRUTHER's document reading,

And thereby put a ftop to his rapid proceeding.

He obferv'd to their LORDSHIPS, he could not fee why

They fhould read any Papers that did not apply——

He faid, he was fure there was no allegation,

To which the faid Papers bore any relation;

That the MANAGERS ought not *to wander at large,*

To feek criminality, not in the Charge.

Then PLUMMY requefted their LORDSHIPS would

    note,

'Twas a *confequent circumftance,* near or remote.

As the HERO appear'd to be heavily preft,

And, for want of an argument, deeply diftreft:

Great EDMUND and CHARLES, when they faw him

    difmay'd,

Like JUNO and PALLAS, came down to his aid.

A bat-

A battle enfued, not with *Piſtols* and *Swords*,
Some DUELS were fought, and the weapons were *Words :*
Three hours they engag'd, without ſtopping or ſtaying,
Each other they *cut*, without *killing* or *ſlaying*.

According to CHARLES, *Miſdemeanour's* a crime,
In proportion to *conſequence, manner*, and *time :*
According to THURLOW, they ſhould not enlarge
The deſcription of Crimes, but go on with the Charge ;
And the granting of Leaſes, for leſs than they ought,
He conſider'd, as making a ſeparate fault,
Which into ſome ARTICLE ſhould have been brought.
But CHARLEY contended, that all aggravations,
Like PELION on OSSA, ſhould load *Allegations* ;
And that, tp eſtabliſh the truth of one faƈt,
You ſhould evidence bring of a *conſequent Aƈt.*
Then the CHANCELLOR ſaid—" 'Twas unuſual to
        " plead,
" Or to *anſwer a Charge* that has *never been made.*

Here EDMUND declar'd—" 'twas improper to draw
" *Regulations* for MANAGERS, out of the Law ;
" That men, who were bleſt with a liberal mind,
" Could not brook the idea of being *confin'd* ;
                              " And

" And as HASTINGS's crimes were not murder or
" treason,
" He could not discover a shadow of reason,
" Why their LORDSHIPS, in mere *Misdemeanour*, should
" bind 'em
" From seeking new Charges, where'er they could
" find 'em;
" And, indeed, I shall think it uncommonly strange,
" If a MANAGER is not permitted to range :
" Reftriction, My LORDS, would our energy damp,
" And our tongues would be hurt by a fit of the *Cramp :*
" But, my LORDS, I've a reason that forces conviction,
" Why a MANAGER should not lie under *reftriction.*
" I've heard it reported, not many days since,
" That HASTINGS intends to forego his defence;
" For, it seems, an idea has enter'd the head
" Of himself, and some others, that ALL we have said
" Amounts to juft nothing, but wafting of time,
" And difburfement of cafh, without reason or rhyme :
" But, My LORDS, I am rather inclin'd to fuppofe
" That the *Pris'ner's* afraid of the MANAGERS' *blows;*
" That the danger of being repeatedly ftruck,
" Has taught him to dive like *a dog-hunted duck :*

" For

" For this reafon, My Lords, are the Managers
      " ftriving
" To bring in new matter, by way of depriving
" The *Rogue* of th' advantage of *ducking* and *diving*.

" My Lords, let him *duck*, if he pleafes ; why then
" *Five and twenty intrepid, invincible men,*
" When he pops up his head, will have at him agen :
" But, My Lords, I befeech you, for fear we fhould not
" Opportunity find of repeating the *fhot*,
" To let us go on with our *firing* and *popping*,
" As faft as we can, till we fee the Bird *dropping*."

In this manner did Edmund his arguments prefs
On the Court, with much *humour* and little fuccefs.
'Twas half after four when their Lordships withdrew,
To confult about what was moft proper to do,
Which as foon as I know, I fhall forward to you.

There was one thing, however, as I underftood,
Which fhews Plummy's heart is furprifingly good ;
Tho' he made it appear, that the Company *gain'd*
Half a Million almoft, yet he loudly complain'd,
With tears in his eyes, of the *lofs* they fuftain'd.

Fare-

Farewell! and rejoice, for the feafon is coming,
When all will go mad to hear CHARLES Fox's fum-
  ming;
For he is the HERO by EDMUND appointed,
For *putting together* what PLUMMY *disjointed.*

April 27th, 1790.

LETTER LV.

I SAID in my laſt that their Lordships withdrew,
To conſider of what was expedient to do;
When the Court re-aſſembled, the Chancellor ſaid,
" That Anstruther's papers ought not to be read;
" That the Managers ought to make no variations,
" Nor the Articles burthen with new accuſations."
Then Charley ſet off with *Calamity's cry*,
That *he did not know* what, that *he could not tell* why:
Then he ſadly lamented their keeping the ground
Of their Judgement from him ſuch a ſecret profound:
He reſolv'd *to ſubmit to it, neverthelefs*,
As no method occurr'd of *obtaining redreſs*.

Plumboso now felt himſelf hurt and defeated,
As the Lords had rejected whatever he ſtated;
He therefore determin'd to do by the *tongue*,
What he could not by *paper*—ſo call'd upon Young.
He wanted to know, whether he underſtood,
The beſt means *to let Lands*, for the Company's good,
And his duty official, as well as he ſhou'd?

X

Then

Then he wifh'd to inquire, if the OFFICE he got

His emolument from, fhould be *broken* or not?

He afk'd, if in making a new BUNDOBUST,

Himfelf or a *Black* were more fit for the *truft*;

And, fuppofing the value of lands were adjufted,

Whether YOUNG, or the RAJAH, were fit to be trufted?

As PLUMMY proceeded, thus certain and flow,

With wifhing to afk, and with wanting to know—

One of HASTINGS's *Counfel* ftood up, to oppofe

The putting fome queftion—then EDMUND arofe;

He faid, " We are plac'd in a ftrange fituation,

" Such as never occurr'd to *one man in this Nation.*

" If a *Queftion* we afk, if a *Paper* we read,

" We muft tell why we do it, before we proceed;

" We muft fay of *what ufe* is the queftion we afk,

" Which is, to be fure, *a moft difficult tafk.*"

This ended, PLUMBOSO declar'd he was going

A ftep further on, with his *ftating* and *fhowing*,

The found of which *pleafant, agreeable news,*

A general happinefs feem'd to diffufe;

Tho' 'twas afk'd in a whifper, Can PLUMMY forget,

That he has not got forward *a fingle ftep* yet?

As PLUMMY this ftep was attempting to go,

He faid to the Witnefs, " I want next to know,

" From

" From what you know of, and concerning the mind

" Of the *Natives* at large, if they ftood *well inclin'd ?*

" That is, if the FARMERS were not difcontented

" On account of the Provinces KELLORAM rented ?

" I mean, can you tell us, *what fort of impreffion*

" Was made on their minds by *this horrid tranfgreffion ?"*

But DALLAS, who thinks 'twere as fafe to confide

In the conftant, and uniform flux of the tide;

As fit to rely on the courfe of the wind;

As it were to depend on the thoughts of mankind,

Begg'd leave to their LORDSHIPS to make a fuggeftion,

That the EVIDENCE *ought not* to anfwer the queftion.

But PLUMMY his queftion refus'd to withdraw,

And 'twas therefore referr'd to the JUDGES *of Law.*

Their LORDSHIPS, of courfe, were oblig'd to adjourn,

And I hope, on next *Thurfday,* to fee them return :

A queftion important will then be adjufted,

Whether public opinion is fit to be trufted ?

You, SIMON, remember, that CHARLEY *once* mov'd,

To create SEVEN KINGS, and the COMMONS *approv'd*

Of the MEN and the MEASURE, and 'twould have

    gone down,

Had the TERROR not fpread thro' each city and town'

That NORTH and CHARLES FOX meant to *feize on*

    the Crown.

X 2

CHARLES

CHARLES has often declar'd, by the force of DELUSION,
PITT and THURLOW occasion'd THAT scene of confu-
    sion;
Common Fame, he affirm'd, was an impudent Jade,
Which had ruin'd his friends, and the Nation betray'd;
But in HASTINGS's case all this doctrine's unsound,
And CHARLEY now builds upon different ground.

There is one thing, *dear* BROTHER, I wish to obtrude
On your patience a moment before I conclude:
You remember, BURKE formerly said to *the* COURT,
That one Mr. PATERSON made *that Report*,
From which he extracted the wonderful things
Perform'd by the cruel, iniquitous SINGS: ·
This Gentleman hearing that BURKE had exprest,
To the high Tribunal, a humble request,
That his own name and PATERSON's, *ty'd by one tether*,
To posterity latest *might go down together*,
Has asserted, but wherefore I cannot conceive,
That he does not like having BURKE *pinn'd to his sleeve:*
He, therefore, has publish'd a strong *Declaration*,
To shew BURKE was guilty of *gross defamation*,
When DEBY SING's crimes were to HASTINGS im-
    puted,
And thus the *whole calumny now stands refuted.*

                         I know

I know there are thofe who fuppofe it a *plot*,

A forgery, done by that treacherous SCOTT;

And, indeed, I muft own, it looks rather fufpicious,

As SCOTT, without doubt, is extremely officious,

And, without the *leaft fcruple*, would offer a fee

To PATERSON, JOSEPH, or even to ME;

And I hear there are fome of the ORATOR's *tribe*,

Who fufpect honeft JOSEPH of *taking a bribe*;

But this *is a ftory* that never can hold,

For the *virtue* of JOSEPH is *proof againft gold—*

Your men of found judgement are apt to fuppofe,

That JOSEPH *the ruin of* EDMUND *foreknows*;

And therefore, in order to make *his efcape*,

Pick'd a quarrel, and got himfelf *out of the fcrape* :

But whate'er be is motive, to me it is hateful,

To fee *human nature* fo very ungrateful;

And tho' *all others* leave him *alone to be hurt*,

I will ever ftick to him *as clofe as his fhirt*.

April 29th, 1790.

X 3

LETTER LVI.

DEAR Simon, the Lords have been pleas'd to de-
    cide,
That in *popular clamour* you should not confide:
This the Managers think is provokingly odd;
As the *Voice* of a *Mob* is the *Voice of their God.*
When the Chancellor stated the Court's Resolution,
That the *Question was foreign to this Prosecution,*
Fox rose, and in passionate language lamented,
That *himself* and his *party* were *all discontented.*
His *disconsolate wailings* I need not go o'er,
As you've had them repeated so often before.

When Charley had given full scope to his tongue,
Plumboso a second time called upon Young.
He had scarce wish'd to ask, (for he wanted to know)
What Effects were observ'd or expected to flow
From Cullan Sing's and from Kelloram's renting—
When up started Law, for the sake of dissenting.
This Law, I've observ'd, is a constant *Dissenter,*
And should bear the *nickname* of the *Question Preventer.*

He

He declar'd that PLUMBOSO was trying *once more*
A proof which the Court had *rejeEted before.*
In aid of ANSTRUTHER, and LAW to oppofe,
A *Trio of Heroes* invincible rofe :
CHARLES faid, there was nothing unjuft or abfurd
In HASTINGS's changing the *Revenue Board ;*
That the *AEt in itfelf* might be proper and right,
But the *Motives,* perhaps, were not very upright ;
That the MANAGERS would be exceedingly glad,
Could they make out a proof that his *motives were bad ;*
And therefore their LORDSHIPS muft not think it ftrange
If the *Crime-hunting* MANAGERS wander and *range.*

In this way, the *invincibles* argu'd and reafon'd,
But their language, it feems, was not *properly feafon'd.*
Then WYNDHAM, that *Metaphyfician* profound,
Arofe and obferv'd, they were *trying the ground,*
And by *tentative inftances* making a trial
To difcover the grounds of their LORDSHIPS' denial;
And having remark'd that the *breaking of rocks,*
Is perform'd by the *quick repetition of knocks,*
He repeated again all the fayings of Fox.
But in fpite of their *new metaphyfical drefs,*
Old arguments fail'd of obtaining fuccefs :
For the CHANCELLOR faid, that the *prefent obtrufion*
Came into the *range* of their *former conclufion.*

X 4

Then

Then BURKE rifing up, began *ringing the changes*
Upon *Bombs, Shots and Shells,* and their *different ranges.*
His fimilitudes pleafantly tended to fhow,
That in battering HASTINGS, their *damnable foe,*
The MANAGERS ought not to narrow their plan,
But *enlarge* and *extend* it as far as they can :
That all *Laws* of *Evidence* fhould be abolifh'd,
Or *fufpended* at leaft, till the *Prifoner's demolifh'd.*

LAW rofe, and requefted permiffion to fay,
That 'twere needlefs to anfwer, except for delay.
Fox anfwer'd, and freely admitted 'twere wrong,
That HASTINGS's Trial continued fo long ;
The PUBLIC, whofe hearts are not iron and fleel,
For the fufferings of HASTINGS now vifibly feel.
The LORDS and the COMMONS are ready to fay,
They fincerely lament, and *condemn the delay.*
'Tis ufual with thofe who are broaching of lies,
To fummon that Witnefs, who feldom replies ;
So CHARLES, who the general fentiment knew
With regard to *delay,* and to whom it is due,
Repeatedly call'd upon GOD to attend,
And to vouch for the truth of himfelf and his friend ;
To bear in perpetual remembrance, that they
Were not inftrumental in caufing delay.

But

But till this Appeal shall produce some effect,

The people, I fear, will be apt to suspect

That the reason of making divine invocation,

Is, because there exists not a man in the Nation,

But looks on *delay* as an artful provision

Against the effects of their LORDSHIPS' decision.

After argument tedious, the *Heroes* withdraw

Their Question, without the decision of *Law*.

As KELLORAM fail'd, the *Invincibles* bring

A new accusation about GOVIND SING,

Whose powers, they said, were so very extensive,

That they trusted their LORDSHIPS would deem it of-
> fensive.

PLUMMY wanted to know, so he made a request,

To ask, if the Natives were ever opprest.

But LAW, who for ever objects to digression,

Would consent to no Question concerning *Oppression*.

He said, as *Oppression* was *not in the Charge*,

On *that* 'twere incompetent now to enlarge;

Nor could words of *Inference* plac'd at the end,

To *substantive acts* of *Oppression* extend.

Then EDMUND and CHARLES, who at some little
> distance

Heard the *cry of distress*, flew to PLUMMY's assistance,

And

And now was another *Tongue Battle* begun—
BURKE faid, that the tying of Father and Son
Was a *fubftantive act* of *Oppreffion*, and more
Than an *Inference* ever admitted before.

But CHARLES, who has often been known to contend
For all manner of Rights, as they *anfwer his end*;
Who is one day for *throwing a Monarchy down*,
And the next ftanding up for the *Rights of the Crown*;
Who, we all well remember, not many months fince,
Was the Advocate bold for *the Rights of the* PRINCE;
Who' once call'd the *People* the *Fountain*, and then
Plac'd the *Fountain* of *Power* in the *Parliament Men* :
Now fays, that the COMMONS may juftly difpenfe
With all Rules of Evidence, Reafon, and Senfe;
That the COMMONS are *Laymen*, and *not Men of Let-*
  ters,
Unus'd to be bound in *Legality's Fetters*;
That proof by them offer'd fhould ne'er be rejected,
But thankfully taken, and highly refpected;
That the COMMONS of ENGLAND not being *Law*
  Readers,
Are not to be treated like *common Law Pleaders*.

  To fettle this Queftion their LORDSHIPS withdraw,
And perhaps will refer it to JUDGES of LAW.

I

I have

I have only to tell you, that BURKE is so nettled
By the manner in which the last Question was settled,
That he's gone back to those who the Trial appointed,
To complain that his *Schemes* are all *crack'd* and *dif-
jointed*.

May 4th, 1790.

LETTER LVII.

MY silence, Dear BROTHER, you muſt not aſcribe
To my want of attention, or *taking a bribe*;
For though to the HALL, I've paid conſtant attention,
I have heard nothing lately deſerving of mention :
E'en EDMUND, great EDMUND, began to deſpair,
As the JUDGES, *he thinks, have decided unfair*;
Theſe grave formal Gentlemen can't be perſuaded
To admit of *formality's being invaded*;
They tell us, that *even* in HASTINGS'S cauſe,
Reſpect ſhould be paid to old cuſtoms and laws;
And that, whether the PRIS'NER's condemn'd or ac-
  quitted,
No *illegal evidence* ſhould be admitted.
Mean time the great ORATOR's daily complaining,
Of neceſſity urgent, for *twiſting and ſtraining*;
Nor can he believe that the law is ſo brittle,
As not to allow of its *twiſting a little*;
And indeed, my Dear BROTHER, with grief I obſerve,
Thoſe inflexible men never vary or ſwerve :
I've read how the feelings of HECTOR diſtreſt,
Awaken'd ſoft pity in JUPITER's breaſt;

How

How the Son of old Telamon mifs'd of his mark,
When he *hurl'd* at the Trojans his fpear in the dark;
How he pray'd to the God *for renewal of light*,
His petition was heard, *and he conquer'd in fight:*
But the Judgrs unmov'd, fee the Orator blunder,
They are equally deaf to his *whifper* and *thunder*;
That is, without pity they fee him defpond,
And, remorfelefs, prohibit his going beyond
The *immoveable line* they think proper to draw,
According to Rule, Jurisprudence, and Law.

Thus fetter'd and hamper'd, I can't but admire
The Orator's ftrength, perfeverance, and fire;
When in his metaphorical manner of fpeaking,
He faid, *though his veffel was bulging and leaking,*
Nay more, notwithftanding he could not help thinking
The whole Fleet *of* Impeachment *in danger finking,*
He would *not* quit *his fhip,* howe'er crazy or crank,
But, like Captain Riou, he would fit on *a plank;*
And for this, t'other day, to *the* House he return'd,
Where his want of fuccefs he lamented and mourn'd;
Then, to cheer up his men, he arofe in his place,
And fung them *a Stanza* from old Chevy Chace.
On their Lordships, *in verfe,* he intreated God's
  bleffing,
Whilft he read them, *in profe,* upon *patience* a leffon.

When

When the HERO had clos'd his *deplorable ditty,*
He said that *three parties* were *objects of pity;*
And that, though three sessions already had run,
Since the glorious *Impeachment* of HASTINGS begun,
The *number of hours* he precisely had counted,
To One Hundred and Eighty and Nine, they amounted,
Which being divided by MANAGERS twenty,
Gave none of them reason to boast of a plenty;
The public, he said, without reason complain'd,
That to answer *no purpose,* their pockets are drain'd;
And whilst they repine at *consumption of wealth,*
WARREN HASTINGS laments *the decline of his health;*
That his *hurt constitution* he wants to repair,
By going abroad, or by changing the air;
But EDMUND supposes the place where he dwells,
Or BAGNIGGE, or TUNBRIDGE, *or some other Wells,*
Might serve for the present his health to restore,
And enable his *spirits to suffer much more.*
Then he said, tho' the *militant* MANAGER's toils
Had ne'er been rewarded by honours or spoils;
Tho' *disgrace* had attended himself and his host,
They were *pity'd the least,* yet *deserv'd it the most.*
He clos'd with a Motion, for *further extension*
Of POWER, and the HOUSE has *increas'd its dimensions.*

And

And now of *fuccefs*, he increafes the hope,

From this beneficial *enlargement of fcope*;

From enlargement of fcope, comes *enlargement of fun,*

And all his *outdoings* will now be *outdone.*

May 18th, 1790.

LETTER LVIII.

THIS DAY the *great* HEROES went on, as before,
In adduction of proof, fo they call'd upon MOORE.
Next, HARWOOD was afk'd, *whether in his opinion*
A COUNCIL PROVINCIAL, *was fit for dominion?*
Which queftion means, whether in HARWOOD's be-
      lief,
He himfelf was a *compctent Revenue Chief?*
The anfwer came out, as might well be expected,
That his *merit was great and fhould not be neglected.*
Then ANSTRUTHER faid, he a paper would read,
To fhew HASTINGS's fyftem *was wicked indeed;*
That the HOUSE was not *bolted* fo very fecure,
As to hinder *Oppreffion* from ent'ring the door.
The paper was read, and it tended to fhow,
That DEBY, whofe ftory you perfectly know,
According to HASTINGS's written confeffion,
Might *poffibly fin,* and *conceal the tranfgreffion.*

PLUMBOSO next faid, he was going to ftate
The tranfgreffions of DEBY, enormoufly great;

But

But LAW, whom repeated experience has taught,
That *sterility's* never a MANAGER's fault;
That when they perceive their own evidence failing,
They supply the defect by invention and railing—
Objected thereto, unless PLUMMY could show him,
That the *Epiſode* made *any part* of the *Poem.*

Then EDMUND, who's always at hand to assist,
When HASTINGS's Counsellors enter the lift,
Who is always prepar'd to renew the attack,
When the *heavy-arm'd* PLUMMY is forc'd to give back;
Like DIOMED, clad in an *armour of braſs,*
Oppos'd his firm breaft, and difputed *the paſs.*
When the conteft was ended, their LORDSHIPS. with-
        drew,
To refolve to which party the victory's due.
They return'd, and declar'd, 'twere improper to bring
Or renew the *old ſtory* about DEBY SING;
Then EDMUND, apparently much difcontented,
Exclaim'd, and the LORDSHIPS' decifion lamented!
He faid, that altho' WARREN HASTINGS, 'tis true,
With *the actions* of DEBY has nothing to do;
Tho' even by us 'tis no longer difputed,
That *another man's crimes ſhould to him be imputed;*
Tho' directly at him we can't poffibly ftrike,
Yet it is our intention to *wound him oblique.*

Y

You

You remember, my LORDS, when I firſt laid before

    ye,

In my *opening oration*, this *horrible ſtory*,

I made it as *gloomy* and *black* as I cou'd,

And the audience allow'd that the painting was good;

Some Ladies of *very high rank* were affected,

Your LORDSHIPS were hurt, and the country dejected;

And now, with permiſſion, as PLUMMY has ſtated,

The ſtory by him ſhall again be related.

    Here LAW, who on EDMUND ſtill fixes his eye,

Aroſe in his place, with intent to reply,

When one of the NOBLES, who thinks *altercation*

Of very ſmall ſervice to *inveſtigation*,

Call'd EDMUND *to order !* and ſaid, 'twere in vain,

Of the COURT's Reſolution for him to complain;

That whether the ſtory was groundleſs or true,

And whether 'twere DEBY's or HASTINGS's due,

'Twere incompetent now upon that to enlarge,

As nothing thereof could be found *in the Charge.*

This keen obſervation more pointed than ſteel,

Through the *Armour of Braſs* made the ORATOR feel;

He ſaid, " The firſt CHARACTER ENGLAND could

    " boaſt

" For juſtice, deſervedly valued the moſt,

        " Had

" Had declar'd, that unless I shall make it appear,

" That the story of DEBY is founded and clear;

" That from HASTINGS the mass of iniquity sprung,

" *I ought to be damn'd for my slanderous tongue:*

" And now we are proving the things DEBY did,

" To proceed with our proof by the COURT we're
   " forbid;

" And HASTINGS, who bully'd us once with denial

" Of guilt, is alarm'd, and now shrinks from the trial."

LAW heard, and indignantly casting his eye

On EDMOND, made this most provoking reply:

" So distant, my LORDS, is my client from *shrinking*

" From trial, so little in danger of *sinking*,

" That what of the COMMONS he once did implore,

" Of the MANAGERS now he solicits once more.

" My CLIENT, indeed, will rejoice and be glad,

" If the MANAGERS now will *an* ARTICLE *add.*—

" If the MANAGERS *now* will an Article frame,

" My CLIENT is ready to answer the same;

" And if he disproves not the whole they have said,

" Let vengeance perpetual fall on his head:

" But, my LORDS, this great Champion now hectors
   " and swaggers,

" In a way that is usual with *Bullies* and *Braggers:*

Y 2

" A *Chal-*

" A *Challenge* they give, but fo cunningly make it,

" That they know 'tis impoffible HASTINGS fhould

  " take it;

" Forefeeing their danger, they *carefully fhun*

" The way, it might yet be *fuccefsfully done.*"

While LAW was pronouncing this *daring* ORATION,

I obferv'd EDMUND's vifage in *vaft agitation*;

He feem'd to be finking with horrors and woes,

And the *bottle* was often applied *to his nofe*;

The MANAGERS all appear'd fadly perplext,

Not knowing *what proof they fhould offer the next*;

They had fcarcely recover'd their fright and confufion,

When the bufinefs of yefterday came to conclufion.

  May 20th, 1790.

LETTER LIX.

DEAR BROTHER, as during the TRIAL's fuf-
  penfion,
No circumftance happen'd deferving of mention,
I was forc'd to be filent; but now I have got
An Anecdote recent relating to SCOTT :
The MAJOR, it feems, in a late publication,
Has wounded my HERO, and his *reputation* ;
A GENERAL fam'd for *Theatrical writing,*
As he formerly was for AMERICAN *fighting,*
In compaffion to EDMUND, advanc'd in the field,
And cover'd his friend with AMERICAN fhield ;
That fhield which at fam'd SARATOGA he won,
Where fo many *heroical actions* were done.
So on Thurfday this gallant *Theatrical fighter,*
Made a motion, *that* SCOTT *was a libellous Writer* ;
And SCOTT, who had boldly acknowledg'd the Work,
Defended himfelf by accufing of BURKE :
He produc'd to the HOUSE a whole *bundle of* LIBELS,
And Volumes as thick as your large *printed Bibles* ;
And

Y 3

And thefe, he declar'd, were not all he could find,
Having left at the leaft *Twenty* VOLUMES *behind*;
All which, by their leave, he was ready to fhow,
Were produc'd by the pens of Great EDMUND and Co.
That if he himfelf had committed a fault,
'Twas owing to BURKE, who the *fcience* had taught:
Then, in order to foften the edge of the fentence,
The HOUSE might inflict, he *affected repentance*.
Then WIGLEY arofe, in fupport of his friend,
And faid, that in juftice they ought to extend
Their inquiry ftill farther, by way of requiting
The merit of BURKE in his *libellous writing*.

Then EDMUND arofe, and began an ORATION,
In defence of his own and his friend's *reputation*;
He faid, that the MAJOR, inftead of repenting,
Had the LIBEL avow'd, and was fpitefully venting
His malice, by making a bold accufation
Of himfelf and his party, by recrimination.
On my friends, I, however, place perfect reliance,
And fet the *laft* SPEAKER and SCOTT at defiance;
According to what Mr. WIGLEY has fpoken,
Our privilege might be diurnally broken;
But if for each breach we commence profecution,
It might poffibly injure our good conftitution;

I   And

And if every Libel and breach is neglected,
The House *of* St. Stephen will not be refpected ;
But I always will tell you whenever 'tis fit
To punifh offenders, as well as acquit ;
Good writers and fpeakers fhould never be ftinted,
And *fpeeches* like mine fhould be carefully printed.

Some *fpeeches* are fit for the public, but not
Such iniquitous fpeeches as utter'd by Scott.
Ten years, Mr. Speaker, have I been *accufing*;
Ten years has the Major myfelf been abufing;
Of the Blacks by *myfelf* I'm appointed *protector*,
And of Guilt by the House I'm appointed *detector*;
Mr. Speaker, by me no refentment was fhown,
Whilft Hastings's *Harpies* bedaub'd me alone;
But their filth is fo bad, I no longer can bear it,
Efpecially now, as my Masters muft fhare it :
And indeed, Mr. Speaker, 'tis vaftly provoking,
To become a *mere butt* of *fatirical joking* ;
Altho' I've been always *a friend to the* Press,
I dread its *Venality* neverthelefs :
And, indeed, Mr. Speaker, I've frequently thought
All the Presses in Europe by Hastings are
      bought.

Now at Hastings my Hero more bitterly rails,
And roundly afferts, all the prifons and jails

That

That ever exifted, could never produce

An object like HASTINGS fo fit for abufe.

Then EDMUND went on, to unravel a plot,

And faid SCOTT was HASTINGS, and HASTINGS was
      SCOTT;

That their influence extended from Region to Region,

And that HASTINGS's name fhould hereafter be
      Legion.

Then he afterwards faid, he was not greatly fmitten

With any thing HASTINGS's party had written;

That their works were deficient in *beauty and wit,*

But fuch as they were, 'twas expedient and fit

That the COMMONS in punifhing fhould not be
      fparing,

Efpecially this, *fo flagitious and daring.*

   In the courfe of his ravings, I could not but fee,

How often the HERO reflected on me;

Since turn'd out of office, I very well know,

He has look'd upon me as a dangerous foe;

His confcience muft whifper, 'tis fhockingly hard,

For SIMKIN to ferve *without fee or reward*;

To attend at the HALL when his HONOR *impeaches,*

And turn into Verfe all his long-winded Speeches.

But

But now an idea has enter'd my head,

On hearing the KING's *Poet Laureat* is dead,

That His MAJESTY might, to reward that devotion,

Which BURKE has neglected, confer this promotion;

And when I have sung of His MAJESTY's *satis*,

I would sing of Great EDMUND and Company *gratis*.

June 1st, 1790.

LETTER LX.

THE day, my DEAR BROTHER, is happily come,
Which has long been expected, for CHARLEY to fum :
Thus the HERO began—" All your LORDSHIPS muft
    " fee,
" That a *difficult tafk* is allotted to me :
" Your LORDSHIPS muft think me *prefumptuous and*
    " *bold*,
" Should I liken myfelf to that SPEAKER *of old*,
" Who faid, that whate'er he thought proper to men-
    " tion,
" Never fail'd of exciting the JUDGES' attention :
" If the JUDGES who heard him *were honeft and good*,
" He was fure he could make himfelf well underftood.
" Thus CICERO fpoke, but your LORDSHIPS well
    " know,
" That with ME and *my Colleagues* the cafe is not fo ;
" We are not afraid of your LORDSHIPS' *decifion* ;
" Do but hear, and we afk *for no other provifion*.
" I know very well that your LORDSHIPS are juft,
" But *your patience is gone*, as it certainly muft.
                               " My

" My Lords, 'tis a great difadvantage to follow
" In fumming, thofe *favourite Sons of* Apollo,
" Who fung of great Rajahs and Nabobs *oppreft*,
" *Of* Princesses *plunder'd,* and Natives *diftreft :*
" How mean is the office that falls to my lot,
" To develope *the wealth* which the Criminal got.
" Lord Clive, 'tis recorded, once folemnly fwore,
" *He had* Money *enough,* and would *never take more :*
" A fimilar oath, I fhall make it appear,
" Was made by Verelst, and by Mr. Cartier ;
" And, therefore, 'tis probable Hastings did take it ;
" And, fuppofing he did, 'twas improper to break it :
" But, My Lords, We, *the* Managers, care not a
      " jot,
" Whether Hastings did really take it or not.
" If he never did take it, he *certainly ought*
" To have done it, *and therefore committed a fault :*
" But fuppofing that Hastings fhou'd fay he did
      " take it ;
" Why then, we fhall prove, he did frequently break
      " it.
" So, my Lords, let him offer whatever he will
" By way of defence, we *fhall prove it was ill."*

Here Charley adverted again to the ftory,
Which I have prefented fo often before ye;

I mean

I mean Nuncomar, who, as Charley contends,

Was *hung on a gibbet* by Hastings's friends.

" My Lords, I aver, as Burke formerly did,

" Notwithstanding my Masters, the Commons,
   " forbid,

" And tho' I may hereafter be censur'd and chid,

" That this Nuncomar on a gallows was hung,

" In order to silence his *garrulous tongue.*"

Then Charley digress'd, and a liberty took

Of stating a crime that was *not in the book.*

He said that one Crofts, in a *certain account,*

Had made a mistake to enormous amount,

And instead of his being from office ejected,

With *wrath* and *disdain,* as might well be expected,

He a Pardon obtain'd, and the *fault* was corrected.

When Burke drew the Charge, he forgot at the time

To make this *forgiveness* a *substantive crime :*

Here a subtle distinction the Orator drew—

A *distinction* to me which was perfectly new ;

From which I discover the wit of the times

Have made *adjective Charges,* and *substantive Crimes.*

The latter, it seems, can stand firmly alone,

But the former are weak, and may soon be o'erthrown.

This incident trifling, I thought fit to mention,

In honour of Charles's *distinctive invention.*

'Twere

'Twere needlefs, DEAR SIMON, for me to go through

Thofe parts of his SPEECH which contain'd nothing

new :

For altho' he fhew'd ftrong *oratorical pow'rs*,

That is, he harangu'd us for more than five hours,

'Twas agreed, by all parties, he faid little more

Than BURKE and PLUMBOSO had told us before.

And, indeed, he confefs'd, he was merely appointed

To colleƐt in a *focus*, what they had *disjointed*.

Howe'er, in the courfe of his *florid Oration*,

He fpoke of *an excellent Adminiftration*;

Whofe praife his own modefty forc'd him to fpare,

Becaufe he himfelf had *the principal fhare*.

Then he put us in mind of his old INDIA BILL,

Whofe remembrance he fofters and cherifhes ftill;

Which, though 'twas rejeƐted, he was not afham'd

To call *the beft* BILL *which had ever been fram'd*.

Once, all of a fudden, on fome ftrange fuggeftion,

He turn'd round, and afk'd for *the fharp goading queftion*;

I heard, and my fpirit prophetic foreboded,

That HASTINGS would foon be confoundedly *goaded*.

At times he endeavour'd to carry conviƐtion,

By fhewing in HASTINGS a flat contradiƐtion;

And that HASTINGS and LARKINS, in many refpeƐts,

Were guilty of *errors*, as well as *negleƐts*.

But

But whilst he was speaking, I made this remark,
That his tongue often stumbled, like one in the dark ;
And had not a PROMPTER been station'd behind,
To *jog* him, and *tap* him, and put him in mind,
We had had little else but *tongue-lapses* and blunders,
Convey'd in *shrill squeaks* and in *loud rolling thunders.*
The HALL, I observ'd, was exceedingly full,
But the LADIES appear'd disappointed and dull ;
And as CHARLES gave but little amusement and sport,
By *Duos*, and *Trios*, they stole out of COURT.
When he saw that but few of the LADIES were left,
He fear'd that the LORDS were of *patience bereft* ;
And perhaps recollected that whilst he *was toiling*
In JUSTICE's service, his *dinner was spoiling* ;
He therefore consented to end *for that day*——
The LORDS appear'd glad, and went bowing away.

June 9th, 1790.

LETTER LXI.

YOU will find, my DEAR BROTHER, on reading
    this Letter,
That the Second Day's Summing was shorter, and
    better:
On the latter we heard WARREN HASTINGS accus'd
Of having a *Present*, when offer'd, *refus'd.*
His Accuser contended, in language sublime,
That *refusing a Gift* was in HASTINGS a *crime,*
Unless he had told the NABOB, what he did
Was because taking Gifts was expressly forbid.
" But, my LORDS, all those fears which the Pris'ner
    " exprest,
" Lest the NABOB should be by refusal distrest,
" Serve only to shew his long habit and use
" To take all which the Natives could ever produce."

Next he talk'd of one JOHNSON, whom HASTINGS
    had try'd
For detention of Assets, which JOHNSON deny'd;
That

That tho' Hastings had harbour'd strong doubts in
    his breast,
That Johnson in *private* the money possest,
Yet having no positive *proof* of the act,
He *acquitted* the person accus'd of the fact.
Charles said, " My opinion is therefore decided,
" That Hastings and Johnson the *money divided.*
" Two points we have prov'd, both of tendency bad,
" The Bribe he refus'd, and the Bribe which he had."

Then Charley went on with a string of *suggestions,*
And making *shrewd answers to self-propos'd questions*;
And hop'd that the Lords would to memory bring
The Names of Crofts, Anderson, and Govind
    Sing;
The latter of whom had been charg'd with a crime,
And therefore from Office dismiss'd for a time;
But the Charge never being prov'd clear to the Board,
He again was employ'd, and to favour restor'd:
But Charley says, being *dismiss'd from a station*
On Suspicion, amounts to Disqualification.

The looks of both Parties which happen'd to hear
This doctrine, discover'd their joy or their fear.
With opposite feelings their minds were impassion'd,
At hearing a doctrine so strange and new-fashion'd;

Awhile

Awhile it created a general confufion,

But at length all concurr'd in the felf-fame conclufion—

That as CHARLES *by the Mob* had been *hooted* and *hifs'd,*

By HIS MAJESTY's order *from Office difmift*

On fufpicion of too much attachment to pelf,

When he very near got *all the Eaft to himfelf,*

He never again can an office enjoy,

But muft dwell in minority out of employ.

To return—CHARLEY faid, " By the Pris'ner's com-
  " mands

" *Aumeens* were appointed to fettle the lands,

" Which having been fettled by competent men,

" 'Twas a *fubftantive* crime to examine again."

Then he told us the manner how HASTINGS o'erthrew

Six Revenue Councils, and made them anew.

This part of the ftory I need not go o'er,

As BURKE and ANSTRUTHER have told it before.

Then my *Hero* return'd with a retrograde fpring

To the ftory BURKE told us about DEBY SING,

And loudly demanded the *vengeance* of GOD,

That *himfelf,* and *not* BURKE, might be *fcourg'd with*
  the rod,

If the ftory BURKE told were not perfectly true,

And the whole of the cruelties HASTINGS's due.

Z

At

At length, when the hearers fuppos'd he was come
To the Summary's end, he proceeded to fum
All the fummary points, which affording no fun,
The whole COURT was rejoic'd, when he faid—*I have
      done.*
But now I muft tell you, that this Revolution,
(The HIGH COURT of PARLIAMENT's now *diffolution,*)
May probably alter both *Meafures* and *Men,*
And that HASTINGS may never be *badger'd* agen.

Great EDMUND declares he is forry to fee
The *fport* is not relifh'd in equal degree;
That tho' he fhall for ever be willing and able
A new *difh of Corruption* to place on the table,
Yet their LORDSHIPS of late are in *ftomach fo cloy'd,*
That none of his difhes are highly enjoy'd.
Befides, BURKE has taken it into his head,
That fuch Letters as SIMKIN's ought not to be read.
He has often expreft his furprife, that *John Bull*
Should relifh Epiftles fo *ftupid* and *dull.*
From a tafte fo deprav'd, it was certain that *John*
Was off at a tangent, and *totally gone.*
But if this be the cafe, it is well worth our knowing,
Why *John* fo departed, and where he is going.*

* BURKE faid in the Houfe of Commons, that the fuffering fuch
facred Speeches as his to be ridiculed, was a certain fign that the
Nation was gone.

'Tis

'Tis hinted that EDMUND defpairs of recalling

The *fugitive* JOHN, by additional bauling;

And therefore to fave his whole Party from laughter,

May fuffer the *Pris'ner* to flumber hereafter.

But fuppofing the Trial fome dozen weeks hence

Once more fhould according to order, commence,

Be affur'd I fhall always be ready to fend

The *proceedings* thereof to my BROTHER and *Friend*.

June 14th, 1790.

LET-

LETTER LXII.

IF SIMKIN, of late, has been lazy and idle,
'Twas becaufe EDMUND's clapper was under the bridle;
For, except when the Houfes of Parliament fit,
No occafion occurs for difplaying his wit.
But now, left he fhould be forgotten by men,
He excites their attention by ufing his pen :
You know, fince he left *Academical Teaching*,
He has bufied himfelf with *Political Preaching*,
And of late fpent the moft of his time in IMPEACHING.
Howe'er, as that bus'nefs is probably ended,
Or, at leaft, till the Parliament meets, is fufpended—
His fortune and fame he expects to advance
By *Impeaching* the NATIONAL COUNCIL of FRANCE.
His book, which had oft' been announc'd to the town,
This morning I bought, and it coft me a crown,
Which being too dear for the fending you down,
The fubftance thereof I intend to rehearfe
(As I frequently do of his fpeeches) in verfe.

It feems a French Gentleman afk'd BURKE's opinion
Of the late REVOLUTION, and Change of Dominion;

To which Burke reply'd, You, perhaps, may fuppofe
That I alfo am one of the number of thofe
Who approve of your conduct, becaufe certain *Scrubs*,
Which form two *Societies*, alias Clubs,
The one for protecting our good *Conftitution*,
The other for praifing the laft *Revolution*,
Have exprefs'd, in a letter, their warm approbation,
Thus giving your actions their fanctification:
But before the *Two Clubs* I proceed to defcribe,
Give me leave to deny being one of the tribe.

The Club Constitutional, feven years old,
Is for buying up books which would never be fold,
And, for charity's fake, to give free circulation
To *Political Pamphlets* all over the Nation;
And 'tis likely that fome of thofe Pamphlets, by chance,
Not faleable here, may be vended in France;
And as liquors grow better by croffing the ocean,
The books may derive much advantage from motion.
But here I am certain, that no information
Has been drawn from this good-natur'd affociation.

Thus much having faid of the Club Constitution,
I now have to fpeak of the Club Revolution:
This laft all their honour and confequence owe
To the praife your Assembly were pleas'd to beftow,

And

And now are a mere SUB-COMMITTEE, to spread
The doctrines deliver'd by you, as their head :
This CLUB, of whose name I had never heard mention,
And which never excited the smallest attention,
Consisted of certain *fantastical Thinkers*,
DISSENTERS by name, in reality DRINKERS,
Who an annual Sermon procur'd from a Vicar,
By way of excuse for indulging in liquor :
No national theme ever enter'd among
These men, save *the Bottle, the Glass*, and *the Song* ;
And whilst from this custom they never departed,
No sober objection could justly be started ;
But now, after farther inquiry, I find
Some political men, of a true *Christian Mind*,
Have lately crept in, for the *good of the Soul*,
Concealing the hand which distributes the dole.
By the bye, my dear SIMON, most people suppose
These true *Christian* men are the CHARLEYS and JOES,
Whose characters now EDMUND gratefully raises,
By way of compensating similar praises ;
This trio of *Worthies*, like FUR and his brother,
Are beholden for character one to the other.

To return—EDMUND says, that he is not a *Paul*,
A *gen'ral Apostle*, for preaching to all ;

And

And his fentiments being of confequence great,

Muft not be divulg'd without leave of the State:

Then he tells his FRENCH GENTLEMAN, he fhould ex-
      pect

That our HOUSE of COMMONS would proudly reject

The moft *fneaking* PETITION that ever was feen,

For an object however contemptibly mean,

If prefented before them with fuch kind of figning,

As appear'd to their COUNSEL fo fplendidly fhining,

And which they accepted with equal parade,

Or greater, perhaps, than could well have been made,

Had our reprefentative, MAJESTY all,

Condefcended to vifit, or give them a call.

But I fhould not, fays EDMUND, have taken offence,

Had *their paper* contain'd either reafon or fenfe;

For had that been the cafe, 1 am free to confefs,

There might be conviction in't, neverthelefs—

As it ftands—'tis a *vote*, nay a mere *refolution*

Of unauthoris'd people, who love REVOLUTION:

Had they all put their names, one might judge of thei
      number,

And diftinguifh *found pieces* from that which is *lumber*.

Now EDMUND a fmall matter alters his ftrain,

And fays, that himfelf is a *Gentleman plain*:

Z 4

(Bu

(But to make his fenfe clearer, I wifh he had faid,
Whether plain in his *perfon* or plain in his *head)*
That, from their proceedings, he's prone to fuppofe,
'Tis a juggle or trick very like fome of Joe's.
Then he flatters himfelf that mankind will agree,
That no man loves Liberty better than He;
Alluding, perhaps, to the *freedom of fpeech,*
When he fpeaks in the House, or is fent to *impeach*—
If fo—Warren Hastings and North will agree,
That Edmund is always *exceedingly free.*

Now, all of a fudden, the hero takes flight,
And foaring aloft, he efcapes from my fight;
He fays, he can give no applaufe to an action,
In the *nakednefs* of *metaphyfic abftraction;*
That Government's good, and fo alfo is Freedom,
According as perfons may happen to need 'em.
As to praife the French *Nation*, he thinks 'twere as well
To give praife to a Madman efcap'd from his cell;
Or give praife to a wretch, who his prifon had left,
Where he had been committed for murder or theft;
" No, no,"—fays the Orator—" praifing fuch men,
" In me, would be *acting* Don Quixote again."

Thus much I have fcribbled, dear Simon, in hafte,
Of Burke's *compofition* to give you a tafte;

You

You muſt judge of its merit and value when known,
That all this is obtain'd from eight pages alone;
That his book is a large *Magazine*, or a *ſtore*,
Containing near Fifty ſuch quantities more,
All which, at my leiſure, I mean to detail,
Unleſs you forbid—or my PEGASUS fail.

————————

POSTSCRIPT.

Since cloſing my Letter, chance brought me a tale,
That the *Second Edition*'s already on ſale;
And the Public, it ſeems, are enabled to fix
Upon Burke playing ſome of the *Bookſelling tricks*;
But the circumſtance you may conſider as worſt,
Is the *Second Edition's preceding* the *Firſt*;
For Saturday morning, with humble ſubmiſſion,
Dodſley offer'd the Public the *Firſt-born Edition*,
But the *Second* came forth on the *Friday preceding*,
And was privately ſold for a Gentleman's reading.

Nov. 1ſt, 1790.

LETTER LXIII.

SOME things which at prefent 'twere needlefs to men-
    tion,
From the PAMPHLET of BURKE turn'd away my at-
    tention;
But now I embrace the firft moment of leifure
To comment thereon—and I do it with pleafure.

It feems, Dr. PRICE, a DISSENTING DIVINE,
A countryman, fure, of Aunt BRIDGET's and mine,
Preach'd a Sermon replete with POLITICAL SENSE,
At which, *loyal* EDMUND took mighty offence.
You know, 'tis the ORATOR's mode to exprefs
His thoughts in *fublime metaphorical drefs*;
So he call'd it—*a fort of a porridge or mefs*
Of POLITICS ftrong—and MORALITY weak—
The laft, milk and water—the former, a leek.
The DOCTOR would make our Nobility preachers,
But BURKE does not like to have *Mefs-Johns* for teachers;
So he reafons, with gravity, fome hundred lines
Againft DUKES and MARQUISSES turning *Divines.*
As the *Wilds of Diffent* are rough, rugged, and dry,
He admits fome improvement might happen thereby;

That

That the town might be pleas'd with a MARQUIS's
        preaching,
For *novelty's* fake, as they were with IMPEACHING.

    After this EDMUND fays—He is loath to acknowledge
PRICE's right to erect an Electoral College
For the chufing of MONARCHS, and, therefore, fhall hope
The DOCTOR will not be ARCHPONTIFF, or POPE ;
And that KINGS may fit fafe on the Thrones they have
        got,
Whether PRICE's *difciples* elect them or not.
Then EDMUND triumphantly feems to rejoice,
That the MONARCHY *here* is not matter of *choice :*
Then knocks the poor preacher with arguments down,
Whilft he proves that a KING has a right to a Crown.
The DOCTOR, fays BURKE, as the reader may fee,
In his SERMON, eftablifhes principles three—
1. Their RULERS, the *mob,* have a right to elect :
2. To cafhier for mifconduct or any defect :
3. For themfelves a new GOVERNMENT they may
        erect.
Then BURKE analizes this new BILL of RIGHTS ;
And puts it in many ridiculous lights ;
Concluding, at laft, that this grand inftitution
Is a CLUB or SOCIETY *for* REVOLUTION.

                            Skipping

Skipping eighty dull pages, with hafte I advance
To EDMUND defcribing the BEGUM of FRANCE.
You muft know, that though BURKE is near fixty years
       old,
In the funfhine of *beauty* his heart is not cold;
And were we to judge from his vigorous pen,
We fhould think his young days coming over again.

You have read how DON QUIXOTE felected a *dame*;
How he languifh'd, and lov'd, and refounded her fame!
For he knew that *Knight Errantry* could not exift,
Unlefs BEAUTY were plac'd at the head of the lift:
In like manner DON EDMUND once folemnly vow'd
He would ftill be the KNIGHT of the BEGUM of OUDE:
He fought all her *battles*, as bound by his duty,
And faid all he could in defence of her *beauty*;
But as lovers too frequently wander and range,
DON EDMUND has fuddenly taken a change.
Now leaving the BEGUM—behold him advance,
And brandifh his *pen*, in the room of a *lance*,
In defence of the prefent QUEEN CONSORT of FRANCE!
" Sixteen years ago, or my *memory* fails,
" The QUEEN, then the DAUPHINESS, was at *Verfailles*:
" When furely (exclaims the old *languifhing* DON,)
" So delightful a VISION, ne'er lighted upon

I

" This

" This ORB; for her *motion* and *gesture* was such,
" Tho' she trod on the ground, she appear'd not to
" touch—
" Above the *horizon*, I saw her appearing,
" The *sphere* of her *movement* enlight'ning and cheering;
" Full of joy, life, and splendour, the Palace adorning,
" She glitter'd and shone like a *star* in the *morning !*"

But here 'tis a difficult task to rehearse,
The effusions of woe from DON EDMUND in verse;
For all of a sudden, he changes his ditty,
And my eyes are, alas! *running over with* PITY.
He tells us the QUEEN was affrighted, and fled,
One night from *her own*, to his MAJESTY's *bed*.
" Oh! how could I dream, that in *fixteen short years*,
" In a nation of HEROES, and *brave* CAVALIERS—
" In a nation of men of high primitive honour,
" A *difafter* like this should have *lighted upon her*;
" Ten thoufand bright swords I suppos'd, but miftook,
" Wou'd leap from their scabbards to punifh a look:
" But, alas! thus continues the sorrowful DON,
" The *age is quite alter'd*, and CHIVALRY's gone;
" *Economifts, Sophifters,* and *Calculaters,*
" *Reformers* of *Kitchens,* and *Parliament Praters,*
" Have fucceeded in spite of my *honeft endeavour*,
" And the GLORY of EUROPE's extinguifh'd for ever.

" Should

" Should *Knight Errantry* ever go quite out of feafon,

" And if men fhould become more *enlighten'd* by reafon,

" Nay, fhould they proceed on this fyftem of things,

" It muft prove in the end inimical to Kings.

" According to their new fophiftical plan,

" A King on his *throne* ftill continues a *man* ;

" And to be but a *woman*, continues a Queen,

" And a *woman's* an *animal* apt to be *mean*."

Thus Edmund the *Empire of Reafon* denies,

In the doing whereof, he's fagacious and wife ;

The intereft of B——, reafon never promoted,

Then wherefore fhould he be to reafon devoted—

All his life waging war againft *reafon* and *fenfe*,

To exterminate both is an *act of defence*.

From a natural principle all men oppofe,

As well *accidental*, as *natural foes* ;

With reciprocal vengeance, men juftly condemn,

Whatever may caft a reproach upon them.

There is one thing in Burke, and I've notic'd it often,

A *pitiful tale*, or *a picture*, can foften

His hard twifted heart, but his ftill harder eye,

Can furvey *real woe*, without even a figh.

I remember when Edmund, the Nation provoking,

Made the *Malady-royal* a *fubject for joking* ;

Lords

2

Lords and Commons (his Colleagues excepted,) pour-
    traying,

Like dogs o'er a carcafe contending and baying.

He faid, that the King God had hurled from his throne,

Had no property left him, no rights of his own—

Sick Majefty making the theme of a *pun*—

To *revile* was a *virtue*, to *laugh at* was *fun* :

But mark how a *foreign King* alters his tone,

For the King thus infulted, alas ! was *his own*.

" Now the man who can fpurn at a monarch fo hurl'd,

" As Louis now is, by the Lord of the world,

" And can tread on a Prince in diftrefs, *is a creature*

" *In morals as ftrange, as a Monfter in nature.*

" Had I laugh'd at the Monarch of France or his Queen,

" At a tragedy how fhould I blufh to be feen

" Shedding tears at Andromache's fufferings in fiction,

" When 'twas known I had fported with *real affliction.*"

'Tis curious enough to obferve, my dear Brother,

How nearly one Tyrant refembles another ;

For as Ed—d reproach'd Doctor Price, that he fhone

By impofing Hugh Peters's words for his own ;

So this fentiment, fine as it is, is no more

Than a * Tyrant of Thessaly utter'd before—

* His name was Alexander. He ufed to few his fubjects in bear
fkins, and have them baited by dogs for his amufement and diverfion.

Perhaps

Perhaps, you will fay, that the *fhedder of blood*,

And the man who would *willingly fhed if he could*,

May both without copy or concert exprefs

Their fimilar feelings in fimilar drefs—

Of the tyrant juft mention'd, I've heard it related,

How he few'd up his fubjects in fkins to be baited—

Not, indeed, to be bark'd at, and torn by himfelf,

But by dogs which were purchas'd and train'd by his
  pelf,

In this inftance to try, if the equipoife fails,

Shall we weigh them in Plutarch's hiftorical fcales?

Afk HASTINGS—he'll fay, they are both of a piece,

The *Lad of Kilkenny* and *Tyrant of Greece*.

He wou'd rather endure, as I heard him once fwear,

To be baited by dogs, and be clad like a bear,

Than to fit, though by Peereffes gaz'd at and Peers,

And be held for five hours at a ftretch by the ears,

With EDMUND's *Cerberean Eloquence* wrung,

And *abufe that like Aconite flows from his tongue*,

Though BURKE ftill laments, and with truth, it is thought,

That his culprit does *not* feel fo much as he *ought*,

And for this to the LORDS, join'd with arguments
  ftronger,

He prays to torment him for *feven years longer*.

  Nov. 11th, 1790.

LETTER LXIV.

This wonderful Book, my dear Simon, imparts
New means of improving the liberal arts;
I faw t'other day, as I happen'd to ftop
In the ftreet, a new Print in a bookfeller's fhop:
On the left there appeared a moft *beautiful Dame*,
Dulcinea's rival, or rather the fame;
All around the horizon a *Glory* was fpread,
Emanating in ftreams from the Goddess's head;
Underneath, an Old Don was exhibited *kneeling*,
Whom Time had in vain try'd to rob of *his feeling*,
For Cupid, young rafcal, determin'd to fcorch
His heart, was come down with his love-lighting torch,
His *fpectacled eyes* were her *beauty* adoring,
And his *wide gaping mouth* was her *favour* imploring;
But the Lady fcarce heeding the *love-fmitten* Don,
Appears on *the wing*, and in hafte to be gone:
She runs to get rid of his *Death* and *Defpair*,
So faft, that fhe treads upon *nothing butair*;
The next thing in courfe, which I muft not forget,
Is the *fcale of precedence*, in payment of debt;

Accor-

According to Edmund, a *bribe* or a *penfion*,
Has of all other debts, the firft claim or pretenfion;
And he thinks yon Assembly was playing the knave,
When they ftruck off the penfions his Majesty gave;
And that they were more fundamentally wrong,
In difcharging *thofe* Debts which were owing too long;
And that he who his cafh to a Government lends,
Should his principal forfeit, by way of amends.
Then he tells us, the *Catholic Clergy* are *flooding*
All France with their *tears*, for the lofs of their *pudding*;
Whofe right to *good living*, our Author fuppofes,
May be fairly derived from a *Chapter* of *Mofes*.

Then Edmund directs the keen point of his pen,
To the *doctrine of Rights* appertaining to men;
No Marius, no Sylla, no *Roman Dictator*,
No *Tribune*, no *Tyrant*, no *grand Devaftator*;
Not Harry the VIIIth, that *immenfe Confifcator*,
Stretch'd forth in like manner Injustice's rod,
As France has of late on the *Servants of* God.

But here, my dear Simon, I ought to relate,
Some things which have paft in this neighbouring State.

It feems that French Parfons by ftuffing and feeding,
Were too *fat* and *fhort-winded* for *preaching* and *reading*;
Befides,

Befides, their high living, as EDMUND confeffes,
Had often occafion'd immoral exceffes.
Hence, the NATIONAL COUNCIL thought fit to reduce
Their income, and render the Clergy of ufe;
THEY thought them mere fervants, receiving the pay
Of the State, and of confequence *bound to obey*;
That whene'er with a *fervant* the *mafter* engages,
He alone has the right of prefcribing the wages;
But EDMUND fuppofes thefe fhepherds and paftors
Have a much better right to the foil than their mafters,
And that the fole purpofe of tending their flocks,
Is to make what *addition* they can to *their flocks*;
That the CLERGY themfelves fhould, in order to render
The LAITY good, live in very great fplendor;
And to give CHRISTIANITY fpirit and vigour,
The Priefthood fhould *cut a moft capital figure.*
Thus he proves, by diffufing his fpiritual light,
That JOHN BULL poffeffes no natural right;
And he gives us at length his decided opinion,
That *Bifhops* and *Lords* fhould inherit dominion.

But indeed, my dear BROTHER, I queftion if JOHN
Will relifh the doctrine deliver'd by DON;
The Priefthood will favour his new *Orthodoxy*,
And give him their votes both in *perfon* and *proxy*.

A a 2

You

You afk me, by whom was *Don* Edmund elected
Chief Juftice, and who his Tribunal erected ?
I anfwer—Pray who was *Don* Quixote's *Elector*,
When he glitter'd in arms, diftrefs'd Beauty's *protector ?*
You afk me, what infatuation of mind
Makes Edmund wage war with the *rights of mankind ?*
By a fimilar queftion I anfwer you ftill—
Pray why did *Don* Quixote encounter *the mill ?*
'Tis afferted in terms unequivocal, flat,
That Edmund look'd up to a Cardinal's *Hat,*
When he wifh'd that his young correfpondent and friend,
Th' Archbishop of Paris to England would fend—
And by way of *Bravado,* and *Mifery ftabbing,*
In exchange he would fend him a *Proteftant Rabbin.*
Believe me, fays Edmund, we fhall not neglect
To treat the Archbishop with proper refpect ;
Provided a plentiful baggage he brings,
Full of *Money* and *Jewels,* and other *good things* ;
I will guard it fo well, if the Prelate be willlng,
That the Treafury here fha'n't confifcate a fhilling.

    Before, for the prefent, I lay down my pen,
As it may be fome time 'e'er I write you again,
I fhall give you a tafte of his *Logical Powers,*
Inftead of a *fniff* of *Rhetorical Flowers.*

2

He

He fays, that the French Revolutionifts fhould,
To render their Government *perfeƈtly good*,
Derive all the claims, and their inftances quote,
From an old race of Anceftors very remote ;
And by holding thofe FATHERS in high veneration,
And with the affiftance of *imagination*,
Afcribe to them Wifdom and Virtue *ideal*,
Which may ferve, for example, as if it were real :
In this manner our great *Metaphyfical* MAN,
For a new CONSTITUTION has fettled a *plan*.

Here then, my *Dear* SIMON, this LETTER I clofe,
And, perhaps, I hereafter may comment in profe.

Nov. 15, 1790.

LET-

LETTER LXV.

IF SIMON, or any *Welch Coufin*, expects
My comment in profe on the *Knight Errant*'s text,
I wifh them to know that the Work I began,
But was forc'd with reluctance to give up my plan ;
For I found EDMUND's profe with fuch melody flowing,
That it *flid into verfe* without thinking or knowing ;
This circumftance fingle, abundantly fhows,
That DON is a capital POET *in profe.*

 The fubject to which I fhall draw your attention,
Is the very laft page, where the AUTHOR makes men-
  tion
Of Himfelf, and the caufe and effect of his writing,
All curious enough to deferve my reciting :
There is *little,* fays BURKE, that can *much* recommend
This Work to my young Correfpondent and Friend,
Except *obfervation* attentive and long,
And a *judgement* that *feldom* or *never goes wrong* ;
It comes from a perfon that follows *no rule,*
Who ftoops not to flatter or ferve as a tool,

Who

Who wifh'd, *if he cou'd have contriv'd it*, to fhun
The departure fo wide, from the courfe he had run,
And belying the whole he had formerly done.

It comes from a man long accuftom'd to ftruggle
For the *freedom* of others, (which now *proves a juggle :)*
From one in whofe breaft no *refentment* or *rage*
Maintain'd its poffeffion for more than an age,
Except when the *object of anger* was fuch,
As he thought could not poffibly *fuffer too much :*
From one who, in concert with other *good* men,
Has long been employing his *tongue* and his *pen,*
Of haughty oppreffion to lower the pitch,
Reducing to *poverty* all who are rich ;
Who fnatch'd from that laudable, good undertaking,
Now and then a few hours, for the purpofe of making
Some *juft* Observations on what you are doing,
And to fave you from total perdition and ruin :
It comes from a man who would like well enough
Diftinctions and *honours,* and fuch *kind of ftuff,*
Who, if offer'd, moft certainly would not reject 'em,
But who does not pretend any *right to expect 'em :*
It comes from a man who defpifes not fame,
Yet fears no *reproach,* and is *proof againft fhame :*
It comes from man who *contention* abhors,
Yet fports an opinion, and *carries on wars :*

From.

From one who is always Consistency's friend,

Yet varies the means to arrive at his end:

It comes from a man, who, by way of preserving

Confiftency, often is guilty of *fwerving*;

But *then*, he departs from *Confiftency*'s line,

For *preferving* the *unity* of his defign.

   This language, Dear Brother, is rather obfcure,

But its meaning, tho' latent, is certain and fure:

Burke formerly thought, 'twas a very good thing,

To lower the *pride* and the *purfe* of a King;

He maintain'd that the State, the whole *Church*, and

      its *Steeple*,

Were nothing, compar'd with the Rights of the Peo-

     ple;

And that the refifting Authority Royal

By American Rebels, was *perfectly loyal*;

He faid that the then House of Commons was venal,

And that North ought to anfwer in *damages penal*:

He compos'd many *Speeches* and *Books* upon *freedom*,

In hopes that the People of England would read

    'em,

And himfelf by *the nofe* be enabled to *lead 'em*,

After forty years labour, he found that the caufe

Of Freedom, brought nothing but *windy applaufe*;

That,

That in fpite of his long, unremitted endeavour,
His pocket remain'd juft as *empty* as *ever :*
He therefore determines to enter the port
Of PLUTUS, by praifing the MEASURES OF COURT :
Thus we fee what he meant, when he faid to his friend,
He would vary *the means,* to arrive at *the end.*

Should you afk, how the CRITICS in general look
Upon this lately publifh'd, this *laudable* BOOK ?
I fhould anfwer, the JUDGES in *parties divide,*
And that Burke from himfelf does not differ more wide,
Than the *fentence* of thofe who *prefume* to *decide.*
Some fay, that the Book is a *Wonder of Wonders !*
Some call it a *Copia Verborum* and *Blunders ;*
Some fay 'tis a *garden* of *beautiful flowers,*
Mix'd with *hemlock* and *weeds* of *mortiferous powers.*
The BISHOPS all fay, that its *merit* is fuch,
That it ne'er can *be read,* or *commended too much,*
And they mean to tranflate it in *German* and *Dutch :*
And fhould fome ORIENTALIST render the work
In *Arabic,* 'twould teach both the MOGUL and TURK.

A *fatyrical* MAJOR, in company fwore,
That EDMUND refembled a black HELLALKHORE ;
Whofe touch would a pearl or an emerald *ftain,*
So much that no HINDOO would wear it again ;

That

That whenever his purpofe *veracity* fuited,
The *brightnefs* thereof was by EDMUND *polluted*;
I can't, altogether, affent to this laft,
For truth is no BRAMIN, and lofes no *caft*;
However, this much, I am free to confefs,
That EDMUND gives TRUTH fuch a highflying drefs;
So colours and daubs her all over with paint,
That fhe looks like a HARLOT inftead of a *Saint.*

(An additional blunder I've lately detected,
Which, indeed, is no more than might well be expected;
DON BURKE's Correfpondent, fo *gentle* and *young,*
Knows little, except his *vernacular tongue*;
Now the *ftile* of *this Book* is fo *fubtle* and *fine,*
That he cannot difcover *the fenfe of one line*;
And BURKE being afk'd to *correct the miftake,*
Has *publifh'd,* in French, for the GENTLEMAN's fake.

NOV. 20, 1790.

L E T-

Y OU remember, dear SIMON, that Curate in Wales,
Who, among other Ecclefiaftical Tales,
Inform'd us how ST. ATHANASIUS difputed,
Without either confuting, or being confuted,
With ARIUS, his Brother; when, laftly, agreed,
Each polemical Bifhop to publifh his Creed ;
Juft fo have difputed our JOSEPHS, and FOXES,
And EDMUNDS, concerning the charms of their *Doxies* ;
Great EDMUND, wound up to infanity's pitch,
Calls the *Doxy* of JOSEPH a *Billingfgate Bitch* ;
Who, by fpreading *falfe Tales*, and creating fufpicion,
Endeavours to ftir up *inteftine Sedition* ;
That her aim is to throw all the world in a flame,
And that *Hetero* fhould be the termagant's name ;
And the *Doxy* of CHARLES, he is apt to fuppofe,
Is a *Vixen*, as ugly, and wicked as JOE's ;
At the fame time the Gentleman fays, that his own,
Call'd ORTHO,'s a Doxy deferving a Throne ;

But

But Joseph inflam'd, can no longer endure
His beloved to fee in a *Caricature*,
And has, therefore, refolv'd on expofing to view
Her picture, in naked *Simplicity* true.

But now, my dear Simon, by way of forfaking
This new metaphorical manner of fpeaking,
Let me tell you that Joe is preparing, with fpeed,
To exhibit in print his *Political Creed*,
Which bright emanation of knowledge divine,
Muft illumine fuch dark underftandings as mine.
The work will be fram'd on the *Moralift's* plan,
As a kind of *Political Duty of Man*;
It will teach us, among other wonderful things,
The Rights of the People, and Duties of Kings;
And many more *Rights*, which I need not rehearfe
Juft now, as I mean to recite them in verfe;
For moft people think, that fuch writings as Joe's
And Edmund's, read better in verfe than in profe.

You faid, in your laft, that my *Taffyland* friends
Are anxious to know what my Hero intends;
You may tell them, that now he the houfe is be-
    feeching,
For a feven year's leave to go on with impeaching;

And

And to PITT he will probably send a petition,

That he and the *Council* will grant him permission,

To bring WARREN HASTINGS once more to *the Bar*,

With whom he is willing and ready to spar,

Like HANNIBAL, swearing perpetual war :

And indeed, my DEAR FRIEND, these political men

May justly be liken'd to JOHNSON and BEN,

MENDOZA and HUMPHREYS, who meet on a stage,

And without provocation each other engage.

I dreamt, t'other night, as I lay on my bed,

With BURKE and *Impeachment* possessing my head,

That a Member of Parliament suddenly rose,

All future proceedings to check and oppose.

He said, that the stories my Hero had told,

For the seven last years, had the Nation cajol'd,

And made them believe, for a very long time,

That HASTINGS committed some *actual crime*;

That thousands and thousands were lavishly spent,

Without even a *chance of the promis'd event*;

That three years had pass'd since the TRIAL begun,

And *only three* CHARGES were *only half done*;

That he strongly suspected 'twas one man's endeavour

To make the said TRIAL *continue for ever*,

By way of providing for this and the other,

(Alluding perhaps to the GENERAL'S Brother);

That,

That, even suppofing the CHARGES were true,
The Pris'ner had fuffer'd much more than was due;
But suppofing no criminal deed were committed,
And that after BURKE's *death* he were fairly acquitted,
What recompence then could his countrymen make,
To the man who had fuffer'd fo much for their fake.

Here the ORATOR waxing exceedingly warm,
And rolling about like *a Ship in a Storm*,
Gave his head a high pitch, and declar'd 'twas a fhame
To defraud the keen hound of his long hunted game.
Eight years had the *ftrong-fcented, deep noted* PACK,
Purfued the *wild* BEAST through his long-winding track;
And now he was juft within reach of their paws,
Muft they give up their chafe, in obedience to Laws?
What Hunter's fo dull, or what well mounted Spark,
In purfuit of the game, would not break thro' a Park?
No, No—let us on, in *Humanity's* caufe,
Regardlefs of Precedents, Cuftoms, and Laws.
Whenever their LORDSHIPS appointed a day,
Did I ever once fhew the leaft *fign of delay*,
Or the fmalleft intention of *leaving my prey?*
If the MINISTER does not begrudge the expence,
Why fhould not the TRIAL *de novo* commence?
If their LORDSHIPS complain they are weary of hearing,
Let 'em take by rotation the days of appearing;

Re-

Relieving each other, as Centinels do,

A method of trial, both ufeful and new.

And if on my Law, they place proper dependance,

The Court may difpenfe with the Judges' attendance;

Nor need at the trouble my Colleagues repine;

They may fit at their eafe, all *the work* fhall be mine;

And as to the Pris'ner, his crimes are fo great,

That he never can fuffer too foon or too late;

For actions *fo foul, fo excefsively wrong,*

He cannot be tortured too much or too long.

Remember *that fhocking, that horrid abufe,*

His receiving ten Lacks for the Company's ufe;

His forcing Cheyt Sing to contribute a fhare

Of expence, which he feem'd fo unwilling to bear;

His advifing the foft-hearted Prince to impofe

On his Mother a fine for affifting his foes.

Such wickednefs how can the Nation forgive,

Or fuffer this *wretch* any longer to live?

He fhould flowly pafs thro' the gradations and ftages

Of mis'ry, protracted for ages and ages;

His mind fhould be tortur'd with dread of conviction,

And of fentence, the moft ignominious infliction.

Purfue him I will to the very laft breath,

Nor fhall any thing fave the *fell* Monster, but death,

Juft

Juſt here, EDMUND ſeem'd in a fit of deſpair,
He threw up his hands and was *thumping the air*;
His horrors, his geſtures extravagant, broke
The *chain of my ſleep*, and I therefore *awoke*.

Dec. 17, 1790.

SPLENDID